3.60

"My name is Templar — Simon Templar."

SIMON TEMPLAR: a/k/a The Saint, the Happy Highwayman, the Brighter Buccaneer, the Robin Hood of Modern Crime.

DESCRIPTION: Age 31. Height 6 ft., 2 in. Weight 175 lbs. Eyes blue. Hair black, brushed straight back. Complexion tanned. Bullet scar through upper left shoulder; 8 in. scar on right forearm.

SPECIAL CHARACTERISTICS: Always immaculately dressed. Luxurious tastes. Lives in most expensive hotels and is connoisseur of food and wine. Carries firearms and is expert knife thrower. Licensed air pilot. Speaks several languages fluently. Known as "The Saint" from habit of leaving drawing of skeleton figure with halo at scenes of crimes.

The Saint

LESLIE CHARTERIS

GETAWAY

LIBRARY OF CRIME CLASSICS®

MISTER E'S
INTERNATIONAL POLYGONICS, LTD.
NEW YORK CITY

GETAWAY

Copyright © 1932 and 1933 by Leslie Charteris.
Reprinted with permission of the author and John
Farquharson Ltd.

Library of Congress Card Catalog No. 90-84280
ISBN 1-55882-084-1

Printed and manufactured in the United States of America.
First IPL printing January 1991.
10 9 8 7 6 5 4 3 2 1

TO
P.G. WODEHOUSE

who had time to say a word for the Saint stories, when he could have written them so much better himself.

THE VILLAINS in this book are entirely imaginary, and have no relation to any living person.

Prologue

WROTE Chief Inspector Teal, of Scotland Yard, grimly refrigerating his personal emotions down to the temperature required of an official report:

The fact that Simon Templar has long since given up even pretending that he is not "The Saint" has never made it any easier to deal with him. In almost every case which has so far come to my notice, he has either made certain that his victim will not dare to charge him, or he has provided himself with an alibi that we cannot upset. He has resources which our organization was scarcely designed to cope with. From the very beginning of his career I have done everything in my power to secure an arrest, but all the evidence we have been able to accumulate so far has been practically valueless. . . .

The tense of the report was past—past and apologetic—though no one would have hated to admit it more than Teal. For, since the epoch to which that prefatory paragraph referred, certain things had changed. The trouble was that they had not changed in any particularly helpful way. This the chief commissioner had made distressingly plain. He did so with what several people considered to be an excessive amount of verbiage, decoration, and detail; but he was a pardonably angry man. Simon

1

Templar, having a more cheerful point of view, put
it to Patricia Holm much more succinctly.

"Somewhere," said the Saint, with the old gay
wave of his hand, and the light of the old Saintly
laughter dancing in his eyes, "somewhere in the
great sprawling mess that constitutes the Official
Drain—Brain—of Scotland Yard—there is a little
more evidence. And at the same time, in the great
palpitating area watched over by the Brain—there is
a lot less Saint. Who cares?"

Well, as a matter of fact, a good many people
cared. And a fat lot of use that was. Wherefore their
tribulation is mentioned merely as a thing of tran-
sient interest, in the same casual way as the Saint
himself would have referred to it.

Gunner Perrigo cared—but his feelings never
seemed to have been considered at any stage of the
proceedings. He languished in Brixton Prison on
remand and meditated gloomily on Life; and the
tenor of his meditations was that Life had handed
him the rawest of raw deals. For he, Gunner Perrigo, could once have claimed a half share in the
largest packet of illicit diamonds ever smuggled into
England, and now the prison inventory of all his
worldly goods made him out to be worth exactly
eight shillings and fourpence cash. Those were the
two cardinal facts of his existence; and no statistician
on earth could have figured them out into a more
comprehensive assortment of permutations and
combinations than he had already elaborated for
himself.

And Scotland Yard cared. Scotland Yard, into
whose Official Ear, as representatively rooted to the
scalp of Chief Inspector Teal, the umpteenth Saintly
flea had neatly been injected, was seriously

annoyed—and that from no motives of sympathy with the bereavement of Gunner Perrigo. And the index of that annoyance could have been calculated from the dour faces of the three dozen bulbous luminaries of its C.I.D. who littered themselves in pairs about strategic points in every port of the United Kingdom, waiting for the anticipated getaway, throughout one clammy week in April. Like the hosts of Midian, they prowled and prowled around, looking tremendously impressive, but achieving nothing more substantial than that. One of them caught a cold, which was just too bad.

And the Saint was away out of England—away ten thousand feet over their heads, in a flying streak of silver droning between the piled red pinnacles of the evening clouds. He was away with Patricia Holm and his freedom, with every penny of the accumulated profits of ten years of buccaneering rescued from a bank that Teal had not been quick enough to find and close against him, with one hundred thousand pounds' worth of illicit diamonds in his pocket, and the wide world before him.

Beyond the Channel they were waiting for him. Out of six police departments in six different countries the humming intercontinental wires conjured forth men to watch for him at Cherbourg, Havre, Dieppe, Boulogne, Dunkirk, Ostend, Hook of Holland—way east as far as Helsingfors and Riga. They glimpsed him over Etaples and were ready for him between Amiens and Paris; but he landed at midnight in the empty wastes of the High Fen behind Monschau, and came to Aachen in a borrowed lorry before the dawn.

And there the trail ended.

Van Roeper, the little blue-eyed Jew who paid

seven hundred thousand gilders for the diamonds, trotted peacefully round Amsterdam on his own business, and saw no reason to come forward with the little help he could have given to the chase. And he was the last man who knew that he had seen the Saint. None of the frontier guards of Europe knew that the Saint had passed them, for Simon Templar travelled his own trails. But it is only a matter of history that one day three weeks later Simon Templar and Patricia Holm walked south from Lenggries, which is in Bavaria, and passed through the woods to Achenwald in Austria by a path which the Saint knew, and so came presently to Innsbruck.

Monty Hayward found him there; and Monty has a lot to do with this story. In fact, the Saint has been heard to say that the whole story was Monty's fault from the very beginning. For they dined together at the Tirol, and afterwards drank beer together; and it was very late that night when the three of them were strolling home along the Rennweg, which runs beside the Inn. And the perfectly priceless part of it was that the Saint had made up his mind to be as good as gold.

1

HOW SIMON TEMPLAR FELL FROM GRACE AND STANISLAUS WAS UNFORTUNATE

IT ALL began to happen with a ruthlessly irresistible kind of suddenness that was as unanswerable as an avalanche. It was like the venomously accurate little explosion that wrecks a dyke and overwhelms a country. The Saint has sworn that he did his level best to get from under—that he communed with his soul and struggled manfully against temptation. But he never had a chance.

On the bridge, scarcely a dozen yards away, the four men swayed and fought; and the Saint stood still and stared at them. He stood with one hand on Monty Hayward's arm and the other on Patricia Holm's, exactly as he had been walking when the astonishing beginning of the fight had halted him in his tracks like the bursting of a bomb, and surveyed the scene in silence. And it was during this silence (if the Saint can be believed) that he held the aforesaid converse with his soul.

The change that had taken place so abruptly in the landscape and general atmosphere of that particular piece of Innsbruck was certainly a trifle startling. Just one split second ago, it seemed, the harmless-looking little man who was now the focal point of the excitement had been the only specimen of humanity in sight. The deserted calm of the Herzog Otto

Strasse ahead had been equalled only by the vacuous repose of the Rennweg behind, or the void tranquillity of the Hofgarten on the port side; and the harmless-looking little man was paddling innocently across the bridge on their right front with his innocuous little attaché case in his hand. And then, all at once, without the slightest warning or interval for parley, the three other combatants had materialized out of the shadows and launched themselves in a flying wedge upon him. Largely, solidly, and purposefully, they jammed him up against the parapet and proceeded to slug the life out of him.

The Saint's weight shifted gently on his toes, and he whistled a vague, soft sort of tune between his teeth. And then Monty Hayward detached his arm from the Saint's light grip, and the eyes of the two men met.

"I don't know," said Monty tentatively, "whether we can stand for this."

And Simon Templar nodded.

"I also," he murmured, "had my doubts."

He hitched himself thoughtfully forward. Over on the bridge, the chaotic welter of men heaved and writhed convulsively to a syncopated accompaniment of laboured breathing and irregularly thudding blows, varied from time to time by a guttural gasp of effort or a muffled yelp of pain. . . . And the Saint became dimly conscious that Patricia was holding his arm.

"Boy, listen—weren't you going to be good?"

He paused in his stride and turned. He smiled dreamily upon her. In his ears the scuffling undertones of the battle were ringing like celestial music. He was lost.

"Why—yes, old dear," he answered vaguely.

"Sure, I'm going to be good. I just want to sort of look things over. See they don't get too rough." The idea took firmer shape in his mind. "I—I might argue gently with them, or something like that."

Certainly he was being good. His mind was as barren of all evil as a new-born babe's. Gentle but firm remonstrance—that was the scheme. Appeal to the nobler instincts. The coal-black mammy touch.

He approached the battle thoughtfully and circumspectly, like an entomologist scraping acquaintance with a new species of scorpion. Monty Hayward seemed to have disappeared completely into the deeper intestines of the potpourri, into which his advent had enthused a new and even more violent tempo. In that murderous jumble it was practically impossible to distinguish one party from another; but Simon reached down a thoughtfully probing hand into the tangle, felt the scruff of a thick neck, and yanked forth a man. For one soul-shaking instant they glared at each other in the dim light; and it became regrettably obvious to the Saint that the face he was regarding must have been without exception the most depraved and villainous specimen of its kind south of Munich. And therefore, with what he would always hold to be the most profound and irrefragably philosophic justification in the world, he hit it, thoughtfully and experimentally, upon the nose.

It was from that moment, probably, that the ruin of all his resolutions could be dated.

Psychologists, from whom no secrets are hidden, tell us that certain stimuli may possess such ancient and ineradicable associations that the reactions which they arouse are as automatic and inevitable as the yap of a trampled Peke. A bugle sounds, and the

old war horse snorts with yearning. A gramophone
record is played, and the septuagenarian burbles
wheezily of an old love. A cork pops, and the mouths
of the thirsty water. Such is life.

And even so did it happen to the Saint.

After all, he had done nothing desperately excit-
ing for a long time. About twenty-one days. His
subconscious was just ripe for the caressing touch of
a few seductive stimuli. And then and there, when
his resistance was at its lowest ebb, he heard and felt
the juicy plonk of his fist sinking home into a nose.

The savour of that fruity squish wormed itself
wheedlingly down into the very cockles of his heart.
He liked it. It stirred the deepest chords of his
being. And it dawned persuasively upon him that at
that moment he desired nothing more of life than an
immediate repetition of that feeling. And, seeing
the nose once more conveniently poised in front of
him, he hit it again.

He had not been mistaken. His subconscious
knew its stuff. With the feel of that second biff a
pleasant kind of glow centred itself in the pit of his
stomach and tingled electrically outwards along his
limbs, and the remainder of his doubts melted away
before its spreading warmth. He was punching the
nose of an ugly man, and he was liking it. Life had no
more to offer.

The ugly man went sprawling back across the
bridge. Then he came in again with his arms flailing,
and the Saint welcomed him joyfully with a crisp
half-arm jolt to the ribs. As he fetched up with a
gasp, Simon picked a haymaker off the ground and
crashed him in a limp heap.

The Saint straightened his coat and looked around
for further inspiration.

The party had begun to sort itself out. A couple of paces away, Monty Hayward was giving the second thug a wholetime job; and right beside him the third hoodlum was kneeling on the inoffensive little man's chest, squeezing his windpipe with one hand and fumbling in his pocket with the other.

Some of which may help to explain why the third hoodlum was so utterly and devastatingly surprised by the next few things that happened to him. Undoubtedly his impression of the events that crowded themselves into the following eight seconds was a trifle hazy. A pair of sinewy hands locked themselves together beneath his chin, and he was conscious of a tall, lean shape leaning affectionately over him. And then he was hurled backwards into the air with a jerk that nearly dislocated his spine. He rolled dizzily over on his knee, reaching for his hip pocket; and the Saint laughed. It was the one move that had not till then been made—the move that Simon had been waiting and hoping for with all the concentrated power of his dismantled virtue—the move that flooded the one missing colour into the angelic beauty of the night.

"Dear heart!" said the Saint, and leapt at him like a panther.

The man was halfway to his feet when the Saint hit him, and his hand was less than halfway out of his pocket. The blow clicked his head back with a force that rocked his cervical vertebrae in their sockets, and he slumped blindly up against the parapet.

Simon piled smotheringly on top of him. Over the man's shoulder he caught a fleeting glimpse of the dark waters of the river hurtling sleekly past and breaking creamily against the broad piers of the bridge—for the Inn is none of your dignified and stately streams, it comes pelting down from the Alps like a young tidal wave—and the little fighting smile that played round the Saint's lips slowly widened to an unholy grin. His right arm circled lovingly round the man's legs. After all—why not?

"Saturday night is bath night, brother," said the Saint.

His left hand pushed the man's face down, and his right arm hauled upwards. The parapet was squarely in the small of his victim's back, and it was easy. The man pivoted over the masonry with an airy grace to which he had contributed no effort at all, and disappeared from view with a faint squawking noise. . . .

For a second or two the Saint gazed beatifically down upon the bubbles that broke the surface of the icy torrent, letting the sweetest taste of battle soak lusciously into his palate. The die was cast. The last, least hope of salvation that he might have had was shredded up and scattered to the winds. He felt as if a great load had been lifted from his mind. The old days had come back. The fighting and the fun had come back of their own accord, without his seeking, because they were his allotted portion—the rescuing of small men in distress, and the welting of the ungodly on the boko. And it was very good that these things should be so. It was a beautiful and solemn thought for a man who had been good for three whole weeks.

He turned around with a happy little sigh, nebulously wondering whether he had by some mischance overlooked any other opportunities of nailing down the coffin of his virtue. But a temporary peace had settled on the scene of strife. The man with the exceptionally villainous face was still in no condition to continue with the argument. The harmless-looking little man was sitting weakly in the gutter with his head in his hands. And on the head of the remaining tough sat Monty Hayward, licking a skinned set of knuckles. He looked up at the Saint with an air of quiet reflection.

"You know," he said, "I'm not sure that a cold bath would do this bird a lot of harm, either."

The Saint laughed suddenly.

"Let's go," he said.

He stooped and grasped the man's ankles. Monty took the shoulders. The man shot upwards and outwards into space like a clay pigeon from a trap. . . .

They turned again. In the middle of the road, the last of the Mohicans was crawling malevolently to his feet; and his hand also, like the hand of his predecessor, was fetching something from his pocket. . . . For the third time, Simon looked at Monty, and Monty looked at the Saint. Their attitudes were sober and judicial; but neither was able to read in the other's eyes the bashfulest suggestion that the good work should go unfinished. . . . The Saint nodded, and they streaked off the mark as one man. The hoodlum was borne away towards the wall. There was a wild whirl of arms and legs, a splash, and a silence. . . .

Simon Templar dusted his coat.

"Somehow or other," he remarked, after a short interval of contented rumination, "we seem to have disposed of the opposition. Let's have a look at Little Willie."

He walked over and hitched the cause of all the trouble to its feet. In the clear light of one of the standard lamps mounted on the parapet, he saw a thin, sallow face from which two dull brown eyes blinked at him dazedly. Simon studied the little man curiously. On closer inspection, the prize he had collected from the lucky dip seemed a rather inadequate reward for the expenditure of so much energy and mental stress; but the Saint had a sublime faith in his good fortune.

"Where were you on your way to, George?" he inquired affably.

The little man shook his head.

"*Ich verstehe nicht.*"

"*Wohin wollten Sie gehen?*" repeated the Saint, translating.

To his surprise, the little man's lips tightened, and a sullen glaze came over his eyes. He almost snarled out his reply.

"*Ich will gar nichts sagen.*"

Simon frowned.

Somewhere a new shrill noise was drifting through the stillness of the night, and he realized that both Monty and Patricia were standing rather tensely at his side; but he paid no attention. His brain registered the impressions as if it received them through a fog. He had no time to think about them then.

A little pulse was beating deep within him, throbbing and surging up in a breathless fever of surmise. The stubborn rigidity of the small man's mouth had started it and the harsh violence of his voice had suddenly quickened it to a great pounding tumult that welled clamorously up and hammered on the doors of understanding. It was preposterous, absurd, fantastic; and yet with an almost jubilant fatalism he knew that it was true.

Somewhere there was a catch. The smooth simplicity of things as he had seen them till that instant was a delusion and a snare. A child of ten could have perceived it; and yet the deception had been so bland and natural that the unmasking of it had the effect of a battering ram aimed at the solar plexus. And it had all been so forthright and aboveboard. A small and harmless-looking little man is hurrying home with his week's wages in his little bag. Three hairy thugs set on him and proceed to beat him up. Like a good citizen, you intervene. You swipe the ungodly on the snitch, and rescue Reginald. And then, most naturally, you approach your protégé. You prepare to comfort him and bathe his wounds, what time he hails you as his hero and sends for the solicitors to revise his will. In your rôle of the compleat Samaritan, you inquire whither he was going, so that you may offer to shepherd him a little further on his way. . . . And then he bites your head off. . . .

The Saint laughed.

"Yes, yes, I know, brother." Very gently and soothingly he spoke, just as before; but way down in the impenetrable undertones of his voice that whisper of soft laughter was lilting about like a mirthful will-o'-the-wisp. "But you've got us all wrong. *Sie haben uns alles falsch gegotten. Verstehen Sie Esperanto?* All those naughty men have gone. We've just saved your life. We're your bosom pals. *Freunde. Kamerad. Gott mit uns,* and all that sort of thing."

The German language has been spoken better. The Saint himself, who could speak it like a native when he chose, would have been the first to acknowledge that. But he computed that he had made his meaning fairly clear. Intelligible enough, at any rate, to encourage any ordinary person to investigate his credentials without actual hostility.

And definitely he had given no just cause for the response which he received.

Perhaps the little man's normal nerve had been blown into space by his adventure. Perhaps his head was still muzzy with the painful memory of his recent experience. These questions can never now be satisfactorily settled. It is only certain that he was incredibly foolish.

With a vicious squeal that contorted his whole face, he wrenched one arm free from the Saint's grip and clawed at the Saint's eyes like a tiger-cat. And with that movement all doubts vanished from Simon Templar's mind.

"Not quite so quickly, Stanislaus," he drawled.

He swerved adroitly past the tearing fingers and pinned the little man resistlessly against the wall; and then he felt Monty Hayward's hand on his shoulder.

"If you don't mind me interrupting you, old man," Monty said coolly, "is that bloke over there a friend of yours?"

Simon looked up.

Along the Rennweg, less than a hundred yards away, a man in an unmistakable uniform was blundering towards them with his whistle screaming as he ran; and the Saint grasped the meaning of the omens that had been drifting blurredly through his senses while he was occupied with other things. He grasped their meaning with scarcely a second's pause, in all its fatal and far-reaching implications; and in the next second he knew, with a reckless certainty, what he was doomed to do.

The Law was trying to horn in on his party. At that very moment it was thumping vociferously towards him on its great flat feet, loaded up to its flapping ears with all the elephantine pomposity of the system which it represented, walloping along to crash the gate of his conviviality with its inept and fatuous presence—just as it had been wont to do so often in the past. And this time there were bigger and better reasons than there had ever been why that intrusion could not be allowed. Those reasons might not have seemed so instantaneously conclusive to the casual and unimaginative observer, but to the Saint they stuck out like the skyline of Chicago. And Simon found that he was no less mad than he had always been.

Under his hold, the little man squirmed sideways like a demented eel, and the attaché case which he was still clutching desperately in his right hand smashed at the Saint's head in a homicidal arc. Lazily the Saint swayed back two inches outside the radius of the blow; and lazily, almost absentmindedly, he clipped the little man under the jaw and dropped him in his tracks. . . .

And then he turned and faced the others, and his eyes were the two least lazy things that either of them had ever seen.

"This is just too soon for our picnic to break up," he said.

He stooped and seized the little man by the collar and flung him over his shoulder like a sack of coals. The attaché case dangled from the little man's wrist by a short length of chain; and the Saint gathered it in with his right hand. The discovery of the chain failed to amaze him: he took it in his stride, as a detail that was no more than an incidental feature of the general problem, which could be analyzed and put in its right place at a more leisured opportunity. Undoubtedly he was quite mad. But he was mad with that magnificent simplicity which is only a hair's breadth from genius; and of such is the kingdom of adventurers.

The Saint was smiling as he ran.

He knew exactly what he had done. In the space of about two minutes thirty-seven seconds, he had inflicted on his newest and most fragile halo a series of calamities that made such minor nuisances as the San Francisco earthquake appear positively playful by comparison. Just by way of an hors-d'œuvre. And there was no going back. He had waltzed irrevocably off the slippery tight wire of righteousness; and that was that. He felt fine.

At the end of the bridge he caught Patricia's arm. Down to the right, he knew, a low wall ran beside the river, with a narrow ledge on the far side that would provide a precarious but possible foothold. He pointed.

"Play leapfrog, darling."

She nodded without a word, and went over like a schoolboy. Simon's hand smote Monty on the back.

"See you in ten minutes, laddie," he murmured.

He tumbled nimbly over the wall with his light burden on his back, and hung there by his fingers and toes three inches above the hissing waters while Monty's footsteps faded away into the distance. A moment later the patrolman's heavy boots clumped off the bridge and lumbered by without a pause.

2

Steadily the plodding hoofbeats receded until they were scarcely more than an indistinguishable patter; and the intermittent blasts of the patrolman's whistle became mere plaintive squeaks from the

Antipodes. An expansive aura of peace settled down again upon the wee small hours, and made itself at home.

The Saint hooked one eye cautiously over the stonework and surveyed the scene. There was no sign of hurrying reinforcements trampling on each other in their zeal to answer the patrolman's frenzied blowing. Simon, knowing that the inhabitants of most Continental cities have a sublime and blessed gift of minding their own business, was not so much surprised as satisfied. He pulled himself nimbly over the wall again and reached a hand down to Pat. In another second she was standing beside him in the road. She regarded him dispassionately.

"I always knew you ought to be locked up," she said. "And now I expect you will be."

The Saint returned her gaze with wide blue eyes of Saintly innocence.

"And why?" he asked. "My dear soul—why? What else could we do? Our reasoning process was absolutely elementary. The Law was on its way, and we didn't want to meet the Law. Therefore we beetled off. Stanislaus was just beginning to get interesting: we were not through with Stanislaus. Therefore we took Stanislaus with us. What could be simpler?"

"It's not the sort of thing," said Patricia mildly, "that respectable people do."

"It's the sort of thing we do," said the Saint.

She fell into step beside him; and the Saint warbled on in the extravagant vein to which such occasions invariably moved him.

"Talking of the immortal name of Stanislaus," he said, "reminds me of the celebrated Dr. Stanislaus Leberwurst, a bloke that we ought to meet some day. He applied his effort to the problems of marine engineering, working from the hitherto ignored principle of mechanics that attraction and repulsion are equal and opposite. After eighty years of research he perfected a *bateau* in which the propelling force was derived from an enormous roll of blotting paper, which was fed into the water by clockwork from the bows of the ship. The blotting paper soaked up the water, and the water soaked up the blotting paper, thereby towing the contraption through the briny. The project was taken up by the Czecho-Slovakian Navy, but was later abandoned in favour of tandem teams of trained herrings."

Patricia laughed and tucked her hand through his arm.

In such a mood as that it was impossible to argue with the Saint—impossible even to cast the minutest drop of dampness on his exuberant delight. And if she had not known that it was impossible, perhaps she would not have said a word. But the puckish mischief that she loved danced in his eyes, and she knew that he would always be the same.

"Where do we make for now?" she inquired calmly.

"The old pub," said the Saint. "And that is where we probe further into the private life of Stanislaus." He grinned boyishly. "My God, Pat—when I think of what life might have been if we'd left Stanislaus behind, it makes my blood bubble. He's the brightest ray of sunshine I've seen in weeks. I wouldn't lose him for worlds."

The girl smiled helplessly. After she had taken a good look at the circumstances, it seemed the only thing to do. When you are walking brazenly through the streets of a foreign city arm-in-arm with a man who is carrying over his shoulder the abducted body of a perfect stranger whom for want of better information he has christened Stanislaus—a man, moreover, who is incapable of showing any symptoms of guilt or agitation over this procedure —the respectable reactions which your Auntie Ethel would expect of you are liable to an attack of the dumb staggers.

Patricia Holm sighed.

Vaguely, she wondered if there were any power on earth that could shake the Saint's faith in his guardian angels, but the question never seemed to occur to the Saint himself. During the whole of that walk back to "the old pub"—in actual fact it took only a few minutes, but to her it felt like a few hours—she would have sworn that not one hair of the Saint's dark head was turned a millimetre out of its place by the slightest glimmer of anxiety. He was happy. He was looking ahead into his adventure. If he had thought at all about the risks of their route to the old pub, he would have done so with the same dazzlingly childlike simplicity as he followed for his guiding star in all such difficulties. He was taking Stanislaus home; and if anybody tried to raise any objections to that manœuver—well, Simon Templar's own floral offering would certainly provide the nucleus of a swell funeral. . . .

But no such objection was made. The streets of Innsbruck maintained their unruffled silence, and stayed benevolently bare: even the distant yipping of the patrolman's whistle had stopped. And Simon was standing under the shadow of the wall that had been his unarguable destination, glancing keenly up and down the deserted thoroughfare which it bordered.

"This is indubitably the reward of virtue," he remarked.

Stanislaus went to the top of the wall with one quick heave, and the Saint stooped again. Patricia felt his hands grip round her knees, and she was lifted into the air as if she had been a feather: she had scarcely settled herself on the wall when the Saint was up beside her and down again on the other side like a great grey cat. She saw him dimly in the darkness below as she swung her legs over, and glimpsed the flash of his white teeth; irresistibly she was reminded of another time when he had sent her over a wall, in the first adventure she had shared with him—one lean, strong hand had been stretched up to her exactly as it was stretched up now, only then it was stretched upwards in a flourish of debonair farewell—and a deep and abiding contentment surged through her as she jumped for him to catch her in his arms. He eased her to the ground as lightly as if she were landing in cotton wool. She heard his voice in a blithe whisper: "Isn't this the life?"

Above her, on her right, towered the cubical black bulk of the old pub—the Hotel Königshof, hugest and most palatial of all the hotels in Tirol, which the Saint had chosen just twelve hours ago for their headquarters. There, with a strategic eye for possible emergencies of a rather different kind, he had selected a suite on the ground floor with tall casement windows opening directly onto the ornamental gardens; and the fact that it was the only suite of its kind in the building and cost above five pounds a minute could not outweigh its equally unique advantages.

"Straight along in, old dear," spoke the Saint's whisper, "and I'll be right after you with Stanislaus."

She started off, feeling her way uncertainly between confusedly remembered flower beds; but he was beside her again in a moment, steering her with an unerring instinct over clear, level turf. The windows of their sitting room were already open, and he found them faultlessly. Inside the room, she heard him opening a door; and when she had found the switch and clicked on the lights the room was empty.

And then he came back through the communicating door of the bedroom, closing it behind him, and gazed at her reproachfully.

"Pat, was that the way I raised you—to let loose all the limes and invite the whole world to gape at us?"

He went over and drew the curtains; and then he turned back, and her rueful excuses were swept away into thin air with his gay laugh.

"In spite of which," he observed soberly, "it's better to be too careful than too optimistic. The results are likely to be less permanently distressing." He smiled again, and slid an arm along her shoulders. "And now what do you think we could do with a cigarette?"

He pulled out his case and sank luxuriously into a chair. Patricia ranged herself on the arm.

"Are you leaving Stanislaus in the bedroom to cool off?"

Simon nodded.

"He's there. You can go in and kiss him goodnight if you like—he sleeps the sleep of the bust. I handcuffed him to the bed and left him to his dreams while we decide what to do with him."

"And what happens if he wakes up and starts yelling his head off?"

The Saint blew out a long, complacent wisp of smoke.

"Stanislaus won't yell," he said. "If there's one thing that Stanislaus won't do when he wakes up, it's yell. He may utter a few subdued bleating cries, but he'll do nothing noisier than that. I've been doing a lot of cerebration over Stanislaus recently, and I'm willing to bet that the din he'll make will be so deafening that you could use it for the synchronized accompaniment of a film illustrating a chess tournament in a monastery of dumb Trappists. Take that from me."

A gentle knock sounded from the outer door of the suite; and the Saint peeped at his watch as he unrolled himself from his chair and sauntered across the room. It was five minutes to three—just thirty-five clocked minutes since they had detached themselves from the Breinössl and set out to ventilate their lungs before turning in, on that idle stroll beside the river which was to lead them into such strange and perilous paths. The night had wasted no time. And yet, if Simon Templar had had any inkling of the landslide of skylarking and song that was destined to be poured into his young life before that night's work had been fully accounted for, even he might have hesitated.

But he did not know. He opened the door three inches, checked up the pleasantly familiar features that surrounded Monty Hayward's small and sanitary moustache and pulled him through. Then he slid the bolts cautiously into their sockets and filtered back into the sitting room with his cigarette tilting buoyantly up between his lips.

"What-ho, troops!" he murmured breezily. "And

how do we all feel after our *culture physique?*"

"I don't think I want to talk to you," said Monty. "You're not nice to know."

The Saint's eyebrows slanted at him mockingly.

"Scarface Al Hayward will now tell us about his collection of early Woolworth porcelain," he drawled. " 'I never wanted a drag in politics or any other racket,' says Scarface Al. 'Art is the only thing that counts a damn with me. Why can't you guys ever leave me alone?' "

Monty laughed, operating the Saint's cigarette case with one hand and a siphon with the other.

"Surely. But still—this sort of thing's all very well for you, old sportsman, seeing as how you've chosen to make it your job; but why d'you want to boot me into it?"

"My dear chap, I thought it would be good for your liver. Besides, you can run awfully fast."

Monty plugged a cushion at him and went over and sat on the arm of the chair which Patricia had taken.

"Do you allow him to do this sort of thing, Pat?" he asked.

"What sort of thing?" inquired the girl blandly.

"Why—inveigling respectable editors into free fights and kidnappings and what not. Haven't you noticed what he's been doing all night? He goes around throwing people into rivers—he grabs people off the streets and runs away with them—he lets his pals be chased all over Europe by hordes of heathen policemen, while he goes and hides—and then he stands around here as happy as a dog with a new flea and can't see anything to apologize for. Is that the way you let him behave?"

"Yes," said Patricia imperturbably.

The Saint picked up a glass and hitched himself

onto the table. He blew Patricia a kiss and looked at
Monty Hayward thoughtfully.

"Seriously, old lad," he aid, "we owe you no small
hand. You drew the fire like a blinkin' hero—just as
if you'd been trained to it from the kindergarten. But
I'm damned sorry if you feel you've been landed in a
place where you ought not to be. There's no one I'd
rather have with me in a spot of good clean fun, but if
you really hear the call of the old hymn book and
hassock——"

Monty flicked ash into the fireplace.

"It's not the hymn book and hassock, you
fathead—it's the Consolidated Press. As I told you at
dinner, I've done a week's job in a couple of days, so
I reckon I've earned five days' holiday. But that's not
going to help me a lot if at the end of those five days
I'm just beginning a fifteen-year stretch in some
beastly German clink. . . . Anyway, what's happened to Stanislaus?"

Simon jerked a thumb towards the bedroom door.

"I dumped him out of the way. When he comes to,
he's going to throw a heap of light on some dark
subjects. I was waiting for you to arrive before I did
anything to speed up his awakening, so that you
could join the interested audience." He stood up
and crushed his cigarette end into an ash tray. "And
in the circumstances, Monty, that seems to be the
very next item on the programme. We'll get together and hear Stanislaus give tongue, and then
we'll have a little more idea of the scheme of events
and prizes in this here rodeo."

Monty nodded.

"That seems a fairly sound notion," he said.

The Saint went over and opened the communicating door. He had taken two steps into the room
when he felt a distinct draught of cold air fanning his

face; and then his eyes had attuned themselves to the darkness, and he saw the rectangle of starlight where the window was. He stepped back without a sound, and his hand caught Monty's fingers on the electric light switch.

"Not for just a moment, old dear," he said quietly. "That was the mistake Pat made."

He vanished into the gloom; and in a little while Monty heard a faint metallic rattle and saw the Saint's figure silhouetted against the oblong of dim light. Simon was closing the window carefully—and Simon knew quite well that that window had already been closed when he dropped Stanislaus on the bed and handcuffed him there. But the Saint was perfectly calm about it. He drew the curtains across the window, and turned; and his voice spoke evenly out of the dark.

"The notion was very sound. Monty—very sound indeed," he said. "Only it was a little late. You can put the light on now."

Light came, drenching down in a sudden blazing flood from the central panel in the ceiling and the alabaster-shaded brackets along the walls. It quenched itself in the deep green curtains and the priceless carpet that had been fitted to a queen's bedchamber, and lay whitely over the spotless linen of the carved oak bed. In the middle of that snowy expanse, the little man looked queerly black and twisted.

The ivory hilt of a stiletto stood out starkly from the stained cloth of his shirt, and his upturned eyes were wide and staring. Even as they looked at him, his right hand sagged lower over the side of the bed, and the attaché case that dangled from his wrist settled on the floor with a dull thud.

2

HOW SIMON TEMPLAR WAS UNREPENTANT, AND THE PARTY WAS CONSIDERABLY PEPPED UP

SIMON unlocked the handcuffs and dropped them into his pocket. He was far too accustomed to the sight of sudden and violent death to be disturbed in any conventional way by what had happened; but even so, a parade of ghostly icicles was crawling down his spine. Death that struck so swiftly and mercilessly was just a little more than he had expected to encounter so early in the festivities. It was a threat and a challenge that could not be misunderstood.

"How did it happen?" Patricia asked, breaking the silence in its sixth second; and the Saint smiled.

"In the simplest possible way," he said. "A member of the ungodly trailed us home, and let himself in here while we were gargling in the next room. Whoever he was, his sleuthing form is alpha *plus*—I was keeping one ear pricked for him all the way, and I never heard a thing. But if you ask me the reason why Stanislaus was bumped, that'll want a bit more thinking over."

The actual physical demise of the little man left him unmoved. They had not known each other long enough to become devoted comrades; and it was doubtful, in any case, whether the little man would

26

ever have been inclined to permit such an affection to burgeon in his breast. The Saint, whose assessment of character was intuitive and instantaneous, judged him to be a bloke whose passing would leave the world singularly unbereaved.

And yet that same unimportant murder wrote a sentence into the story which the Saint could read in any language.

Across the bed, his clear blue gaze levelled into the eyes of Monty Hayward with a glimmer of new mockery, and that reckless half smile still rested on his lips. Onto his last speech he tacked one crackling question:

"Anyone say I wasn't right?"

"Right about what?" Monty snapped.

"About abducting Stanislaus," came the Saint's crisp reply. "You both thought I was crazy—thought I was jumping to conclusions, and jumping a damned sight too far. But since there was nothing else you could do, you gave the jump a trial. Now tell me I haven't given you the goods!"

Monty shrugged.

"The goods are there all right," he said. "But what are we supposed to do with them?"

"Get on with what's left of our sound notion," said the Saint. "Carry on finding out as much as we can about Stanislaus—then we may have some more to talk about."

Already he was examining the little man's attaché case. His first glance showed him that the leather had been half ripped away, doubtless by some other sharp instrument in the hands of the recent visitor; and then he saw what was inside, and grasped the reason for the bag's extraordinary weight. The little attaché case was nothing but a flimsy camouflage:

inside it was a blued steel box, and it was to this box itself that the chain was riveted through a neat circular hole cut in the leather covering. A couple of shrewd slits with a penknife fetched the covering away altogether, and the metal box was comprehensively revealed—one of the compactest and solidest little portable safes that the Saint had ever seen.

Simon ran over its smooth surface with an expertly pessimistic eye. The lid fitted down so perfectly that it required the perspicacity of a lynx to spot the join at all. The edge of a razor couldn't have sidled into that emaciated fissure—much less the claw of the finest jemmy ever made. The only notable break that occurred anywhere in that gleaming case-hardened rhomboid was the small square panel in one side where the combination lock showed narrow segments of its four milled and lettered chrome-steel wheels—and even those were matched and balanced into their aperture so infrangibly that a bacillus on hunger strike would have felt cramped between them.

"Can you open it?" asked Monty; and the Saint shook his head.

"Not with anything in my outfit. The bloke who made this sardine can knew his job."

He snapped open one of his valises, and produced a bulging canvas tool-kit which he spread out on the bed. He slid out a small knife-bladed file, tested it speculatively on his thumb, and discarded it. In its place he selected a black vulcanized rubber flask. With a short rod of the same material he carefully deposited a drop of straw-coloured liquid on one of the links of the chain, while Monty watched him curiously.

"Quieter and easier," explained the Saint, replacing the flask in his holdall. "Hydrofluoric acid—the hungriest liquor known to chemistry. Eats practically anything."

Monty raised his eyebrows.

"Wouldn't it eat through the sardine can?"

"Not in twenty years. They've got the measure of these gravies now, where they build their strong-boxes. But the chain didn't come from the same factory. Which is just as well for us. I can't help feeling it would have been darned embarrassing to have to wade through life with a strong-box permanently attached to the bargain basement of a morgue. It's not hygienic."

He lighted a cigarette and paced the room thoughtfully for a few moments. On one of his rounds he stopped to open the communicating door wide, and stood there listening for a second. Then he went on.

"One or two things are getting clearer," he said. "As I see it, the key to the whole shemozzle is inside that there sardine can. The warriors who tried to heave Stanislaus into the river wanted it, and it's also one of the three possible reasons for the present litter of dead bodies. Stanislaus was bumped, either (a) because he had the can, (b) because he might have made a noise, (c) because he might have squealed—or for a combination of all three reasons. The man who knifed him tried to grab the contents of the attaché case and was flummoxed by the sardine can within. Not having with him any means of opening it or separating it from Stanislaus, he returned rapidly to the tall timber. And one detail you can shunt right out of your minds is any idea that the contents of the said can are respectable enough to be mentioned in law-abiding circles anywhere."

"Bank messengers have been known to carry bags chained to their wrists," Monty advanced temperately.

"Yeah." Simon was withering. "At half-past two in the morning, the streets are stiff with 'em. Diplomatic messengers have the same habits. They're recruited from the runts of the earth; and one of their qualifications is to be so nit-witted they don't know a friend when they see one. When they're attacked by howling mobs of hoodlums, they never let out a single cry for help—they flop about in the thickest part of the uproar and never try to get saved. Stanislaus must have been an ambassador!"

Monty nodded composedly.

"I know what you mean," he said. "He must have been a crook."

The Saint laughed and turned back to the bed. After one appraising scrutiny of the link on which he had placed his drop of acid, he twisted the chain round his hand and broke it like a piece of string.

With the steel box weighing freely in his hand, he lounged against a chest of drawers; and once again he looked across at Monty Hayward with that mocking half smile on his lips.

"You hit the mark in once, old lad," he said softly. "Stanislaus was a crook. And who bumped him off?"

Monty deliberated.

"Well—presumably it was one of the birds we threw into the river. A rival gang."

Simon shook his head.

"If it was, he dried himself quickly enough. There isn't one damp spot on the carpet or the bed, except for Stanislaus's gore. No—we can rule that out. It was a rival gang, all right, but a bunch that we haven't yet had the pleasure of meeting. Their representative was obviously on the set the whole time, unbeknownst, only the Water Babies forestalled him. But who were the Water Babies?"

"Do you know?"

"Yes," said the Saint quietly. "I think I know."

Mechanically Patricia Holm took a cigarette from her case and lighted it. She, who knew the Saint better than anyone else living, saw clearly through the deceiving quietness of his voice—straight through to the glinting undercarry of irrepressible mirth that weaved beneath. She caught his eye and read his secret in it before he spoke.

"They were policemen," said the Saint.

The words flicked through the room like a whisk of rapturous lightning, leaving the air prickling with suspense. Monty froze up as though his eardrums had been stunned.

"What?" he demanded. "Do you mean——"

"I do." The Saint was laughing—a wild billow of helpless jubilation that smashed the suspense like dynamite. He flung out his arms shakily. "That's just it, boys and girls—I do! I mean no more and nothing less. Oh, friends, Romans, countrymen—roll up and sign along the dotted line: the goods have been delivered C.O.D.!"

"But are you sure?"

Simon slammed the strong-box on the chest of drawers.

"What else could they have been? Stanislaus never shouted for help because he knew he wouldn't get it. I thought that was eccentric right from the start, but you can't hold up a first-class rough-house while you chew the cud over its eccentric features. And then, when Stanislaus gave me the air, I knew I was right. Don't you remember what he said? *'Ich*

will gar nichts sagen'—the conversational gambit of
every arrested crook since the beginning of time,
literally translated: 'I'm saying nothing.' But what a
mouthful that was!"

Monty Hayward blinked.

"Are you telling me," he said, "that all the time
I've been risking my neck to save some anæmic little
squirt from being beaten up by three hairy toughs,
and then cheerfully heaving the three toughs into
the river—I've actually been saving a nasty little
crook from being arrested, and helping you to murder three respectable detectives?"

"Monty, old turbot, you have so." Once more the
Saint bowed weakly before the storm. "Oh, sacred
thousand Camemberts—stand by and fill your ears
with this! . . . And you started it! You lugged me
into the regatta. You led these timid feet into the
mire of sin. And here we are, with the police after
us, and Stanislaus's pals after us, and the birds who
bumped Stanislaus off after us, and a genuine corpse
on the buffet, and an unopenable can of unclaimed
boodle on the how's-your-father—and I was trying
to be good!"

Monty put down his glass and rose phlegmatical-
ly. He was a man in whom the Saint had never in his
life seen any signs of serious flusterment, but just
then he seemed as close to the verge of demonstration as he was ever likely to be.

"I never aspired to be an outlaw myself, if it comes
to that," he said. "Simon, I simply loathe your sense
of humour."

The Saint shrugged his shoulders. He was unre-
pentant. And already his brain was leaping ahead
into a whirlwind of surmise and leaving that involuntary explosion of rejoicing far behind it.

He had summarized for Monty everything that he knew or guessed himself—in a small nutshell. He had divined the situation right from the overture, had been irrevocably confirmed in his suspicion in the first act, and had turned his deductions over and over in his mind during the interval until they had taken to themselves the coherence of concrete knowledge. And in his last sentence he had epitomized the facts with a staccato conciseness that lammed them together like a herd of chortling toads.

They failed lamentably to depress him. Never again would he mourn over his lost virtue. What had to be would be. He had angled for adventure, and it had been handed to him abundantly. Admittedly the violent decease of Stanislaus complicated matters to no small extent, but that only piled on proof that here was the authentic article as advertised. Whoever the gangs were that he was up against, they had already provided prompt and efficient evidence that they were worthy of his steel. His heart warmed towards them. His toes yearned after their posteriors. They were his boy friends.

His brain went racing on towards the next move. The other two were watching him expectantly, and for their benefit he continued with his thoughts aloud.

"If anybody is wanting to get out," he said, "this is the time to go. The birds who bumped off Stanislaus are going to have lots more to say before they're through, and it's only a question of hours before they say it. The guy who did the bumping has gone home to report, and the only thing we don't know is how long they'll take to get organized for the come-back. Even now——"

He broke off and stood listening.

In the silence, the gentle drumming on the outer door of the suite, which had commenced as an almost inaudible vibration, rose slowly through a gradual crescendo until they could all hear it quite distinctly; and the Saint's brows levelled over his eyes in a dark line. Yet he rounded off his speech without a tremor of expression

"Even now," said the Saint unemotionally, "it may be too late."

Monty spoke.

"The police—or Stanislaus's pals—or the knife experts?"

Simon smiled.

"We shall soon know," he murmured.

There was a gun gleaming in his hand—a wicked little snub-nosed Webley automatic that fitted snugly and inconspicuously into the palm. He slipped back the jacket and replaced it in his pocket, keeping his hand there, and crossed the room with his swift, swinging stride. And as he reached the door, the knocking stopped.

The Saint halted also, with the furrows deepening in his forehead. Not once since it began had that knocking possessed the timbre which might have been expected from it—either of peremptory summons or stealthy importunity. It had been more like a long tattoo artistically performed for its own sake, with a sort of patient persistence that lent an eerie quality to its abrupt stoppage. And the Saint was still circling warily round the puzzle when the solution was launched at him with a smooth purposefulness that made his heart skip one beat.

"Please do nothing rash," said a mellifluous voice in perfect English.

The Saint spun round.

In the communicating doorway of the sitting room stood a slim and elegant man in evening dress, unarmed except for the gold-mounted ebony cane held lightly in his white-gloved fingers. For three ticked seconds the Saint stared at him in dizzy incredulity; and then, to Monty Hayward's amazement, he sagged limply against the wall and began to laugh.

"By the great hammer toe of the holy prophet Hezekiah," said the Saint ecstatically—"the Crown Prince Rudolf!"

2

The prince stroked his silky figment of moustache, and behind his hand the corners of his mouth twitched into the shadow of a smile.

"My dear young friend, this is a most unexpected pleasure! When you were described to me, I could scarcely believe that our acquaintance was to be renewed."

Simon Templar looked at him through a sort of haze.

His memory went careering back over two years—back to the tense days of battle, murder, and sudden death, when that slight, fastidious figure had juggled the fate of Europe in his delicate hands, and the monstrous evil presence of Rayt Marius, the war maker, had loomed horribly across an unsuspecting world; when the Saint and his two friends had fought their lone forlorn fight for peace, and Norman Kent laid down his life for many people. And then again to their second encounter, three months afterwards, when the hydra had raised its head again in a new guise, and Norman Kent had been remembered. . . . Everything came back to him with a startling and blinding vividness summed up and crystallized in the superhuman repose of that slim, dominating figure—the man of steel and velvet, as the Saint would always picture him, the stormy petrel of the Balkans, the outlaw of Europe, the man who in his own strange way was the most fanatical patriot of the age; marvellously groomed, sleek as a sword-blade, smiling. . . .

With a conscious effort the Saint pulled himself together. Out of that maelstrom of reminiscence, one thing stood out a couple of miles. If Prince Rudolf was participating in the spree, the soup into which he had dipped his spoon was liable to contain so little poppycock that the taste would be almost imperceptible. Somewhere in the environs of Innsbruck big medicine was being brewed; the theory of ordinary boodle in some shape or form, which the Saint had automatically accepted as the explanation of that natty little strong-box, was wafted away to inglorious annihilation. And somewhere behind that smiling mask of polished ice were locked away the key threads of the intrigue.

"Rudolf—my dear old college chum!" Mirthfully, blissfully, the Saint's voice went out in an expansive hail of welcome. "This is just like old times! . . . Monty, you must let me introduce you: this is His Absolute Altitude, the Crown Prince Rudolf himself, who was with us in all the fun and games a year or two ago. . . . Rudolf, meet Saint Montague Hayward, chairman of the Royal Commission for Investigating the Incidence of Psittacosis among Dromedaries, and managing editor of *The Blunt Instrument*, canonized this very day for assassinating a reader who thought a blackleg was something to do with varicose veins. . . . And now you must let us know what we can do for you—Highness!"

The prince glanced down with faint distaste at the bulge of the Saint's pocket. Grim, steady as a rock, and unmistakable, it had been covering him unswervingly throughout that gay cascade of nonsense, and not one of the Saint's exaggerated movements had contrived to veer it off its mark by the thousandth part of an inch.

"I sincerely trust, my dear Mr. Templar," he remarked, "that you are not contemplating any drastic foolishness. One corpse is quite sufficient for any ordinary man to have to account for, and I cannot help thinking that even such an enterprising young man as yourself would find the addition of my own body somewhat inconvenient."

"You guess wrong," said the Saint tersely. "Corpses are my specialty. I collect 'em. But still, we're beginning to learn things about you. From that touching speech of yours, we gather that you belong to the bunch who presented me with the first body. Izzat so?"

The prince inclined his head.

"It distresses me to have to admit that one of my agents was responsible. The killing was stupid and unnecessary. Emilio was only instructed to follow Weissmann and report to me immediately he had reached his destination. When Weissmann was first arrested, and then rescued and abducted by yourself, the ridiculous Emilio lost his head. His blunder is merely a typical example of misplaced initiative." The prince dismissed the subject with an airy wave of his hand. "However, the mistake is fortunately not fatal, except for Weissmann—and Emilio will not annoy me again. Is your curiosity satisfied?"

"Not so's you'd notice it," said the Saint pungent-
ly. "We're only just starting. Our curiosity hasn't got
its bib wet yet. Who was this Weissmann bird,
anyway?"

The prince raised his finely pencilled eyebrows.

"You seem to require a great deal of information,
my dear Mr. Templar."

"I soak up information like a sponge, old
sweetheart. Tell me more. What is the boodle?"

"I beg your pardon?"

"Granted. What is the boodle? You know. The
jack—the swag—the loot—the mazuma—the stuff
that all this song and dance is about. The sardines in
that ingenious little can. Goshdarn it," said the
Saint, with exasperation, "you used to understand
plain English. What's the first prize in the
sweepstake? We've paid for our tickets. We're inquisitive. Let's hear you tell us what it's all about."

For the merest fraction of a second, a glitter of
expression skimmed across the prince's eyes. And
then it was gone again, and his sensitive features
were once more as impassive as a Siberian sea.

"You appear," he said suavely, "to be forgetting
your position."

"You don't say."

The prince's stick swung gracefully from his
fingertips.

"You forget, my impetuous young friend, that I
am the visitor—and the dictator of the conversation.
You are inquisitive, but you may or may not be so
ignorant as you wish me to believe. The point is
really immaterial. Except that, if you are honestly
ignorant, I can assure you—from nothing but my
personal regard for you, my dear Mr. Templar—I

can assure you that it will be healthier for you to remain in ignorance." He glanced at his watch. "I think we have wasted enough time. Mr. Templar, when you abducted Weissman, he was carrying a small steel box. I see that you have detached it from him. That box, Mr. Templar, is my property, and I shall be glad to have it."

The Saint lounged even more languidly against the wall.

"I'll bet you'd love it—Highness."

Simon's voice was dreamy. And right down behind that drawling dreaminess his brain was sizzling with the knowledge that somewhere the interview had sprung a leak.

In no way whatsoever had it taken the line he had subconsciously expected of it, and not one of his deliberate discourtesies had been able to startle it back into the way it should have gone. The Saint felt like a second-rate comedian frantically pumping the old oil into a frosted audience, and feeling all the inclement draughts of Lapland whistling back at him to roost below his wishbone. The badinage was going hideously flat. He caught the prince's gaze on him with a quiet wraith of humour in it.

"In a few minutes more, my friend, I shall believe that your ignorance is genuine. Or possibly your intelligence has deteriorated. Such things have been known to happen. I will admit that, when I decided to call on you myself, I had my doubts about the wisdom of the proceeding. A natural curiosity of my own persuaded me to take the risk. Now the risk has been justified, and I have been disappointed. It is a pity. But perhaps one cannot have everything. . . ."

"Allow me," murmured the Saint genially, "to

mention that I'm doing my utmost to oblige. What, after all, is one corpse more or less between friends? Of course, my shooting isn't what it was, and as a matter of fact it never has been, and if you feel like taking a chance on it——"

"I rarely feel inclined to take chances," said the prince calmly. "But perhaps I have been distracting your attention."

He made a slight signal with his right hand.

Just for an instant, the movement seemed to be nothing more than a meaningless gesture; and the Saint was deceived. And then the scales fell from his eyes—just that one instant too late.

He had forgotten that drumming on the front door of the suite. When it had stopped for the arrival of the prince he had thought no more about it. He had taken it for nothing more than an elementary ruse to enable the prince to make his entrance unobserved through the sitting-room windows; he had cursed himself silently for being so simply taken in, and thereafter had dismissed it from a mind that was fully occupied with other problems.

And now he grasped his error.

It was literally thrust upon him—jabbed firmly and incontrovertibly into his spine, and purposefully left there. Before that, in his irregular and energetic life, he had experienced the identical sensation. The feel of a gun muzzle in one's back leaves an indelible imprint on one's memory.

Simon stood quite still.

"Disappointing, in its way," said the prince silkily, "but satisfactory in most respects. I can recall the days when you would have been more troublesome."

Unhurriedly he crossed the room and picked up

the strongbox, and the Saint watched him coldly. There were two chips of white-hot sapphire in the Saint's eyes, twin lights of concentrated wrath that blazed through a thin crust of glacial immobility. The memory of the old days was seething through his tissues like an elixir of hot gall. The prince was right. Simon Templar had never been so easy.

The Saint's mouth writhed into a grimly tightening line. The softness had gone out of him. He felt as if he had just woken up—as if he had been fumbling feebly through a stifling fog, and suddenly the fog had vanished and he was stretching limber muscles and gulping down great lungfuls of clear mountain air. His brain was as pellucid as an Alpine pool. It had room for only one idea: to get his hands on to the contemptuous faces of the party that had made a fool of him, and hit them. Hit them, and keep on hitting. . . .

The prince was smiling at him.

"I can only repeat my assurance, Mr. Templar, that there are times when ignorance is bliss and curiosity may be an expensive pastime. Particularly in one whose hand has lost its cunning."

Simon Templar drew a deep breath.

Then he fired from his pocket.

His gun, with a half-charged cartridge in the chamber, gave no more than an explosive little cough, which merged into the sharp smack of the bullet crashing home into the single electric light switch by the door; and the room was plunged into impenetrable blackness.

The Saint hurled himself sideways. Right behind him he heard the dull plop of an efficiently silenced gun, but he was untouched. He twisted like an eel, and his hand brushed a pair of legs. They heard his grim chuckle in the darkness. There was a gasp, a strangled cry, and a terrific thud that mingled with the slamming of a door.

And after that there was a queer stillness in the room; and in the stillness someone groaned harrow-ingly. . . .

Monty Hayward dipped in his pocket and found a box of matches. He struck one circumspectly, and looked about him.

Patricia Holm was standing quietly beside the bed; and on the floor the horse-faced gun-in-the-back guy was giving a lifelike imitation of a starfish in its death agony. But the Crown Prince had gone—and so had Simon Templar.

3

HOW SIMON TEMPLAR MADE A JOURNEY, AND PRINCE RUDOLF SPOKE OF HIS APPENDIX

THE Saint went through the sitting-room window in a flying leap that landed him on the turf beyond like a crouching puma.

He paused there for a moment with his eyes and ears alert, sifting the shadows for the tell-tale movement which he knew he would find somewhere. And while he paused he felt his spirits soaring upwards till they knocked their heads against the stars.

The bouncing of the gun artist had done him good—more good even than the initial encounter with the thugs who had been heaved in error into the river. On the whole, those three had only been common, or garden, thugs; whereas the gun artist had prodded his gun into the Saint's spinal purlieus, thereby occasioning him considerable discomfort, uneasiness, and inconvenience. Well, things had happened to the gun artist which ought to learn him. The Saint had picked him up by his ankles, bounced him halfway to the ceiling, and allowed him to return to earth under his own steam.

And after that, the temptation to repeat the performance with Prince Rudolf had been almost overwhelming. Only an epic triumph of brains over

43

brawn, a positively prodigious magnificence of will, the Saint modestly believed, had made it possible to withstand the succulent allurements of the idea. But his better judgment, borne up on a wave of Saintly inspiration, told him that the time for playing ball with Rudolf was not yet.

Ten yards away, down by the sheer black walls of the hotel, a blurred glimpse of white showed for the twinkling of an eye, a glimpse that was there and gone again, like the pale belly of a shark turning fathoms deep in a midnight lagoon; and the Saint smiled contentedly. He slipped noiselessly into the murk beside the wall, and followed along on toes that hardly seemed to touch the grass.

The figure ahead was not so stealthy. Simon could hear the soft rustle and pad of thin shoes hurrying over the ground, and once he caught the dry rustling of leaves as the prince scraped past a laurel bush. To a man with the Saint's ears, those sounds were of more value than all the sun arcs in Hollywood: they told him everything he wanted to know, without making his own presence so obvious. Flitting inaudibly behind them, he closed on his quarry until he could actually hear the prince's steady breathing.

A second later, the sudden squeak of a metal hinge fetched the Saint up all standing. Immediately in front of him he could make out an arched opening in the gloom, and for a moment the prince's silhouette was framed in the gap. Then the hinge squeaked its second protest, and the silhouette was gone.

Simon frowned. Laurel bushes he could cope with, dead twigs likewise, and similarly any of the other hazards of night-stalking; but squeaking gates were a notch or two above his form. And the Saint

knew that when once a gate has made up its mind to
squeak it will surely get its squeak in somehow, even
though the hand that shifts it has a touch like gos-
samer.

Thoughtfully he stepped back.

Seven feet up, the wall through which the arch
was cut ended in a flat line of deeper blackness
against the dense obscurity of the sky. That seemed
to be the only hope; and the Saint went for it with a
quick spring and a supple pull on his fingers that
brought him to the top of the wall like an athletic
phantom. He drew his feet up after him without a
sound—and stopped there motionless.

Right underneath him a big limousine was parked
with its lights out and its engine whispering, barely
discernible in the faint luminance which filtered
down the alley from an invisible street lamp somewhere in the road at the far end. A man in some sort
of livery was closing the door, and Simon heard the
prince murmur a curt order. The chauffeur hurried
round and climbed in behind the wheel. There was a
dull click as he engaged the gears; and the headlights
cut a wide channel of radiance out of the darkness of
the lane.

Without a moment's hesitation, the Saint stepped
out into space and spreadeagled himself silently on
the roof.

He was aware that he was doing the maddest of
mad things. For all he knew, that car might be
preparing to hustle to the other end of Europe. If it
chose to do so, it could easily travel two hundred
miles before it made its first stop; and every one of
those miles would have its chance of hurling him off
to certain injury and possible death—apart from the
ever present risk of discovery. And back in the Hotel

Königshof he had left Monty and Pat to keep their
ends up with a corpse and a prisoner, and not one
clue between them to indicate what he expected
them to do.

But they would have to pull their own weights in
the boat, even as the Saint was pulling his. Patricia
he knew like his own hand; and Monty Hayward was
a veritable tower of strength. They would find their
own solution to the revised problem—even if that
solution consisted of nothing more desperate than a
policy of masterly inaction.

Meanwhile, fully three quarters of his own talents
were taken up with the business of maintaining his
present strategic position. At the first trial, the roof
of the car had seemed most conveniently propor-
tioned to enable him to curl his toes over the rear
corners and his fingers over the front ones, thereby
stabilizing his equilibrium over a wide base; but
after the first five minutes he discovered that his
position was unpleasantly reminiscent of the lunch
hour in a mediæval torture chamber. If he had been
able to talk, he would have aired his heartfelt sympathy with the venerable sportsmen who allowed
their heights to be increased on the six-inches-
while-you-wait machine, while the jailers went
round the corner to get gay with a butt of mulled
sack. The car dodged and bucked round every available corner, heading eastwards out of the town onto
the Salzburg road; and at every corner he had to
exert all his strength to avoid being flung into the
scenery like a pea off a gyroscope. Even when they
were clear of the town he was no better off; for the
Inn Valley road, for its own mysterious reasons,
switches over a series of bridges from one side of the
river to the other at every conceivable opportunity

and a few others which only an engineering genius could have invented. Moreover, it is covered to a depth of three inches with a layer of fine white dust; and as the car increased its speed the Saint found himself enveloped in a whirling cloud of pulverized rock which invaded his nostrils and turned the lining of his throat into a lime kiln—a form of frightfulness which the mediæval connoisseurs had omitted to include in their syllabus of entertainment. The Saint clung on like a limpet, breathing through his ears, and dreaming wistfully of feather beds and beer.

After a while he began to get adjusted to the peculiar requirements of his position—for what that was worth. At least, he felt sufficiently secure to try and take a peek at what there was to be seen in the *de luxe* quarters of the vehicle. Locating a merciful straight stretch of road in front of them, he let go one hand and squirmed himself gingerly round to shoot one eye through the miniature skylight under his belt buckle.

At the four corners of the rear compartment, clusters of tiny frosted bulbs illuminated the interior. By their light Simon could see the prince reclining in the sybaritic upholstery with the portable safe balanced on his knee. He was idly twiddling the wheels of the combination, and a tranquil smile was gliding over his face. Presently he put the strongbox down on the cushions beside him and rested his chin on his hand, wrapped in inscrutable contemplation.

The Saint grabbed for a hold and flattened himself out again in time to take the next corner. And he also meditated.

The view he had had of the tableau under his tummy was definitely encouraging. Pondering it between the racking strains on his muscles, he elaborated it into a direct and diagnostic confirmation of his theory. The facts as he knew them so far had to link up somehow, and the Saint felt that he could do the linking. That was why he was suffering his present martyrdom.

He tacked the clues concisely together in his mind.

"Emilio was tailing Stanislaus to report when he made the home base. When I collared Stanislaus, Emilio didn't try to rescue him; he knifed him instead. After which, Rudolf tools in and lifts the sardine can. Simple."

The big car sped on; and time became nothing but a meaningless succession of aches. They passed through a jolly-sounding place called Pill, swung right at Schwaz, and began to climb into the mountains. Shortly afterwards, the so-called "first-class" road petered out, and they were jolting over a kind of glorified mule track which boxed the compass along the brink of a contorted precipice. The chauffeur, whose nervous system must have been nothing more than an elementary apparatus rigged up from a few assorted icicles and bits of string, kept his foot hard down on the accelerator and took the hair-pin turns on two wheels; and after the first mile of it the Saint buried his face in his sleeve and lost interest in the route. Every few minutes he felt the car heel drunkenly over to one side or the other, while the tires skidded horribly over the loose, treacherous surface; and the Saint felt the flesh crawling on the back of his neck and wondered if any art of surgery would ever induce his bones to settle back into their tortured sockets.

Eventually, with a terrific bump which the Saint

at first assumed to be the inevitable end, the car crabbed onto a comparatively level driveway and began to slow down.

Simon raised his head with the feelings of a drowning man who finds himself unexpectedly coming up for the fourth time, and endeavoured to absorb the salient features of the landscape.

Straight in front of him he could see a pitch-black pile rearing up its serrated battlements out of the shrouded dark. The headlamps of the car splashed a wide oval of light over the bleak stone entrance flanked by semicircular bastions, and picked out the gaunt figure of the janitor, who was at that moment hurrying to open the huge wrought-iron gates. To left and right of the archway the forbidding walls of the castle stretched sheer and unbroken to the squat round towers at the corners fifty yards away.

The car moved slowly forward again and the Saint pulled himself cautiously up onto his toes and fingertips. The gatekeeper was temporarily blinded by the headlights; and Simon knew that that was his only chance. Once the car had passed within the walls, the odds on his being spotted would leap up to twenty-five to one; and having travelled so far, he had no urge to gamble his hopes of success on any bet like that.

The gateway was the vulnerable point in the fortifications, with a bare yard of masonry rising over it. As the car passed underneath, Simon set his teeth, gathered his cracking muscles, and jumped. He caught the top of the stonework, and wriggled over with an effort that seemed to split his sinews.

He found himself on a sort of narrow balcony that spanned the archway and disappeared into the turrets on each side. In the courtyard below him he could see the car swinging round to pull up beside a massive door over which a hanging lantern swayed in the slight breeze. The car stopped, and the prince stepped quickly out; as he did so, the door was flung open, and a broad beam of light cast the grotesquely elongated shadow of a footman down the steps. The prince stepped inside, pulling off his gloves; and the door closed.

Simon's eyes roved thoughtfully up the walls above the door. Higher up he could see a narrow streak of light sneaking through a gap in the curtains of a window; while he watched, the window next to it suddenly appeared in a yellow square of radiance.

"Which seems to be our next stop," opined the Saint.

He moved along to the turret on his left, and found a flight of spiral stone stairs running upwards and downwards from the minute landing where he stood. After a second's cogitation, he decided on the upward flight, and emerged onto a broader promenade which ran round the entire perimeter of the walls.

Simon kissed his hand to the unknown architect of that invaluable veranda, and hustled round it as quickly as he dared. A matter of three minutes brought him to a point which he judged to be vertically over the lighted windows; leaning dizzily over the battlements, he was able to make out a dimly illuminated sill. And right under his hands he could feel the thick, gnarled tendrills of a growth of ivy that must have been digging itself in since the days of Charlemagne.

With the slow beginnings of a Saintly smile touching his lips, Simon flexed his arms, took a firm grip on the nearest tentacles, and swung his legs over the low balustrade.

And it was at that moment that he heard the scream.

It was the most dreadful shriek that he had ever heard. Shrill, quavering, and heart-sickening, it pealed out from beneath him and went wailing round the empty courtyard in horrible strident agony. It was a scream that gurgled out of a retching throat that had lost all control—the shuddering brute cry of a man crucified beyond the endurance of human flesh and blood. It tingled up into the Saint's scalp like a stream of electric needles and numbed his belly with a frozen nausea.

2

For a space of four or five seconds that haunting cadence quivered in the air; and then silence came blanketing down again upon the castle—a silence throbbing with the bloodchilling terror of that awful cry.

The Saint loosed one hand and wiped a smear of clammy perspiration from his forehead. He had never reckoned himself to be afflicted with an unduly sensitive set of nerves, but there was something about that scream which liquefied the marrow in his bones: He knew that only one thing could have caused it—the pitiless application of a fiendish refinement of torture which he would never have believed existed. Recalling his flippant reflections on the subject of mediæval dungeon frolics, he found the theme less funny than it had seemed a quarter of an hour ago.

His heart was beating a little faster as he worked his way down the wall. He went down as quickly as he dared, swinging recklessly from hand-hold to

hand-hold and praying consistently as he descended.

Down in that lighted room below him things were
blowing up at eighty miles an hour for the showdown
which he had laboriously arranged to attend in person. Down there was being disentangled the enigma
of the sardine can, and he wanted a front fauteuil for
the climax. He figured that he had earned it. Only
with that tantalizing bait in view had he been able to
deny himself the pleasure of picking up Rudolf by
the hoosits and punting him halfway to Potsdam.
And the thought that he might be missing the small-
est detail of the unravelling sent him slithering
down the scarp at a pace that would have made a
monkey's hair turn grey.

A dead strand of creeper snapped under his
weight, and for one vertiginous instant he pen-
dulumed over the yawning jaws of death by the
fingers of his left hand. Looking down into the Sty-
gian chasm as he swung there, he sighted a nebulous
shaft of luminance just underneath his feet and knew
that he was only a few inches from his goal. He
snatched at a fresh hand-hold, wrapped himself
featly sideways, and went on. A moment later he was
steadying his toes on the broad sill of the open
window and peeping into the room.

In a high-backed, carved-oak chair, at one end of a
long oak table placed in the geometric centre of a
luxuriously furnished library, sat the prince. A thin
jade cigarette holder was clamped between his
teeth, and he was sketching an intricate pattern on
the table with a slim gold pencil. At the opposite end
of the table a big flabbily built man sat in an identical
chair: he was clothed only in his trousers and shirt,
and his bare wrists were locked to the arms of the
chair by shining metal clamps. And the Saint saw

with a dumb thrill of horror that his head was completely enclosed in a spherical framework of gleaming steel.

The prince was speaking in German.

"You must understand, my dear Herr Krauss, that I never allow misguided stubbornness to interfere with my plans. To me, you are nothing but a tool that has served its purpose. I have only one more use for you: to open this little box. That must be a very small service for you to do me, and yet you can console yourself with the thought that it will be an exceedingly valuable one. It will relieve me of the trouble and delay of having it opened by force, and it will save you an indefinite amount of physical discomfort. Surely you will see that it is absurd to refuse."

The other twisted impotently in his chair. There was a trickle of blood running down his arm where one of the clamps which held him had cut into the flesh.

"You devil! Is this what you did to Weissmann?"

"That was not necessary. The egregious Emilio —you remember Emilo?—was careless enough to kill him. Weissmann had actually reached Innsbruck when the police waylaid him. He was rescued, curiously enough, by a young friend of mine —an Englishman who used to be extremely clever. Fortunately for us, his powers are declining very early in life, and it was a comparatively simple matter for me to retrieve your property. You should visit my young friend one day—you will find that you have much in common. When a once brilliant man is passing into his second childhood, it must be a great relief to be able to exchange sympathy with another who is undergoing the same unenviable experience."

The prisoner leaned forward rigidly.

"One day," he said huskily, "I will make you sneer with another face. One day when you have learned that the old fox can still be the master of the young jackal——"

Prince Rudolf snapped his fingers.

"These 'one days,' my friend! How often have I listened to prophecies of what the cheated fox would do 'one day'! And it is a day which never comes. No, Herr Krauss—let us confine ourselves to the present, which is so much less speculative. You have been very useful to me—unwittingly, I know; but I appreciate your kindness just the same. I appreciate it so much that the most superficial courtesy on your part would induce me to let you leave this castle alive—after you have performed me this one service. I could even forget your threats and insults, which have done me no great harm. I have no profound desire to injure you. Your dead body would only be an encumbrance; and even the mild form of persuasion which you have compelled me to apply does not amuse me—the noise you make is so distressing. So let us have no more delays. Do what I ask you——"

"*Du–du Schweinhund!*" The tortured man's voice rose to a tremulous whine. "You will have to wait longer than this——"

"My dear Herr Krauss, I have already waited long enough. Your plot to obtain the contents of this box was known to me three months ago. At first I was annoyed. I regret to say that for a time I even contemplated the advantages of your meeting with a fatal accident. And then I devised this infinitely better scheme. Since we both coveted the same prize, I would retire gracefully. You should have the field to yourself. Your own renowned cunning and audacity should pull the chestnuts out of the fire. It was sufficient for me to stand back and admire your workmanship. And then, when your organization had obtained the prize, and it had been successfully smuggled across Europe to where you were waiting to receive it—when all the work had been done and all the risks had been survived—why, then it would be quite early enough for any accidents to happen. That was the plan I adopted, and it has been rewarded as it deserved to be." The prince removed the cigarette holder from his mouth and tapped the ash from it with an elegant forefinger. "Only one obstacle now detains us: the secret of the combination which keeps our prize inside this rather cumbersome box which I really do not require. And that secret, I am sure, you will not hesitate to share with me."

"Never!" gasped the man in the opposite chair throatily. "I would die first——"

"On the contrary," said the prince calmly, "you would not die till afterwards. But that eventuality need not concern us. In order to refresh your memory, we will let Fritz turn the little screw again."

He signed to the man who stood behind the other's chair, and leaned back at his ease, lighting another cigarette. His face was absolutely barren of expression, and his unblinking eyes were fixed upon his captive with the dispassionate relentlessness of frozen agates. As the man Fritz took hold of the steel cage which encircled the prisoner's head, the prince raised one hand.

"Or perhaps," he suggested smoothly, "the redoubtable Herr Krauss would like to change his mind."

The prisoner's breath came through his teeth in a

sharp hiss. The knuckles showed white and tense on his clenched hands.

"*Nein.*"

The prince shrugged.

Watching half-hypnotized through the window, Simon Templar saw Krauss stiffen in his chair as the screw control of that foul instrument was slowly tightened. A low groan broke from the man's lips, and his heel kicked spasmodically against the table. The prince never moved.

Simon struggled to fight free from the trance of horrible fascination that held him spell bound. He pulled himself further onto the sill, slipping the automatic from his pocket, and felt his temples throbbing. And then the prince raised his hand again.

"Does your memory return, my dear Herr Krauss?"

The other shook his head slowly, as if he had to call on all his forces to find strength to make the movement.

"*Nein.*"

The whisper was so low that the Saint could scarcely hear it. And the prince smiled, without the slightest symptom of impatience. He sat forward and pushed the strong-box along the table; and then he leaned back again in his chair and replaced the cigarette holder in his mouth.

"You will find the box within your reach as soon as you are ready for it," he said benevolently. "You have only to say the word, and Fritz will release one of your hands. I should prefer you to do the actual opening, in case the lock should hold some unpleasant surprise for the unpractised operator. And directly the box is open you will be free to go."

Again the man Fritz twisted the screw; and suddenly that dreadful cry of agony rang out again.

The Saint gritted his teeth and balanced himself squarely on the sill. Ordinary methods of "persuasion" he could understand; they were part of the grim game, and always would be; but to stand by in cold blood and watch the relentless tightening of that ghoulish machine was more than he could stomach. His finger tightened on the trigger, and he sighted the prince's face through a red haze.

And then he saw the man Fritz step quickly round from the control screw, and Krauss's hand clawed tremblingly at the box on the table. He was fumbling frantically with the wheels of the combination, and his shrieking had died down to a ghastly moaning noise. While the Saint hesitated, the box sprang open with a click; and then Simon vaulted into the room.

The man Fritz spun round with an oath and stepped towards him; and with a feeling akin to holy joy the Saint shot him in the stomach and watched him crumple to the floor.

Then he faced round.

"I should keep very still, if I were you, Rudolf," he stated metallically. "Otherwise you might go the same way home."

The prince had risen to his feet. He stood there without the flicker of an eyelid while the Saint sidled round the table towards Krauss, who had fallen limply sideways in his chair; and the smoke went up from the long jade holder in a thin, blue line that never wavered.

Simon found the control wheel of that diabolical mechanism and unscrewed it till it fell out of its socket.

"I assure you, my dear Mr. Templar," said the prince's satiny voice, "the device is really most humane. There is no lasting injury inflicted——"

"Is that so?" Simon clipped his answer out of a mouth like a steel trap. "I thought it looked interesting. The opportunity of experimenting with it on the inventor is almost too good to miss, isn't it?"

The prince smiled.

"Was that the object of your visit?"

"It was not, Rudolf—as you know. But maybe you're right. Business is business, as the actress was always having to remind the bishop, and pleasure must come second." A ray of carefree mockery came back into the Saint's inclement gaze. "What a jolly chat you'll be able to have with Comrade Krauss after I've gone, won't you? You will find that you have much in common. When a once brilliant man is passing into his second childhood, it must be a great relief to be able to exchange sympathy with another who is undergoing the same unenviable experience—mustn't it?"

The prince inhaled slowly from his cigarette.

"I did not know you spoke German, Mr. Templar," he remarked.

"Ah, but there are so many things one never knows till it's too late," murmured the Saint kindly. "For instance, you never knew that I'd be listening in to your dramatic little scene, did you? And yet there I was, perching outside your window with the dicky-birds and soaking up knowledge with both tonsils. . . . Well, well, well! We all have our ups and downs, as the bishop philosophically observed when the bull caught him in the thin part of the pants."

"I think I owe you an apology," said the prince quietly. "I underrated your abilities—it is a mistake I have made before."

Simon beamed at him.

"But it was so obvious, wasn't it? There was I with that bonny little box of boodle, and no means of opening it. And there were you announcing yourself as the guy who could open it or get it opened. At first I was annoyed. I regret to say that for a time I even contemplated the advantages of your meeting with a fatal accident. Since we both coveted the same prize——"

"Spare me," said the prince, with faint irony. "The point is already clear."

The Saint glanced whimsically at the open strong-box. Then his gaze flicked cavalierly back to the prince's face.

"Should I say—thank you?"

Their eyes clashed like crossed rapiers. Each of them knew the emotions that were scorching through the other's mind; neither of them betrayed one scantling of his own thoughts or feelings. The barrage of intangible steel seethed up between them in an interval of tautening silence. . . . And then the prince looked down at the glowing end of his cigarette.

"Your half-charged cartridges are very useful, Mr. Templar. But suppose I were to cry out—you would gain nothing by killing me——"

"I don't know. I should gain nothing by not killing you. And you'd look rather funny if you suddenly felt a piece of lead taking a walk through your appendix. It's that element of doubt, Rudolf, which is so discouraging."

The prince nodded.

"The psychology of these situations has always interested me," he said conversationally.

He had picked the stub of cigarette out of his holder, and the movement he made was so smooth and natural, so perfectly timed, that even Simon Templar was deceived. The prince was reaching languidly for the ash tray while he spoke . . . and then his hand shot past its mark. The lid of the open strongbox fell with a slam; and the prince was smiling.

"By the way," he said coolly, "my appendix is in Budapest."

He must have known that his life hung by a hair, but not a muscle of his face flinched. There was sudden death in the Saint's eyes, cold murder in the tenseness of his trigger finger; but the prince might have been talking polite trivialities at an Embassy reception. . . . And suddenly the Saint laughed. He couldn't help it. That exhibition of petrified nerve was the most breath-taking thing he had ever witnessed. He laughed, and scooped in the box with his left hand.

"Some day you'll sit on an iceberg and boil," he predicted flintily. "But you don't want to take another chance like that this evening, sweetheart. Get back against that wall and put your hands up!"

The prince obeyed unhurriedly. With his back to a bookcase and the Saint's gun focusing on his waistline, he spoke in the same passionless tone:

"My humane little invention is still at your disposal, my dear Mr. Templar. What a pity it is that it fails to meet with your approval. . . ."

"Believe me," said the Saint.

He hooked a chair round with his foot, and drew

the telephone towards him. With one elbow propped on the table, and the strong-box parked alongside, he slid one eye onto the combination panel and kept the prince skewered on the other.

"Innsbruck achtundzwanzig neun dreizehn."

The number clacked back at him from the receiver. And a great wide grin of pure beatitude was deploying itself round his inside. Even Rudolf could still make his mistakes; and it seemed to Simon that the exchange of errors was piling itself up beautifully on the side of righteousness and the Public School Code. But for once he deliberately chose to let the opportunity of chirruping go by.

And then he was through to his own suite at the Königshof.

"Hullo, Pat, old angel! How's the world? . . . Where have I been? Oh, toddling here and there. Wonderful amount of Alp there is in Austria. The place is simply bulging with it. . . . Well, don't rush me. I've been touring the great open spaces, Pat, where men are men and women wear flannel next the skin. Rudolf has been doing the honours. But that'll keep. Shoot me the news from home, old darling. . . . Whassat? . . . Well, I will be teetotal and let it snow!"

His forehead was crinkling as he listened, while the receiver rattled and spluttered with a recital that began by making his hair stand on end. For fully five minutes his granitic silence was punctuated only by an infrequent monosyllable that sizzled into the transmitter like a splinter of hot quartz.

And then, as the tale went on, he began to smile. His interruptions wafted through the air on a breath of inward laughter. And the concluding sentence of the story fetched him half out of his chair.

"Did you say that? . . . Oh, Pat, my precious cherub—get me that scaly humbug on the wire!"

He looked at his watch. It was twenty minutes to five, with barely an hour to go before the dawn. Then another familiar accent answered him.

"H'lo, Monty!" The Saint's voice was sparkling. "So you're the man who wanted to be good! . . . Well, I've got something here for you to take back to the Bible class. You couldn't have arranged it better. This is Simon Templar speaking from a Grade A *schloss* with whiskers on its chest, and he also feels the emigrating urge. Your job is to push out and freeze onto the fastest automobile you can get your fists on, and meet me on the road to Jenbach. All I've got here is the second worst car in Europe, but I ought to get that far. Now jump to it——"

The Saint's gun cracked. He was a second late—his bullet split a thick wedge of wood out of the angle of the dummy bookcase that was closing behind the prince, and then the hidden door had slammed back into place. He heard Monty's sharp question and laughed shortly.

"That was Rudolf on his way, and I missed him. Don't worry—travel!"

He dropped the receiver on its hook and stood up. The strong-box fitted bulkily into his poaching pocket. He darted out into the empty passage and saw another room on the other side. From the window he could locate an eighteen-inch ledge of stone running just beneath it. He swung himself over the sill and went two-stepping along the brink of sticky death.

4

HOW MONTY HAYWARD CARRIED ON

THE apotheosis of Monty Hayward did not actually trouble the attention of the Recording Angel until some time after the Saint had catapulted himself through the open windows and batted off into space on his own business.

Displaying remarkable agility for a man of his impregnable sang-froid, Monty Hayward possessed himself of the weapon which had fallen from the disabled gunman's hand, seized its badly winded owner by the collar, and lugged him vigorously into the sitting room, where the lights were still functioning. There he proceeded methodically to handicap the wounded warrior's recovery by dragging up a massive Chesterfield and laying it gently on the wounded warrior's bosom. Then he lighted a cigarette and looked gloomily at Patricia, who had followed him in.

"Why don't you scream or something?" he asked morosely. "It would help to relieve my feelings."

The girl laughed.

"Wouldn't it be more useful to do something about Ethelbert?"

"What—this nasty piece of work?" Monty glanced down at the gunman, whose groans were becoming a fraction less heartrending as his paralyzed respiratory organs creaked painfully back towards normal. "I suppose it might be. What shall we do—shoot him?"

"We might tie him up."

"I know. You tear the curtains into strips, and blow the expense."

"There's a length of rope in Simon's bag," said Patricia calmly. "If you'll wait a second I'll get it for you."

She disappeared into the bedroom and returned in a few moments with a coil of stout cord. Monty took it from her gingerly.

"I suppose there isn't anything of this sort that Simon ever travels without," he commented pessimistically. "If you've got a gallows in the cabin trunk, it may save a lot of mucking about when the police catch us."

The gunman was still in no condition to make any effective resistance. Monty endeavoured to adapt a working knowledge of knots acquired in some experience of week-end yachting to the peculiar eccentricities of the human frame, and made a very passable job of it. Having reduced his victim to a state of blasphemous helplessness, he dusted the knees of his trousers and turned again to Pat.

"I seem to remember that the next item is a gag," he said. "Do you know anything about gags?"

"I have seen it done," said the girl unblushingly. "Lend me your handkerchief. . . . And that other one in your breast pocket."

She bent over the squirming prisoner, and a particularly vile profanity subsided into a choking gurgle. Monty watched the performance with admiration.

"You know, I couldn't have done that," he said. "And I've been editing this kind of stuff all my life. The stories never give you the important details. They just say: 'Lionel Strongarm bound and gagged his captive'—and the thing's done. Where did you learn it all?"

Patricia laughed.

"Simon taught me," she said simply. "If there's anything that makes him see red, it's inefficiency. He explains a thing once, and expects you to remember it for the rest of your life. Your brain's got to be on tiptoe from the time you get up in the morning till the time you go to bed at night. He's like that himself, and everyone else has got to be the same. It nearly sent me off my rocker till I got used to it; and then I began to see that I'd been half asleep all my life, like eighty per cent of other people. He was right, of course."

Monty went over and poured himself out a drink.

"This is a new line on the private life of an adventurer," he murmured. "Did he ever explain what one should do when stranded in a hotel with a corpse on the bed and a gun artist under the sofa?"

"That," said the girl composedly, "is supposed to be an elementary exercise in initiative."

Monty grimaced.

"Some initiative is certainly called for," he admitted. "Simon may be away for a week, and then Stanislaus will begin to smell."

He wandered pensively back into the bedroom and wished that he felt suitably depressed. Two hours ago he would have expressed no desire at all to find himself in such a situation. Its potentialities in the way of local colour would have left him uninspired. Four years in France had left him with a profound appreciation of the amenities of peace. On several occasions he had told the Saint that he was always pleased to hear or read of stirring exploits anywhere, but that as far as he personally was con-

cerned he could enjoy enough violence to keep his
glands active from an armchair. And if he had to be
decoyed into that sort of thing, he most unequivo-
cally wanted it to be gradual. A minor job of shop-
lifting, if necessary, or an evening out with a
pickpocket, would have satisfied his craving for excitement for a long time.

But since he had been blamelessly landed up to
his neck in a kind of thieves' picnic in which the
disposal of corpses and gagged gunmen was supposed to be merely an elementary exercise in initiative, he found himself taking an interest in the
affair which he tried to persuade himself was purely
morbid. He frisked Weissmann's clothes with an
almost professional callousness and brought a selec-
tion of papers back with him to the sitting room.

"While you're getting your initiative tuned up,"
he said, "it might be helpful if we knew something
more about Stanislaus."

Patricia came and looked over his shoulder as he
ran through the meagre supply of documents. There
were a couple of letters on heavily scented pink
notepaper, addressed to Heinrich Weissmann at the
Dôme, Boulevard Montparnasse, Paris, which disclosed nothing of interest to anyone wishing to have
the strength of ten; a letter of credit for two thousand
marks, issued by the Dresdner Bank in Köln; the
counterfoil of a sleeping-car ticket from Zürich to
Milan; and a receipted bill from a hotel in Basle.

"He certainly did his best to shake off the hue and
cry," said Monty; "but does it tell us anything else?"

"What about that?" asked Patricia, turning over
one of the pink envelopes.

On the flap was a pencilled line of writing:

Zr λ 2 H Königshof

"Room Twelve, Hotel Königshof," Monty translated promptly. "Looks as if this was the very place he was making for."

The girl bit her lip.

"It'd be a frightful coincidence——"

"I don't know. Those squiggly marks in the corner—they're just the sort of pattern a fellow draws at the telephone. Stanislaus would naturally have some note of the place where he was supposed to deliver the boodle. And there's no reason why it shouldn't be here. This is the most slap-up hotel for miles around—the very place that a super crook would make his headquarters——" Monty slewed round in his chair and regarded her expectantly. "Suppose the Big Noise was sitting right over our heads?"

Patricia jumped up.

"But that's just what he is doing, if that address is right! Room Twelve is on the first floor. When we came here they offered us Eleven, but Simon wouldn't have it. He tried to get Twelve, which has a fire escape outside, but it was taken yesterday——"

"I don't see that it's anything to get excited about, anyway," said Monty soothingly. "If it's true, it only means that another bunch of toughs may be crashing in here at any moment to commit a few more murders."

"I'm going to run up the fire escape and see if I can see anything."

Monty looked at her in frank amazement.

For the first instant he thought she was bluffing. He had instinctively salted down her laconic description of the Saint's inexorable training. And then he saw the recklessness of the smile that parted her fresh lips, the eager vitality of her slim body, the devil-may-care light in her blue eyes; and the ban-

tering challenge that trembled on the tip of his
tongue went unuttered. There was a living embod-
iment of Saintliness in her that startled. He smiled.

"If you don't mind my saying so," he remarked
soberly, "Simon's a damned lucky man. And you
won't run up the fire escape, because I'm going to."

He went out onto the lawn, located the stairway
on his left, and groped his way up the narrow iron
steps. There was only one window on the first floor
which could possibly answer the vague description
he had been given, and no light showed through it.
He paused on the grating beside it and wondered
what on earth he should do next. To scale an awkward species of ladder at that hour of the morning in
order to inspect a room, and then to return with the
information that it possesses a window constructed
of square panes of glass, struck him as being an
extraordinarily inane procedure. And he could see
nothing inside from where he was. There seemed to
be only one alternative, and that was to insert himself surreptitiously into the room.

Fortunately one of the casements was ajar, and he
opened it wide and clambered over the sill with a
silent prayer that he might be able to pretend successfully that he was drunk.

Every movement he made appeared to shake the
hotel to its foundations. The loose change clinked in
his pockets like a dozen sledge hammers knocking
the hell out of a cracked anvil, his clothes rustled like
a forest in a gale, and the sound of his breathing
seemed loud enough to wake the Seven Sleepers of
Ephesus. The jaws of the prison yawned on every
side. He could hear them.

Then his right shin collided with something hard.
He felt around for the offending object, and pres-

ently discovered it to be a chair lying on its side. Peering puzzledly into the gloom, he made out the white outline of the bed. He strained his eyes at it for some seconds; and then, with a sudden inspiration, he walked straight across the room and switched on the light. . . .

Three minutes later he was back in the suite below.

"I don't profess to understand anything that's happening tonight," he said, "but the bird upstairs has flown. Flown in a hurry, too, because he's gone without his coat and tie."

Patricia stared.

"But—surely he must have gone to the bathroom."

"Not unless he intends to spend the night there. His door was shut, and the key was on the table by the bed. That's what they call deduction."

The girl sat down on the arm of the Chesterfield with a frown of perplexity wrinkling her forehead. The development required some thinking over.

One thing was as plain as a pikestaff, and she phrased it undemonstratively:

"If we sit around here doing nothing, we're just asking to be shot at."

"Look here, Pat," said Monty Hayward, buttressing himself against the mantelpiece, "we're between several fires. Don't forget that the police have got it in for us as well. And one of the chief essentials in a mess like this seems to be to have the door open for a clean getaway. Now, what would be the Saint's idea about that?"

"He'd say that the main thing was to leave no evidence."

"Right. Then the only serious piece of evidence is

that stiff in the next room. Whatever happens, we can't leave him lying about. And since we know where he was going, and the coast is clear, I should think the best thing we could do is to help him finish his journey."

Patricia looked at him thoughtfully.

"You mean, plant him in the room upstairs——"

"Exactly. And let the gang he belongs to take care of him. It's about time they had some worries of their own."

"And what about Ethelbert?"—she indicated the prisoner with a movement of her cigarette.

"Put a knife beside him and let him do the best he can. Even if they catch him, I don't think he'll have anything to say. For one thing, Stanislaus seems to have been no friend of his; and besides, if he wanted to clear up the mystery, he'd have to give an account of what he was doing in here, which wouldn't be too easy for him."

The argument seemed flawless. Patricia herself could offer no improvements on the scheme; and she realized that every wasted minute increased the danger.

She led the way into the bedroom and produced an electric flashlamp to light Monty on his gruesome task. Luckily the external bleeding had been comparatively slight, and no blood had penetrated to the bedclothes. Monty picked up the rigid body in his arms and went out without another word, and she stayed behind to straighten the sheets and coverlet.

The feelings of Monty Hayward as he climbed the fire escape for the second time were somewhat disordered. He insisted to himself, on purely logical grounds, that he was scared stiff; but the emotion somehow failed to connect amicably with another stratum of his immortal soul which was having the time of its life. He began to ask himself whether perhaps he had been missing something by steadfastly burying himself in a respectable existence; and immediately he reflected that the prospect of being hanged by the neck for other people's murders was a damned good thing to miss anyway. He solemnly vowed that the next time he saw a harmless-looking little man being set on by a gang of thugs, he would raise his hat politely and pass by on the other side; and simultaneously he felt rather pleased with himself for the efficiency with which he had laid out his opponent. It was all very difficult; and he pushed himself and his grisly luggage through the first floor window with some doubts of whether he was really the same man who had been placidly quaffing Pilsener at the Breinössl two hours ago.

After a moment's deliberation, he laid the little man artistically down beside the overturned chair, rubbed the chair with his sleeve to remove any fingerprints, and stood back to examine his handiwork. It looked convincing enough. . . . And it was then that the Recording Angel shuddered on his throne and upset the inkpot; for Monty Hayward gazed at his handiwork and grinned. . . .

Then he switched out the light. He hopped over the window sill and trotted down the escape with a briskness that was almost rollicking. The glorious company of the Apostles held their breath.

He was three steps from the bottom when he saw a shadow move in the darkness just below, and a hoarse voice challenged him:

"Wer da?"

Monty's stomach took a short stroll round his interior.

Then he stepped down to the ground.

"Hullo, ole pineapple," he hiccoughed. "Ishnit lovely night? Are you the lighthoushkeeper? Bacaush if you are——"

A light was flashed in his face, and he heard a startled exclamation:

"Gott im Himmel! Der Engländer, der mich in den Fluss geworfen hat—"

Monty understood, and gasped.

And then, even as it had happened earlier to Simon Templar, the tattered remnants of his virtue were swept into annihilation like chaff before a fire. If he were destined for the scaffold, so let it be. His boats had been burned for him.

He flung up his arm and knocked the light aside. As it flew into the air, he had a fleeting glimpse of the battered face of the man he had tackled on the bridge, with his one undamaged eye bulging and his bruised mouth opening for a shout. He crowded every ounce of his strength into a left hook to the protruding chin, and heard the man drop like a poleaxed ox.

Monty picked him up and carried him into the sitting room. Monty was smiling. He considered that that left hook was a beauty.

"We were only just in time," he said. "This hotel is getting unhealthy."

The girl looked at him open-mouthed.

"Where was he?"

"Standing at the bottom of the fire escape, waiting for me. He's one of the blokes we threw into the river. I think I can guess what happened. If the police were waiting to pinch Stanislaus, they may have been nearly as hot on the trail of the man upstairs. They came dashing along here as soon as they'd reported to headquarters and borrowed a change of clothes—you can see this chap's uniform is too tight for him. The other two are probably interviewing the management and preparing to break in the door. This one was posted in the garden to see that their man didn't make a getaway through the window."

Patricia took a cigarette from her case and lighted it with a steady hand.

"If that bloke's uniform is too tight for him," she remarked evenly, "it should just about fit you."

Monty raised one eyebrow.

After a moment's silence he bent a calculating eye on the unconscious policeman. When he looked up again there was a twinkle in his gaze.

"Is that what the Saint would do?" he asked quizzically.

She nodded.

"I can't see any other way out."

"Then I expect I could manage it."

He knelt down and began to strip off the policeman's uniform and accoutrements. The trousers went on over his own, with his coat-tails inside—he foresaw possible difficulties in the way of parting permanently with his own garments—and then Patricia was ready for him with the tunic. Tailored for the more generous figure of a Teutonic gendarme, it fitted him perfectly over his own clothes. Monty was transformed.

He was buckling on the cumbersome sword belt when the telephone began to ring.

"If that's the Saint," he said, "tell him I never want to speak to him again."

Patricia threw herself at the instrument.

"Hullo. . . . Simon—where have you been? . . .

Oh, don't play the fool, boy. We must know quickly.
. . . Well, the police are here. . . . The police—
the men you and Monty threw in the river. Keep
quiet and let me tell you."

5

HOW SIMON TEMPLAR CHASED HIMSELF, AND MONTY HAYWARD DID HIS STUFF

SIMON TEMPLAR deposited himself neatly on the roof of the car as it flashed underneath him and settled himself down to wallow in the side-splitting aspects of the ride.

The humour of the situation struck him as being definitely rich. To have first induced a wily old veteran like Prince Rudolf to transport you personally to his secret lair, and then, after you have butted violently into an up-and-coming conversazione, plugged his gentleman's gentleman in the lower abdomen, pulled His Elegant Elevation's leg, shot a hole in the air an inch from his elevated ear, snaffled a large can of boodle, and made yourself generally unpopular in divers similar ways, to be taking precisely the same route back to the long grass was an achievement of which any man might have been justly proud. And yet that was exactly what the Saint was doing.

The inspiration had come to Simon while he was listening to Patricia's story on the telephone, and he had put it into effect without a second's hesitation. Sprawling tenaciously on his unstable perch, he reviewed the dazzling casualness with which he had scattered all the necessary bait—the mythical car which he had waiting for him, and the rendezvous on the road to Jenbach—and marvelled at his own astounding brilliance. And after that had been done the elopement of Prince Rudolf mattered not at all. In fact, it saved a certain amount of trouble. The Saint had scarcely reached his point of vantage over the archway of the castle when he saw the prince's car pulling out for the pursuit; and one minute later he was being bowled along on the most hilarious getaway of his eventful life.

It was the very first time in his tempestuous career that he had ever tacked himself to the lid of an unfriendly limousine and helped enthusiastically to chase himself; and the overpowering Saintliness of the idea made him so weak with laughter that he was barely able to save himself from being bucked off into the surrounding panorama when the car jolted over the ridge that place it on the mountain road.

If the voyage to the castle had been hectic, the return journey was the most delirious peregrination in which the Saint ever wanted to take part. How the car itself managed to hold the road at all was more than the Saint could account for by any natural laws. The only conclusion he could come to was that it had been born and bred in a circus and had subsequently been fitted with tires manufactured from a hitherto unknown form of everlasting glue. Half the time, it seemed to be running with two of its wheels skating about on the loose scree and the other two gyrating airily over the unfathomable abyss. The fact that it would probably have done the very same thing if the Saint had been driving it himself was a consolation that could be ignored. The difference between one's own masterly manœuvres at the wheel and the hare-brained antics of a total stranger is one which no practical motorist has ever been able to misunderstand. Besides which, a comfortably upholstered seat inside a vehicle, however suicidally driven, is not and never can be quite so awe-inspiring as a smooth and slippery roof on which you have to maintain your crucified posture largely by the adhesive qualities of your eyelids. For Simon Templar there ensued an interval of fifteen or twenty minutes in which he had no further leisure to enjoy the gorgonzolan ripeness of the jest.

The only merit he could see in that breakneck pace was that it approximately halved the duration of the agony. And by some miracle he found himself still breathing and alive when the precipitous track began to level itself out for the run down to Schwaz.

With a wry grin of triumph, the Saint moistened his dry lips and eased the tension on his crippled thews.

The car was slowing up doubtfully. Simon squeezed his ear against the roof, and heard the prince speaking impatiently.

"Go on further, blockhead! He drives like the devil, but we must be close behind him. The road to Jenbach——"

Simon crooked his toes and fingers and clung on, and the car lurched round a corner and raced on towards the east.

On another furlong of straight road he convoluted himself round again to peep in at the prince, and what he saw made him flop limply down in a renewed paroxysm of mirth.

The prince was sitting tensely forward in his seat, staring fixedly along the road ahead. One hand was clutching something in his pocket, while the other beat a monotonous tattoo on his left knee. Apart from that regular tapping of his fingers he was as

motionless as a painted statue, and his pale, finely
modelled face was as expressionless as ever; and yet
the contrast between him as he was sitting then, and
the inscrutable exquisite whom the Saint knew so
well, was as inconsistent a transfiguration as the
Saint had ever seen. It was not really funny—it was
perhaps the most ominous possible reminder of the
dour realities that had been glossed over so
smoothly with the sheen of airy badinage—but it
was only the fantastic bathos of the whole performance which appealed to him.

"Oh, go down, Moses!" he hallooed. "That's the
stuff to give 'em. Stamp on the gas, Adolphus—don't
let him get away! Yoicks!"

He restrained himself with difficulty from thumping the roof in his excitement, and turned his mind
to the amazing awakening of Monty Hayward.

Monty had acquitted himself like an old stager,
but the breaks had been against him. In spite of
everything he had done, a malicious fluke had
dented the polish of their alibi. Their reputations
were tarnished beyond repair. The thwarted spleen
of the entire Austrian police force would be thrown
into the international ill-will that trailed behind
them. The righteous wrath of one more country
would be thirsting for their blood. . . . And
strangely enough the Saint laughed again.

He took the time from his watch and made a rapid
mental calculation. If Monty had wasted no unnecessary minutes, he should be less than a quarter
of an hour behind them—so long as the car he had
chosen hadn't elected to break down. Given luck
and a warm engine, he might be even closer than
that; and it was essential for the Saint to be waiting
for him when he caught up. Simon looked at the road

on either side hurtling beneath him at sixty miles an hour, and decided against any attempt to step quietly off and send the prince his compliments by post. But he glimpsed a milestone skimming by which indicated only two kilometers more to Jenbach; and he realized that, much as he was still enjoying his little joke, the time had come to share its beauties with the prince.

He drew the gun from his pocket, wriggled to the edge of the roof, and took leisurely aim at the centre of the near-side rear mudguard. The rap of his gun was drowned in the explosive flattening of the tire, and the car listed over and lost speed bumpily.

Simon dropped lightly off behind it just before it stopped. He coiled himself down in the shadow of the hedge two yards away, and watched the chauffeur run round and peer at the pancaked wheel. The chauffeur felt it and prodded it, and went back to describe its devastating flatness to the prince. The prince climbed out. He also peered at the wheel and prodded it. It was indubitably flat.

"It must have been a nail in the road, *Hoheit*," said the chauffeur.

The prince stood absolutely still, looking down the road along the bright beam of the headlights. For a time he made no answer. It was in that time that a lesser man would have been fuming and cursing impotently, but the prince might have been a man carved in stone. There was something terrifying in his inhuman immobility.

When he spoke, his voice was perfectly level—as level and measured as a flow of molten lava.

"Change the wheel."

The words fell through the air like glistening globules of acid; and then the Saint judged that a few

lines of cheery chatter might relieve the tenseness of
the dialogue.

He stepped out into the dim glow of the tail light,
with his automatic ostentatiously displayed, and
cleared his throat.

The two men by the car whirled round as if they
had been stabbed with electric needles. And the
Saint smiled his most winning smile.

"Dear me!" he murmured. "Isn't it odd how we
keep running up against each other? You know, if we
go on like this, you'll begin to think I'm following
you about."

Slowly the prince relaxed. For the moment even
his tempered nerves must have been shaken by the
uncanny promptness of the Saint's return. But even
while he relaxed, his face remained set in a stony
mask in which only the eyes seemed alive.

"I cannot think how we missed you, my dear Mr.
Templar," he said quietly. "Has your car also met
with an accident?"

"My car is yours," said the Saint lavishly. He
grinned gently at the prince's moveless puzzlement.
"To tell you the truth, old dear, it always was. And
while we're on the subject, in case you should be
thinking of giving me a lift some other time, I wish
you'd have something done about that roof. A couple
of good strong coffin-handles would make a heap of
difference; and if you had enough money left after
that to stand me an air-cushion——"

"So!" There was a gleam like the lustre of white-
hot metal in the prince's narrowed eyes, and the
same lustrous malignity in his soft utterance of that
trenchant syllable. "Do I understand that you have
been with us all the time?"

Simon nodded.

"Sweetheart, I hope you do." He smiled again, with captivating sweetness. "Well, well, well—we none of us grow younger, do we? But how the old Borstal boys will chortle over this! Turn round, Rudolf, and let me have your gun—there's a nasty look in your eye which makes me think you might do something foolish at any moment."

He whizzed the prince's automatic neatly from his pocket and went on to disarm the chauffeur in the same way. With their artillery transferred to his own person, he leaned on the side panel of the limousine and regarded the two men affectionately.

"This has been what I call a really jolly little evening," he drawled. "I suppose we've all lost a certain amount of sleep, but you can't have it both ways." He tapped the strong-box which he carried under his left arm. "Would you like me to send you a price catalogue of the boodle when I've had time to look it over? You might like to buy one of the items as a souvenir."

For a while the prince stared at him in silence. And then he also smiled.

"You win, my dear Mr. Templar. Accept my congratulations." After a moment's hesitation, he drew a crocodile-skin case from his breast pocket. "If I were not afraid you would laugh at me," he said apologetically, "I should ask you to accept a cigar as well."

"Don't tempt me, Rudolf," said the Saint amiably. "You know my sense of humour."

The prince laughed.

"All the same," he said, "I wish you could believe that there are depths of childishness to which even I have not yet descended." He extended the case diffidently. "In the circumstances, this is the only sporting gesture I can make."

Simon glance down disparagingly.

And at that instant, before he could make a movement to protect himself, a jet of liquid ammonia struck him squarely between the eyes, and everything was blotted out in an agonizing intensity of blindness. It seared his eyeballs like the caress of red-hot irons, and his gasp of pain sucked the acrid fumes chokingly down into his lungs. He staggered sideways and fired twice as he did so; and then the gun was torn out of his hand and he was flung to the ground under a crushing weight.

A vise-like constriction of thick, powerful fingers fastened on his windpipe. He struck out savagely and tore at the throttling hands; but he was half paralyzed with pain, and his chest seemed to be filled with nothing but the stinging vapour of ammonia. The blood roared in his ears, and he felt everything receding from him. . . .

And then he heard the prince's infinitely distant voice.

"That will be sufficient, Ludwig."

Almost imperceptibly, it seemed, the pressure was loosened from his throat, and the air flowed back into his lungs. The weight lifted from his chest, and he rolled away with his hands covering his eyes.

Presently, out of the spangled darkness, he heard the prince speaking again.

"An unfortunate necessity, my dear young friend. I have never felt comfortable in such a position as the one in which you place me. But your distress, I assure you, is only temporary."

Simon lay still, with his lungs heaving. He heard

the striking of a match and thought he could distinguish the light of it from the pungent flashes of colour that kaleidoscoped across his optic nerves.

"I think you had better enter the car," said the prince urbanely—and Simon could visualize him vivdly, with his cigarette glowing in the long jade holder and his dark eyes satirically veiled. "I fear that your present attitude might provoke undue curiosity."

It was the chauffeur who dragged Simon to his feet and hustled him into the limousine.

The Saint went without resistance. He knew the futility of squandering any more of his strength at that moment, while he was still half blinded and unarmed. He allowed himself to be bundled roughly into a corner, and felt the prince's weight sinking onto the cushions beside him, and the muzzle of the prince's gun thrusting into his ribs. And then the Saint managed to open one of his twingeing eyes, and saw the lights of a car coming down the road.

2

"I need not bother to tell you," murmured the prince's velvety intonation, "what would happen if you were so unwise as to endeavour to attract attention."

Simon said nothing.

The headlights of the approaching car shone straight into the limousine, bathing the tableau in a garish blaze. Certainly there was nothing whatever about it to arouse suspicion. Prince Rudolf and the Saint, two amicable orphans of the storm, were patiently waiting to continue their fraternal journey; what time their chauffeur, diligently bent double

over the hind quarters of the chariot, was working to
repair the mishap that had delayed them. A mournful and pathetic scene, no doubt, but by no means so
uncommon that it should have imbued the innocent
wayfarer with anything but thankfulness for his own
better fortune. . . . And yet the other car was slowing up as it went past them, and through the rear
window of the limousine they could see it pull in to
the side of the road a few yards further on. . . .

Prince Rudolf looked at the Saint again, and
spilled a short cylinder of ash deliberately into the
tray beside him.

"If this should be your friend," he said, "your
actions will have to be extraordinarily discreet."

A man was walking towards them from the other
car. As he drew nearer, a glint of light shimmered on
his helmet and flickered over the trappings of his
uniform. He came to the side of the limousine and
opened the door, standing stiffly in the opening. His
face was in the shadow.

"Entschuldigen Sie mich, mein Herr—"

The Saint never moved a muscle; and yet the
whole of his inside was singing. For the stilted accent was impeccable, but the voice was Monty
Hayward's.

"Excuse me, sir, but do you know this man?"

He addressed the prince, and indicated Simon
with a curt movement of his head. The prince smiled
faintly.

"I cannot say," he answered, "that he is a friend of
mine."

"Your name, please?"

The prince took out his wallet and extracted a
card. Monty carried it to one of the side lamps and
studied it. When he came back, he clicked his heels.

"I beg your Highness's pardon. Perhaps your Highness does not know the identity of his guest?"

"I should like to be informed."

"He is a desperate criminal who calls himself the Saint. He is wanted on many charges. He has already to-night thrown three detectives into the river."

For a fraction of a second the prince paused.

And then, with a deprecatory shrug, he showed his gun.

"I am not surprised," he said calmly. "As a matter of fact, he has also attempted to rob me." He placed one hand on the strong-box which lay on the seat beside him. "I have some family heirlooms with me which would naturally attract a thief of his calibre. But happily my chauffeur and myself were able to overpower him. We were about to take him to the Polizeiamt; but possibly you could save us the trouble."

Simon had to admire the consummate skill with which the part was played. It was an accomplished feat of impromptu histrionics which won the unstinted applause of his artistic soul. The prince was a past master. His unruffled frankness, his engaging modesty, his felicitous rendering of the whole poise of royalty accidentally embroiled in the sordid excitements of common lawlessness—every delicate touch was irreproachable.

Again Monty clicked his heels. The Saint knew that he had had three years at Bonn in which to perfect his German; but this performance revealed a new Monty Hayward, in the guise of yet another gifted actor lost to the silver screen.

"I shall be honoured to relieve your Highness of further inconvenience."

And then the Saint pushed himself forward.

"It is nothing but lies!" he protested furiously. "His Highness is attempting to rob me. That box is mine. I can take you to his Highness's castle and show you things that will make you believe me——"

"Silence!" thundered the policeman magnificently. "It will not help you to insult the nobly born." He turned to the prince. "Your Highness shall not be troubled any longer."

The prince produced a couple of notes from his wallet.

"You will understand," he said, "that I do not wish for any vulgar publicity."

The policeman bowed.

"It is understood. Your Highness's name need not be mentioned. I am proud to have assisted your Highness." He turned again to the Saint. "Outside, you scum!"

"But, for God's sake, listen!" cried the Saint desperately. "Will you not understand that if you let his Highness go, I shall never see my property again? At least you must take him to the Polizeiamt with me, so that the ownership of the box can be properly settled——"

"The ownership of the box is settled to my satisfaction," said the policeman stoically.

Simon clenched his fists.

"But that is only right!" he said, with savagely direct emphasis. "You cannot take me without the box. I have risked everything to keep it!"

"It will be no use to you in the prison," replied the policeman imperviously. "Will you come outside or must I take you?"

"I refuse——"

Simon stopped short. The policeman's revolver was pointed menacingly at his chest.

"Heraus!"

The Saint grabbed the gun and hurled the policeman back. And then the chauffeur's muscular arms wound round his own below the elbows. While they swayed and struggled in the road, he felt two bands of steel snapped on his wrists. Then he was released. He stood wrestling with the handcuffs while the policeman went back to the door of the limousine.

"Your Highness's servant."

The policeman returned. He seized the Saint by the shoulder and pushed him roughly onwards. Fuming and cursing the Saint suffered himself to be manhandled back to the waiting automobile. He was forced into the front seat. The policeman stepped in beside him and took the wheel. The car, with its engine still running, went into gear and gathered speed.

They had travelled a mile before the Saint spoke.

"The hell of a fine partner in crime you are," he said sourly.

Monty kept his eyes on the road.

"And a hell of a fine crook you are," he said acidly. "If this is your usual form, it beats me why there's ever been any fuss about you at all. It's a wonder they didn't lock you up the day after you stole your first sixpence. That's what I think about you. You prance about and get into the most hopeless messes, and expect me to get you out of 'em——"

Patricia leaned over from the back seat.

"Don't you see, boy? We had to get you away somehow, and Monty did the only thing he could. I think he worked it marvellously."

Simon hammered the handcuffs on his knee in a frenzy.

"Oh, Monty was wonderful!" he exploded bitter-

ly. "Monty was Mother's Angel Child! Make your
getaway at any cost—that's Monty. Throw up every
stake in the game except your own skin. Damn the
boodle that we've all been chancing our necks
for——"

"It'll do you good," said Monty. "Next time, you
won't be in such a hurry to get your friends into
trouble."

"But—damn your daft eyes! We had the game in
our hands!"

"What game? What is this boodle that all the
shindy's about, anyway? You keep us up all night
chasing that wretched little box, and I don't suppose
you've any more idea what's inside it then I have.
For all you know, it's probably a couple of floating
kidneys."

Simon sank back in his corner and closed his eyes.

"I can tell you what they were. I've seen 'em.
They're the larger half of the Montenegrin crown
jewels. They disappeared on their way to Christie's
six weeks back. I was thinking of having a dart at
them myself. And we could have had 'em for the
asking!"

"They wouldn't be any use to me," said Monty,
unmoved. "I've given up wearing a crown." He
locked the car round a corner and drove on. "What
you ought to be doing is thanking God you're sitting
here without a bullet in you."

Simon sighed.

"Oh, well," he said—"if you don't want any boodle, that's O.K. with me."

He twisted his hands round and gazed moodily
upwards at the stars.

"You know," he said meditatively, "it's extraordinary what bloomers people make in moments of

crisis. Take dear old Rudolf, for example. You'd
think he'd have remembered that even when you
shut a combination lock that's just been opened, you
still have to jigger the wheels round to seal it up.
Otherwise the combination is still set at the key
word. . . . But he didn't remember, which is
perhaps as well."

And Simon Templar took his hands from his coat
pocket; and the car swerved giddily across the road
as Monty Hayward stared from the scintillating
jumble of stones in the Saint's hands to the laughing
face of the Saint.

6

HOW MONTY HAYWARD SLEPT UNEASILY, AND SIMON TEMPLAR WARBLED ABOUT WORMS

"NEXT on the left is ours," sait the Saint mildly. "I don't think we'll take the corner till we get there, if it's all the same to you."

Monty straightened the car up viciously within a thumb's breadth of the ditch, and slackened the pressure of his foot on the accelerator. His eyes turned back to the road and stayed there ominously.

"Let me get this clear," he said. "Are you telling me that you've still got the whole total of the boodle?"

"Monty, I am."

"And the Crown Prince is chasing back to his *schloss* with an entirely empty box."

"You said it."

"So that apart from the police being after us for assault, battery, murder, and stealing a car, your pal Rudolf will be turning round to come after us and slit our throats——"

"And with any luck," supplemented the Saint cheerfully, "Comrade Krauss will also be raising dust along the warpath. I left him with a pretty easy getaway in front of him; and if he roused up at any time while the complete garrison was occupied with the business of hallooing after me, the odds are that he made it. Which ought to keep the entertainment from freezing up."

This third horn on the dilemma was new to Monty and Patricia. Simon Templar explained. He gave a vigorously graphic account of his movements since he had left them to paddle their own canoes at the Königshof, and threw in a bald description of the mediæval sports and pastimes at the Crown Prince's castle which sent a momentary squirm of horror creeping over their scalps. It took exactly five lines of collocution to link up Comrade Krauss with the man who had vanished from the fateful Room Twelve above the Saint's own suite; and then the whole tangled structure of the amazing web of circumstance in which they were involved became as vividly apparent to the other two as it was to the Saint himself. And the Saint chuckled.

"Boys and girls, my idea of a quiet holiday is just this!"

"Well, it may be your idea of a quiet holiday, but it isn't mine," said Monty Hayward morosely. "I've got a wife and three kiddies in England, and what are they going to think?"

"Wire 'em to come out and join you," said the Saint dispassionately. "We may be wanting all the help we can get."

Monty glowered along the track of the headlights, holding the car steadily on its northward course. They had whizzed through Maurach while Simon was talking, and now they were speeding up the eastern shore of the Achensee. The moon had come up over the mountains, and its strengthening light burnished the still waters of the lake with a sheen like polished jet. Far beyond the lake, behind the black hump of the nearer slopes, an ice-capped peak reared its white head like an enormous beacon, towering in lonely magnificence against a vivid gun-metal sky, so brilliant and luminous that the six forlorn lights that burned in Pertisau looked like ridiculous yellow pinpoints beneath it, and their trailing reflections in the water seemed merely niggling impertinences. The night had put on a beauty that was startling, a splendour that only comes to the high places of the earth. The Saint was filling his eyes. It was a night such as he had seen high up in the Andes above Encantada, or again on the Plateau d'Alzo in the heart of Corsica, where the air may be so clear that the mountains ten miles away seem to be leaning over to fall upon you on the broad ridge that will bring you presently to the Grotto des Anges. The queer streak of paganism in him that took no count of time or occasion touched him with its spell. Patricia was unlocking the handcuffs from his wrists; as they fell away, she found her hands caught in one of his.

"The crown of the world," he said.

And, knowing her man, she understood. The clear blue of the night was in his eyes, the gorgeous madness that made him what he was thrilled in his touch. His words seemed to hold nothing absurd, nothing incongruous—only the devil-may-care attar of Saintliness that would have stopped to admire a view on the way to its own funeral.

She smiled.

"I love you when you say things like that," she said.

"I never have loved him," said Monty Hayward cold-bloodedly; "but I might dislike him a little less if he left off gaping at the scenery and told us where we're supposed to be making for."

Simon lighted a cigarette and inspected his watch under the shielded bulb on the dash. He leaned forward, with his face chiselled out in lines of gay alertness, and his mouth curved to a smile.

"The frontier, of course," he said. "That's the first move, anyway; and praise the Lord there's only a few miles to go. Besides, it might have the practical advantage of keeping the cops a little way behind. You wouldn't believe how I'm devoted to the police, but I don't think we want to get intimate with them to-day."

He had begun to work away on the jewels while he talked. With the blade of his pocketknife he was prising the stones loose from their settings and spilling them into a handkerchief spread out on his lap. Under his swift fingers, rubies, pearls, sapphires, and diamonds cascaded down like drops of frozen fire, carelessly heaping themselves into a coruscating little molehill of multicoloured crystals which the Saint's expert eye valued at something in the neighborhood of a cool quarter of a million. The Maloresco emeralds flopped solidly onto the pile, ruthlessly ripped from their pendant of gold filigree—five flawless, perfectly matched green lozenges the size of pigeons' eggs. A couple of dozen miscellaneous brilliants and three fifty-carat sapphires trickled down on top of them. The Ullstein-bach blue diamond, wedding gift of the Emperor Franz Josef to the Archduke Michel of Presc, slumped into the cluster with a shimmer of azure flame. It went on until the handkerchief was sagging under the weight of a scintillating pyramid of relucent wealth that made even Simon Templar blink his eyes. Shorn of their settings, the stones seemed to take on a lustre that was dazzling—the sheer lambent effulgence of their own naked beauty.

But these things he appreciated only transitorily, much as a surgeon can only transitorily appreciate the beauty of a woman on whom he has been called to perform an urgent operation. And the same unswerving professional thoroughness was visible in the way he wielded his knife, deftly twisting and cutting away the priceless metal-work and flicking it nonchalantly over the side of the car. Every setting was a work of art, but that very quality made each one too distinctive to be trusted. The size and perfection of the jewels themselves were more than hall mark enough for the Saint's unobtrusive taste in articles of vertu; and, besides, the settings were three times as bulky as the gems they carried. With the frontier only a few minutes distant, Simon Templar felt in his most unobtrusive mood. The speed and skill with which he worked were amazing: he had scarcely finished his cigarette when the last scrap of fretted gold vanished into the darkness, and the accumulation was complete.

He looked up to find Patricia staring at the stones over his shoulder.

"What are they worth, boy?" she whispered.

The Saint laughed.

"Enough to buy you a new pair of elastic-sided boots and an embroidered nightcap for Monty," he said. "And then you could write two cheques for six figures, and still have enough change left to stand yourself two steam yachts and a Rolls. That is, if you could sell the loot in the open market. As things are, Van Roeper'll probably beat me down to a lousy couple of million guilders, which means we shall have to pass up one of those cheques and Monty's nightcap. But all the same, lass, it's Boodle with the peach of a B!"

He knotted the corners of his handkerchief diagonally over the spoils, tested the firmness of the bundle, and tossed it effervescently into the air. Then it vanished into his pocket, and he helped himself to another cigarette and settled down in his corner to enjoy the drive.

Monty Hayward was the only one who seemed to have escaped the Saint's own contagious exhilaration. He concentrated his eyes on the task of guiding the car and thought that it was all a pretty bad show. He said so.

"If you'd only left that jewellery as it was, you chump," he said—having only just thought of it himself—"we might have been able to tell the police we'd found it on the road and were on our way to return it."

Simon shook his head.

"We couldn't have told them that, Monty."

"Why not?"

"Because it wouldn't have been true," answered the Saint, with awful solemnity.

"You owl!" snarled Monty Hayward; and relapsed into his nightmare.

It was a nightmare in which he had been groping about for so long that he had lost the power of protesting effectively against anything that it required him to do. Presently, at the Saint's bidding, he stopped the car for a moment while he removed his police uniform, which went into the nearest clump of bushes. Then he suffered himself to be told to drive unhesitatingly up to the frontier post which showed up in the glare of their head-lights a few minutes later, where he obediently applied his brakes and waited in a kind of numb resignation while the guards stepped up and made their formal inquisitions. Every instinct that he possessed urged him to turn tail and fly—to leap out of the car and make a desperate attempt to plunge unseen into Germany through the darkness of the woods on their left—even, in one frantic moment, to let in the clutch again and smash recklessly through the flimsy barrier across the road into what looked like unassailable security beyond. That he remained ungalvanized by all these natural impulses was due solely to the paralytic inertia of the nightmare which had him inextricably in its grip. His, it appeared, not to reason why; his but to sit still and wait for somebody to clout him over the bean—and a more depressing fate for anyone who had passed unscathed through the entire excitement of the last war he found it difficult to imagine. He sat mute behind the wheel, endeavouring to make himself as invisible as possible, while the Saint exhibited passports and answered the usual questions. The Saint was as cool as a cucumber. He chattered affably throughout the delay, with an impermeable absence of self-consciousness, and smiled benignly into the light that was flashed over them. The eternity of prickling suspense which Monty Hayward endured passed over the Saint's unruffled head like a soothing zephyr; and when at last the signal was given and they moved on, and the Saint leaned back with a gentle exhalation of breath and searched for his cigarette case, his immutable serenity seemed little less than a deliberate affront.

"I suppose you know what you're doing, brother,"

said Monty Hayward, as quietly as he could, "but it seems pretty daft to me."

"You bet I knew," said the Saint, and to Monty's surprise he said it just as quietly. "It was simply a matter of taking a chance on the clock. If you hadn't hit that cop at the Königshof quite so hard, it wouldn't have been so easy; but we had to hope we were still a length or two in front of the hue and cry. There's no point in jumping your fences before you come to them. But, believe me, I had that patrol covered from my pocket the whole time, and what might have happened if we'd been unlucky is just nobody's business."

Monty Hayward readjusted his impressions slowly and reluctantly. And then suddenly he shot one of his extraordinarily keen glances at the sober face of the man beside him—a glance that was tempered with the ghost of a smile.

"If we kept straight ahead and drove in relays," he said, "we might make the Dutch frontier to-day. But one gathers that it wouldn't be quite so simple as that."

"Solomon said it first," assented the Saint bluntly. "We shan't take any more frontiers in our stride, and I don't think we shall enjoy much more friendly flapjaw with the constabulary. That was just our break. But there won't be a policeman in Central Europe who doesn't know our horrid histories by lunchtime; and if our pals among the ungodly can't raise a fleet of cars with the legs of this one you may call me Archibald. You were thinking we'd finished—and we've only just begun!" All at once the Saint laughed. "But shall I tell you?"

Monty nodded.

"I'll give you a new angle on the life of crime," said

the Saint lavishly. "I'll hand it you for nothing, Mont—the angle that your bunch of footling authors never get. Every one of 'em makes the same mistake, just like you made yourself. Take this: Any fool can biff a policeman on the jaw. Every other fool can swipe a can of assorted *bijouterie* that's simply dropped into his lap. And any amount of mutts can throw a bluff that'll get by—once, for a ten-minute session. Believe it or not. And then you think it's all over bar the anthem. But it isn't. It's only just started on its way."

Monty accepted the proposition without comment. After a moment's consideration, the uncompromising accuracy of it was self-evident.

He drove on in silence, squeezing the last possible kilometer per hour out of the powerful engine. From time to time he stole a glimpse at the driving mirror, momentarily expecting to see the darkness of the road behind bleached with the first faint nimbus of pursuing headlights. It was strange how the intoxication of the chase, following on the turbulent course of that night's unsought adventure, had sapped his better judgment—stranger still, perhaps, how the foundations of his cautious common sense had been undermined by so much eventful proximity to a man whom in normal times he had always regarded as slightly, if quite pleasantly, bugs. The rush of the wind stroked his face with a hypnotic gentleness; the hum of the machine and the lifting sense of speed soothed his conscience like an insidious drug. For one dizzy moment it seemed to him that there must be worse ways of spending a night and the day after it—that there were more soul-destroying things in a disordered world than biffing policemen on the jaw and flying from multiple vengeance on the hundred horses of a modern highwayman's Mercedes Benz. He thought like that for one moment of incredible insanity; and then he thought it again, and decided that he must be very ill.

But a tincture of that demoralized elation stayed with him and lent an indefinable zest to the drive, while the sky paled for the dawn and the stolen car slid swiftly down the long slopes of the Bavarian hills towards Munich. Beside him, Simon Templar calmly went to sleep. . . .

The rim of the sun was just topping the horizon, and the air was full of the unforgettable sweet dampness of the morning, when the first angular suburbs of the city swam towards them out of the bare plain; and the Saint roused and stretched himself and felt for the inevitable cigarette. As the streets narrowed and grew gloomier, he picked up his bearings and began to direct the edging of their route eastward. It was full daylight when they pulled up before the Ostbahnhof, and an early street car was disgorging its load of sleepy workmen towards the portals of the station. Simon swung himself over the side and piled their light luggage out on the pavement. He touched Monty on the shoulder.

"I think we're a bit conspicuous as a trio," he said. "But if you hopped that street car it'd take you to the Hauptbahnhof, and the Metropole is almost opposite. We'll see you there."

And once again Monty Hayward found himself alone. He made his way to the hotel as he had been instructed, and found Patricia and the Saint waiting for him. Monty felt a little bit too tired to argue. Left to himself, he would have kept moving till he dropped, with the one idea of setting as many miles as possible between his own rudder and the wrath to come. And yet, when he rolled into bed half an hour later, he had a comfortable feeling that he had earned his rest. There is something about the lethargy of healthy physical fatigue, allied with the appreciation of dangers faced and survived, a sense of omnipotence and recklessness, which awakes the springs of an unfathomable primitive contentment; something that can stupefy all present questions along with all past philosophic doubts; something that can wipe away the strains of civilized complexity from a man's mind, and give him the peace of an animal and the sleep of a child.

Monty Hayward would have slept like a child if it had not been for the endless stream of street cars, which thundered beneath his window, rattling in every joint, clanging enormous bells, blowing hooters, torturing their brakes, crashing, colliding, spraying their spare parts onto large sheets of tin, and generally straining every bolt to uphold the standard of nerveshattering din of which the continent of Europe is so justly proud.

He surrendered the unequal contest towards midday and went in search of a bathroom. Shaved and dressed, and feeling a little better, he descended on the dining room in the hope of finding some relics of breakfast with which to complete the restoration of his tissues; and his apologetic order had scarcely been executed when the Saint sauntered in and joined him, looking so intolerably fresh and fit that Monty could have assaulted him.

"Get those *Spiegeleier* inside you quickly, old lad," he said, "and we'll be on our way again."

"Have you pinched another car?" asked Monty

resignedly. "And if so, what was wrong with the last one?"

Simon laughed.

"Nothing. Only stolen cars are notified, and that never makes things easier. Besides which, it isn't every day that you knock off a car complete with its tryptique and general documents of identity, and if you hadn't pulled off that fluke yesterday we should have had a long walk from the frontier. No—I've been over to the station and unearthed a pretty good train, and I don't see why we should turn it down."

Monty carved an egg.

"Where's Pat?"

"Having breakfast in bed. She was asleep when I went out."

"She must be stone deaf," said Monty, glumly. "No one who wasn't could sleep here in the daytime. There were four thousand trams outside my room, and they took every one of them to pieces. I think they used several large hammers and a buzz-saw. Then they threw all the bits through the window of a china-shop and laughed like hell." Monty Hayward sliced a rasher of bacon with meditative brutality and finished the dish in silence. "Where do we go to-day?" he inquired.

"Cologne," said the Saint. "Where they make the *Eau*." He was lighting a cigarette and gazing into the mirror on the wall above Monty's head, watching the two men who had just entered the room. They were, in their way, a brace of the most flabbergasting phenomena that he had seen for a long while; and yet they oiled into the inexorable scheme of things with a smoothness that was almost wicked. And the Saint's face was utterly sterile of emotion as he tacked onto his opening announcement the one sweeping qualification that the arrival of those two men implied. "If we get away at all," he said.

2

With the cigarette slanting between his lips and a slow drift of smoke sinking thoughtfully down into his lungs, Simon Templar lounged back in his chair and watched the two detectives coming up behind him.

The convex surface of the ornamental glass condensed their imposing figures into the vague semblance of two trousered sausages seen through the wrong end of a telescope; but even so, the grisly secret of their calling was blazoned across their bosoms in letters that the Saint could read five hundred yards away with his eyes closed. That was the one disastrous certainty which emerged unchallenged from the chaotic fact of their arrival. Not once since the first instant when they had bulked ponderously through the doors of the deserted *Speisezimmer* had the Saint allowed himself to luxuriate in any sedative delusions about that. When one has played ducks and drakes with the Law for ten hectic years, and, moreover, when one has been fully occupied for the last three of those years with the business of being the most coveted fox in the whole western hemisphere, one's nose becomes almost tediously familiar with the scent of hounds. And if ever the Saint had sniffed that piquant odour, he could smell it then—one breast-high wave of it, which spumed aromatically past his nostrils with enough pungency to make a salamander sneeze.

How those detectives had got there was still an

inch or two beyond him. Granted that in the last twelve hours the purlieus of Innsbruck had been the location of no small excitement, in the course of which a quite unnecessary little man had been violently shoved on out of this world of woe, and an unfortunate misunderstanding had caused the three policemen who should have arrested him to be dumped painfully into the cold waters of the Inn— granted, even, that the estimable Monty Hayward was most unjustly suspected of having personally shoved on the aforesaid little man, and was most accurately known to have taken part in the assault and bathing of the police, to have subsequently assaulted one of them a second time, to have appropriated his uniform, and to have stolen a large car— well, a few minor disturbances like these were a small price to pay for the quarter of a million pounds' worth of genuine crown jewels. And the Saint had most emphatically done his best to avoid any superfluous unpleasantness. His mind flashed back over the details of the getaway; and at the end of the flash he had to admit that the Law was playing a fast ball. Their passing had been reported from the frontier, of course, as soon as the alarm was raised: that was inevitable; but after that the trail should have petered out—for several hours, anyway. A police organization which, in the short time that had been at its disposal, could discover an abandoned car, and then, by an essentially wearisome system of exhaustive inquiries, could trace its fugitive passengers through the separate and devious routes which they had taken to the hotel, argued that somewhere in Munich there were a few devoted souls with no little energy left over from the more important business of assimilating large quantities of Löwenbräu. It ar-

gued a strenuous efficiency that was as upsetting as
anything the Saint had seen for many years.

Across the table, Monty Hayward was staring at
him puzzledly, with the last fork-load of egg and
bacon poised blankly in midair. And then, for a
second, his gaze veered over the Saint's shoulder;
and he began to understand.

The Saint's eyes tore themselves away from the
queer fascination of the mirror. On its surface the
figures of the men behind had swollen in grotesque
distortion, until he knew that they were only a yard
or two away. He felt their presence even more vividly after he had ceased to watch them, in an infinitely gentle little shiver that twitched up his back as
if a couple of spiders had performed a rapid polka
along his spine. It slithered coldly along his gan-
glions in a tingle of desperate alertness, an instinc-
tive tautening of nerves that was beyond all human
power to control.

He took the cigarette from his mouth and looked
Monty Hayward squarely in the face. Within that
yard or two of where they sat, the menace of the Law
had loomed up again, with a suddenness that took
the breath away—a menace which it had always
been so fatally easy to forget, even if the Saint himself had never quite forgotten. And Monty Hayward
looked back at a man who, in some guises, still
seemed a stranger to him. The Saint's eyes were as
hard as flints, cold and blue and mercilessly clear;
and yet somewhere in their grim depths there was a
tiny glitter like shifting sunlight, a momentary
twinkle of mockery that loved the wild twists of the
game for their own sake.

"For many years, Monty," said the Saint very
quietly and distinctly, "I've been meaning to tell you

the Illuminating History of Wilbraham, the Wonderful Worm. Wilbraham was in the very act of
becoming the high tea of a partridge named
Theobald, when the cruel bird was brought down by
a lucky shot from the gun of a certain Mr. Hugglesboom, who was a water-diviner by profession and
generally considered to be eccentric. I said a lucky
shot, because Mr. Hugglesboom believed that he
was aiming his weapon at a rabbit that was nibbling
his young lettuces. On retrieving the bird, Mr.
Hugglesboom discovered Wilbraham in its beak.
Being a kind-hearted gentleman, he released the
unhappy reptile; and he would have thought nothing more about it, if Wilbraham had not had other
views. Wilbraham, in fact, being overcome with
gratitude to his deliverer, followed Mr. Hugglesboom home, and showed such symptoms of devotion that Mr. Hugglesboom's heart was touched. A
lonely man, he adopted the small creature, and
found much companionship on his solitary travels,
in which Wilbraham would follow him like a faithful
dog. Shortly afterwards Wilbraham thought that he
might assist Mr. Hugglesboom in his work. He took
it upon himself to spy out, by tireless burrowing, the
land which his master was commissioned to survey;
with the result that in course of time Mr. Hugglesboom attained such eminence in his vocation——"

Monty Hayward's face had run through a se-
quence of expressions that would have made a movie
director skip like a young ram with joy; and then it
had gone blank. The meaning and purpose of that
astonishing cascade of imbecility were utterly
beyond him. There came to him the hysterical belief
that Simon Templar must have gone suddenly and
irrevocably haywire. The strain of recent happen-

ings had been too much for a brain that had never in its life been truly stable.

He looked up dumbly at the two men who were now standing by the Saint's oblivious shoulder, and in their faces he saw the beginnings of an answering blankness that fairly kicked him between the eyes. It was so staggering that for a space of time he doubted the evidence of his own senses.

And then it dawned upon him that the two men were also listening, and at the same time running through a gamut of emotions similar to his own. As the Saint's beautifully articulated phrases reached their ears, their heavy-footed and purposeful advance had waned away. They had ended up behind the Saint's chair as if they were walking over pins; and there they stood, with their mouths hanging open, sucking in his driveling discourse with both ears. Their awed entrancement was so obvious that for an awful interval Monty Hayward began to wonder whether after all it was his own brain that had slipped its trolley.

"The climax came," said the Saint, with that flute-like clarity which did every single thing in its power to render the words comprehensible to anyone whose knowledge of English might leave much fluency to be desired, "at a garden party organized by Lady Tigworthy, at which Mr. Hugglesboom was to give a demonstration of his art by finding a receptacle of water which had been carefully hidden in the grounds. Keeping his usual rendezvous behind the refreshment tent, Mr. Hugglesboom was duly accosted by a worm who gave him explicit instructions; and shortly afterwards, being a dim-sighted man, he faithfully made his find directly over a shiny pink globe which showed on the lee side of a grassy knoll.

This was discovered to be the head of Lord Tigworthy, who was enjoying an afternoon siesta. Mr. Hugglesboom was expelled from the fête in disgrace; and the worm, which was reclining in an intoxicated condition under the tap of a barrel of mild ale, was thrown after him. It was not until he reached home that Mr. Hugglesboom perceived that this worm was not Wilbraham"—the Saint was looking Monty rigidly in the eyes—"but *Wilbraham's twin brother,* who, filled with jealousy of his luckier relation, had gone out of his way to discredit an unblemished record of unselfish service. Mr. Hugglesboom——"

Behind him, one of the detectives cleared his throat apologetically, and the Saint glanced round.

He glanced round absolutely at his leisure, as if he were noticing the presence of the detectives for the first time. He did it as if they meant nothing whatever in his life, and never could—with a smilingly interrogative composure which cost him perhaps more effort than anything he had done in the last twenty-four hours.

The detective coughed.

"Excuse me, gentlemen," he said, in excellent English. "I am a police officer, and I have to ask you to give an account of yourselves."

Monty Hayward had an insane desire to laugh. The contrast between the detectives' confident march across the room, and the almost ingratiating tone of that opening remark, was so comical that for a moment it made him forget the tightness of the corner from which they had still to make their getaway.

Coolly the Saint shifted his chair round, and waved an obliging hand.

"Sit down, Sherlock," he murmured, "and tell us all your troubles. What's the matter—has somebody declared war, or something?"

Somewhat uncertainly the detective lowered himself into a seat, and after a second's hesitation his companion followed suit. They looked at one another dubiously, and at length the spokesman attempted to explain.

"It is in the matter of a crime that was committed in Innsbruck last night, *mein Herr*. We received proof that the criminals had reached Munich, and afterwards we believed that we had traced them to this hotel. Their descriptions were telegraphed to us from Innsbruck. You will pardon me, gentlemen, but the resemblance . . ."

Simon raised his eyebrows.

"Good Lord! D'you mean we're going to be arrested?"

His startled innocence was beyond criticism. Every line of it was etched into his face and his voice with the touch of a consummate artist. And the detective shrugged.

"Before I spoke to you, I permitted myself to listen to your conversation. I hoped to learn something that would help us. But after I had listened——"

"As far as I remember," said the Saint puzzledly, "I was beguiling the time with a highly moral and uplifting anecdote about a worm named——"

"Vilbraham?" suggested the detective, with a tinge of humour in his homely features. "I admit I did not appreciate all the—the——*die Bedeutung*—the what-do-you-say of the story?" He looked appealingly at the Saint, but Simon shook his head. "It is not important. But it is my experience that a man who had committed a crime so soon ago, and who would expect every minute to be arrested, would not talk like that. His mind is too worried. Also you did not translate *die Bedeutung* for me, which would have been very clever of you if you were one of the criminals, because both of them speak German like I do."

Simon gazed at him with admiration.

"That was cunning of you," he said ingenuously. "But I suppose that's part of your job." He dropped his cigarette into a coffee cup and beckoned a passing waiter. "Have a spot of Schnapps and let's see if there's anything we can do to clear up the difficulty."

The detective nodded.

"You have your passports?"

The Saint took a blue booklet from his pocket and dropped it on the table. The detective turned courteously to Monty Hayward. Something hard was jabbing into the side of Monty's thigh; he slipped his hand quite naturally under the table and grasped it. He was wide awake now; the whole purpose of the Saint's two-edge bluff was plain to him, and his brain was humming into perfect adaptation.

He slid the passport round behind him and produced it as it from his hip pocket. Where it had come from he had no idea, and he had even less idea what information it contained; but he watched it across the table while the detective turned the pages, and gathered that he was George Shelston Ingram, marine architect, of Lowestoft. The photograph was undoubtedly his own—he recognized it immediately as the one from his own passport, and the evidence of the Saint's inexhaustible thoroughness amazed him. The Saint must have put in an hour's painstaking work before breakfast on that job alone, faking up the missing part of the Foreign Office embossments which linked the photograph with the new sheet on which it had been pasted.

The examination was concluded in a few minutes, and the detectives returned the passports to their respective claimants with a slight bow.

"I have apologized in advance," he said briefly. "Now, Mr. Ingram, will you please tell me your recent movements? One of our men saw you at the Ostbahnhof this morning, besides the one who happened to see you arrive at the hotel. They remembered you when the descriptions were received; and it was near the Ostbahnhof that the car in which our criminals escaped was found."

"I think I can explain that," Monty answered easily. "I've been walking around the country in this neighbourhood, and last night I ended up at Siegertsbrun. After dinner I had a telegram from my brother asking me to meet him in Munich this morning, and saying it was a matter of life and death. So after thinking it over I caught a very early train and came straight here."

"Your *brother?*"

The detective seemed suddenly to have gone out of control. He sat forward as if he could scarcely contain his excitement. And Monty nodded.

"Yes. He's my twin. If you didn't grasp the point of my friend's story, I can tell you that he was being extremely rude."

"*Donnerwetter!* And where would he meet you—*Ihr Herr Bruder?*"

"He said he'd meet me here at ten o'clock; but he hasn't turned up yet——"

"You have this telegram?"

"No—I didn't keep it. But——"

"From where was it despatched?"

"From Jenbach." Monty's resentment had plainly been boiling up against the hungry rattle of questions, and at that point he exploded. "Damn it, are you suggesting that my brother is a crook?"

The detective hunched his shoulders. An inscrutable hardness had crept in under the amiable fleshiness of his face. He retorted with the dehumanized bluntness of official logic.

"It is a matter of probability. You are so much alike. Also this telegram was sent from Jenbach, where the criminals have last been seen. For them it is certainly a matter of life and death."

In the silence that followed, the waiter returned and set up the drinks which had been ordered. Simon flicked a note onto his tray and dismissed him with curt gesture. He slid the glasses round in front of the detectives and looked from them to Monty and then back again.

"This is serious," he said. "Are you quite sure you haven't made a mistake?"

"That is to be discovered. But it is strange that Mr. Ingram's brother has not yet arrived."

The reply was unexceptionably polite. And just as incontestably it declined to be drawn into abstract argument. It slammed up one stark circumstance, and invited explanations that would convince a jury—nothing less.

Simon took a fresh cigarette from the packet on the table and slouched back in his pew, watching the two detectives like a hawk. There was not an atom of tension in his poise, not one visible quiver of a muscle to flash hints of danger to a suspicious man, and under the smooth, level brows his eyelids drooped no more than thoughtfully against the smoke; but behind that droop the eyes were alive with frozen steel. His right arm was crooked lazily round the chair back, but the hand hung less than an inch from his gun pocket.

"It does seem odd," he drawled.

The keen gaze of the detective who had done all the talking searched his face.

"Were you travelling with Mr. Ingram?" he inquired.

"Yeah."

The Saint picked up his glass and turned the stem between his fingers. The hand that held it was rockfirm, and he returned the chief detective's direct stare without a tremor; and yet his heart was putting in perhaps two extra beats per minute above its normal rhythm. He knew to the millionth part of an inch how slender was the thread by which their getaway still hung. The crisis of their bluff was pelting into them with less than a handful of split seconds left to run—and he had known all the time that it was coming. It had been on its way from the first word with all the inevitability of an inrushing tide. Simon had expected nothing else. He had won the only stakes it had been played for—the fifteen minutes' grace which had been given, the awakening of doubts in the detectives' minds, the vital cue to Monty and the two police officers sitting there quietly at the table.

"You came here from Siegertsbrun together?"

The eyes had never wavered from the scrutiny. Neither had Simon Templar's.

The Saint raised his glass.

"Cheerio," he said.

Almost mechanically the other groped around and

took up his own drink. His colleague did the same. Both of them were looking at the Saint. He could see the ideas that were working simultaneously through their minds. They had recovered from the first stunning confusion of the bluff, and now in the reaction they were thinking on top gear—turning the defense over under the searchlights of habitual incredulity, probing remorselessly into its structure, reading behind it into the balance of probabilities.

And yet they drank. They ignored the customary clinking of glasses, and their perfunctory bows were so slight as to be almost imperceptible.

"Ihre Gesundheit!"

Simon put down his glass and drew thoughtfully on his cigarette. At that moment he could have laughed.

"No, brother," he said gently. "We missed Siegertsbrun. But we had a swell time in Innsbruck." He smiled sweetly at the startled bulging of the detectives' eyes, and on the tablecloth their empty glasses seemed to rise on tiptoe and cheer for him. "It's been lovely meeting you, and I hope this chat won't get you into trouble at headquarters."

The nearest man half rose from his chair, and the Saint stepped swiftly up and caught him as he went limp.

Simon wrung him affectionately by the hand. He slapped him on the back. He gripped him by the shoulders and bade him an exuberantly· cordial farewell. And in so doing he settled the man carefully back into his chair, lumped him forward, propped his chin up on his hand, and left him huddled in a lifelike pose of contemplation.

"Be good, brother," said the Saint, "and remember me to auntie. Give my love to Rudolf"—out of the corner of his eye the Saint saw that Monty had arranged the other detective in a similar position—"and tell him I hope it chokes him. Tootle pip."

They walked quickly across the dining room and paused to glance backwards from the door. The two detectives at the far corner table, with their backs turned to the room, appeared like a couple of Bavarian Buddhas wrapped in immortal meditations.

Simon smiled again.

"Such is life," he whispered.

Then he moved out into the vestibule. As they emerged into the hall the Saint glanced casually about him, and in that same casual way his glance rested for a long moment on the back of a man who was leaning over the janitor's desk by the main doors. He was talking earnestly to the head porter, and a long jade cigarette holder was tilted up in the fingers of one sensitive white hand.

7

HOW SIMON TEMPLAR BORROWED A CAR AND AGREED TO BE SENSIBLE

SIMON'S long arm shot out and grabbed Monty by the shoulder, halting him in his stride and spinning him half round. The Saint's eyes were debonair.

"Steady, old scout," murmured the Saint blithely. "This is where you go home!"

Monty's brow crinkled. And the Saint laughed. The laugh was almost silent; and not one syllable of what he said could have been heard a yard away.

"Buzz up and collect Pat and all the luggage," said the Saint quietly. "Get down by the fire escape— you're good at that. And I'll see you at the station." He jerked a thin sheaf of reservations from his pocket and thrust them neatly into Monty's hand. "If you want to know why, you can peep back on your way up the stairs. You might even listen for a bit— but I shouldn't wait too long. The train goes in fifteen minutes. Happy landings!"

The same shoulder-hold sped Monty on; and the Saint circled slowly on his heel and continued his stroll across the floor.

Looking back from a flight of stairs that was partly screened by the iron grille of the elevator shaft, Monty had an angle view of him coming up behind the man who was still standing by the porter's desk. The Saint's hands were in his pockets, and his step was airy. He stopped just one pace from the desk, and his voice floated softly up across the hall.

"What ho!" said the Saint.

The man at the desk turned.

It was typical of his iron self-restraint that he placed the tip of the long cigarette holder between his teeth before he moved. He turned round without a trace of hurry or excitement, and his recognition of the Saint was the merest flutter of a pencilled eyebrow.

"My dear Mr. Templar!"

The Saint's hands sank deeper into his pockets.

"My dear Rudolf!" There was a suggestion of sardonic mimicry in the Saint's reply, "Are you staying here?"

The cigarette glowed evenly in its jade setting.

"I was looking for a friend," said the Crown Prince.

Simon gazed at him mockingly. He had hardly expected to renew his acquaintance with the prince quite so soon; and yet the conversation he had had with the detectives who now slept peacefully in the dining room had illuminated many mysteries. It had indicated, amongst other things, that Rudolf was a worker with a classic turn of speed in his own class—if the Saint had required any enlightenment on that subject. Certain facts had been mentioned in that conversation which could never have been known to the police without Rudolf's assistance. And Simon was wondering what new subtleties were being corkscrewed into the delicate tangle—what new stratagems were unwinding themselves behind the statuesque placidity of the smiling chevalier opposite him. But the Saint's face showed nothing.

"Have you any friends?" he asked guilelessly.

The prince laughed. He took Simon engagingly by the arm.

"There is a quiet corner over there where we can talk. It would be worth your while."

"D'you think so?" drawled the Saint.

He sauntered indulgently towards an alcove adorned with three glass-topped tables and a litter of old newspapers, and the prince stayed beside him. As they went, the Saint sidled an eye up the stairway and saw that Monty had disappeared. In the same glance, the hands of a clock hanging on one wall came into his field of view; and the position of them printed itself on his memory in a sector of remorseless warning. Two minutes had ticked by since he left the dining room, which gave him six minutes more at the outside before the effects of the dope which had splashed a lurid semicolon into the purplest passage of the official pursuit would be wearing off—even if no interfering waiter uncovered the deception before that. Six hazardous minutes in which to squeeze what he had to learn out of the brain of that man of polished marble, and to select his own riposte. . . . And then Simon felt the light hand of the prince stroking up inside his arm into his armpit and slipping back to his elbow just as lightly, and he knew that the possible hiding-places for jewels on his own person had been comprehensively investigated. Rudolf also had much to learn. It would be a cake-walk of a race with a whirlwind sprint at the finish, but the Saint could find nothing to complain about in that. He chuckled and sank into an armchair.

"Must you do these things?" he inquired mildly. "You know, I'm rather ticklish, and I might scream."

The prince settled down and crossed his legs.

"You must not let me detain you too long," he remarked solicitously. "Your time must be valuable."

"Have you anything really interesting to say?" murmured the Saint bluntly.

The prince looked at him.

"This is the third time that you have chosen to meddle in my affairs, Mr. Templar. I have told you before that your persistence might compel me to think of methods of permanent discouragement. Believe me, my dear friend, it will only be your own obstinacy which may cause me to take steps which I should genuinely regret."

"Such as—handing over the vendetta to a couple of overfed policemen? You don't know how disappointed I am about you, Rudolf."

"That was an unfortunate necessity. You had to be found without delay, and the police have facilities which are denied to ordinary people like ourselves."

The Saint smiled.

"I see. While you hang around in the offing as the righteous citizen what's been robbed. Well, well, Rudolf," said the Saint tolerantly, "the notion was passably sound, though I won't say I hadn't heard of it before. And what would you have done if I'd actually been collared with the boodle—gone home and burst into tears?"

"That possibility had been considered," admitted the prince calmly. "In fact, I had anticipated it. You may have forgotten that my name carries some weight in this country. I do not think I should have found my task difficult." He shrugged. "But you were always enterprising, my dear Mr. Templar."

"That past tense makes me feel all Tolstoy," said the Saint plaintively.

The prince fingered his moustache.

"You are the unknown quantity which is always disconcerting," he said; and Simon blew out two leisured smoke rings.

"Have you lost your voice, Rudolf?"

"Why?"

"There must be some more policemen in Munich. From what I've seen I shouldn't think there was room for many, but you might find one or two. You could try yodelling for 'em."

"I doubt whether that would be so expedient," said the prince, tapping a length of ash from his cigarette—"now that we know that the jewels are no longer in your possession."

Simon sat up. That was a new one on him— straight from the bandbox and dolled out with ribbons. It caught him slap in the middle of his complacency and made him blink.

"Yeah?" he said automatically. "I haven't seen any corpses carried out."

"Would that be a corollary?"

"It would be if any of your birds tried to go scratching round my room. There's not only two guns in it—there's a girl who can shoot the pips out of a razzberry keeping 'em warm, and she doesn't sleep on her feet. Now think up something else that'll cure hiccoughs!"

The prince showed a glimmer of pearly teeth.

"In that case," he said imperturbably, "we must feel thankful that the porter is an observant man with a good memory."

"Meaning exactly?"

"You went out at eleven o'clock this morning with a parcel, and you came back without it."

Simon raked him with crystalline blue eyes. He

had an instant recollection of the scene in which he had surprised the prince, and in the same flash he understood the significance of it. The very words that must have been spoken trickled almost verbatim through his imagination. His Sublime Eminence's dear young friend had promised to deliver a small package for him. It was vitally important that it should be sent off before midday. Had anything been done about it? The package would be about so big. His dear young friend was inclined to be forgetful. Could the porter remember if he had seen the gentleman leaving the hotel with such a package as had been described? . . . The interrogation would have been simplicity itself to a man of the Crown Prince's magnetic geniality, once he had realized that such a contingency was on the cards. And if it had proved fruitless there would have been no harm done. Mentally the Saint raised his hat to that effort of inductive speculation.

"I won't deceive you," said the Saint. "We have ceased to hold the baby."

"Others have also found it dangerous," murmured the prince.

"That's just how it struck me," said the Saint with equanimity. "So I got rid of it. I went out and bought three fat packets of German cigarettes. I came home and loaded the swag into 'em, and jammed it tight with cotton wool. I tied the boxes up in brown paper and stuck on a label. And then I went out and shoved the whole works into the post office across the way—just ordinary parcel post, and no registration or anything. It'll be waiting for me where I want it." The Saint pushed his hands back in his pockets and stared at the prince seraphically through a veil of smoke. "Got any more to say?" he purred.

Up on the wall the clock gathered its creaking springs and chimed the quarter. The margin of time was closing in; and Simon had learned nearly everything he required to know. There was only one thing more to come—an inkling of the counter attack which must have been spinning its swift web between the lines of that entertaining little chat. And the Saint was keyed up for it like a tiger crouching for the kill.

The Crown Prince leaned forward.

"My friend, we are in danger of cutting our own throats. You have disposed of the jewels temporarily, but you will have still to recover them. It would be awkward for you if you were arrested—and I admit that it would be inconvenient for me. For the time being we have your interests in common. And yet you must acknowledge that you have not one chance in ten thousand of making your escape."

"That sounds depressing," said the Saint.

"It is a matter of fact. In England you have your Scotland Yard, which is the model of the whole world. Perhaps you are tempted to think that our European police organizations are inferior. You would be foolish—very foolish. You have many hundreds of miles still to travel, and every frontier will be watched for you. Every mile, every minute, will see the dice loaded more heavily against you. You have temporarily disposed of the detectives who were sent here; I do not ask how you accomplished it, but I assure you they were only a beginning. Our police do not easily forget being made to look stupid. Your arrest will be a point of honour with every detective in Germany."

"Well?"

Simon's prompting monosyllable rapped into the

prince's silence like the crack of an overstrained fiddle string.

The prince tapped his cigarette holder thoughtfully on a pink-tinted thumbnail. He met the Saint's eyes with a survey of deliberate appraisal.

"I offer you an alliance. I offer you protection, hiding, influence, a practical certainty of escape. I have told you that in this country I am a person of some importance. Mr. Templar, we have been enemies too long. I offer you friendship and security—at the price of a division of the spoils."

The Saint's eyes never moved; but his lips smiled.

"And how would this partnership begin?" he queried.

"My car is outside. It is at your disposal. I promise you safe conduct out of Munich—for yourself and your friends."

For two seconds the Saint gazed at the red tip of his cigarette, with that tentative half-smile playing round his mouth.

And then he screwed the cigarette into an ash tray and stood up.

"I think I should like to use your car," he said.

He drifted towards the street doors with his quick, swinging stride, and the prince went beside him. As they stepped out into the blazing sunshine of the Bayerstrasse the Saint's hardened vigilance scanned the street, left and right, expertly dissecting the apppearance of every loiterer within sight. He eliminated them all. There was a man selling newspapers, another sweeping the street, a one-armed beggar with a tray of toys, a weedy specimen idling in front of a shop window—no one who could by any stretch of imagination be invested with the

aura of bullnecked innocence which to the initiated
observer fizzles like a mantle of damp squibs around
the elaborately plain-clothed man in every civilized
corner of the globe. It was just a little more than the
Saint had seriously hoped for: it showed that the full
measure of his iniquity had not yet been fully revealed to the phlegmatic myrmidons of the German
police, and in any other circumstances he would
have felt that the fact paid him no compliments. He
had been ready for further opposition—squads of
it—and his right hand had never left the gun in his
pocket. The risk had to be taken.

"You are very wise," said the prince suavely.

Simon nodded curtly, without turning his head.

His eyes swept the car that was drawn up by the
curb with its engine pulsing almost inaudibly—an
open, cream-coloured Rolls, upholstered in crimson
leather, with the Crown Prince's coat of arms displayed prominently on the coach work. A liveried
chauffeur held the door open—Simon recognized
him as the man who had done his best to strangle
him in the dark hours of that morning, and favoured
him with a ray of that slight, sweet smile.

"Let me drive," said the Saint.

He twitched the door from the man's hand and
slammed it shut. In one more smooth movement he
whipped open another door and dropped into the
driving seat.

As he flicked the lever into gear, the man's hand
clutched his shoulder. For an instant Simon let go
the steering wheel. With the faintest widening of
that Saintly smile, the Saint's steely fingers brack-
eted themselves lovingly round the man's promi-
nent nose and flung him squealing back into the

prince's arms. A second later the car was skimming down the street under the flanks of the most startled tram in Munich.

2

The journey which Monty Hayward made from the hotel to the station was one which he ranked ever afterwards as an entirely typical incident in the system of unpleasantness which had enmeshed him in its toils.

It would have made his scalp crawl uneasily even if nothing had happened to disturb his breakfast; but now the certain knowledge that his description had been circulated far and wide, and that it was graphic enough for him to have been identified from it three times already, made any excursion into the great outdoors seem tantamount to a lingering mortification of the flesh. He was certain to be hanged anyway, he felt, and it seemed painfully unnecesary to have to keep pushing his head into a series of experimental nooses just to get the feel of the operation.

Patricia laughed at him quietly. She produced one of the Saint's razors.

"You'll look quite different without your moustache," she said, "and horn-rimmed glasses are a wonderful disguise."

Monty scraped off his manhood resignedly. He went out into the brightness of the afternoon with many of the sensations of a man who dreams that he is rushing through a crowded street with no trousers on. Every eye seemed to ferret out his guilt and glare ominously after him; every voice that rang out a semitone above normal pitch seemed like a yell of denunciation. His shirt clung to him damply.

If there were no detectives posted anywhere along the short route they had to take, there were two at the platform barrier. They stood beside the ticket inspector and made no attempt to conceal themselves. Monty surrendered the suitcases he carried into the keeping of a persistent porter and looked hopelessly at the girl. With their hands free, they might stand a chance if they cut and run. . . . But the girl was stone blind to his mute entreaty. She dumped her bag on the porter's barrow and strode on. A touch of black on her eyebrows, and an adroit use of lipstick, had created a complete new character. She walked right up to the ticket inspector and the two detectives, and stood in front of them with one arm akimbo and her legs astraddle, brazening them through tortoise-shell spectacles larger even than Monty's.

"Say, you, does this train go to Heidelberg?"

"*In Mainz umsteigen.*"

"Whaddas that mean, Hiram?"

Her accent would have carved petrified marrowbones. It was actually one of the detectives who volunteered to interpret.

"In Mainz—exchange trains."

"*Bitte, die Fahrkarten,*" said the inspector stolidly.

Monty swallowed, and delved in his pocket for the reservations.

They were passed through without a question. Monty could hardly believe that it had been so simple. He stood by and watched the amused porter stowing their bags away in the compartment, tipped him extravagantly, and subsided weakly into a corner. He mopped his perspiring forehead and looked at Patricia with the vague embryo of a grin.

"Do you mean to tell me this is a sample of your everyday life?" he asked.

"Oh, no," said the girl carelessly. "Sometimes it's very dull. You just happen to have dropped into one of the high spots."

"It must be an acquired taste."

Patricia laughed, and passed him her cigarette case.

"You're having the time of your life, really, if you'd only admit it. It's a shame about you, Monty—you're wasted in an office. Simon would give you a partnership for the asking. Why don't you stay in with us?"

"I think I am staying in with you," said Monty. "We shall probably go on staying together—in the same clink. Still, I'm always ready to listen to any proposals you have to make." He struck a match and held it out for her. "Are you included in the good-will of the business?"

She smiled.

"I might let you hold my hand sometimes."

"And I suppose as a special treat I could kiss your toes when I'd murdered someone you didn't approve of."

"Maybe you might even do that."

"Well," said Monty definitely, "I don't think that's nearly good enough. You'll have to think of something much more substantial if you want me to be tempted."

The girl's blue eyes bantered him.

"Aren't you a bit mercenary?"

"No. It's the Saint's fault for leaving us alone

together so often. I assure you, Patricia, I'm not to be trusted for a minute."

"We'll ask Simon about it," said the girl wickedly, and stood up.

She went over to the window and glanced up and down the platform. Her watch showed less than a minute to the time they were scheduled to start: already the crowd was melting into its compartments, doors were being slammed, and the late arrivals were scurrying about to find their seats. . . . Behind her, a benevolent old clergyman with a pink face and white side-whiskers stopped in the doorway and peered round benignly: Monty leered at him hideously, and he departed. . . . An official came in and checked their tickets without paying them the least attention. . . .

Patricia was tapping one sensibly rounded brogue on the low heel of the other. She turned and spoke over her shoulder:

"Any idea what can have kept him?"

"I could think of several," said Monty, with a callousness which scarcely attempted to ring true. "The silly mutt ought to have got away with us instead of hanging around talking to Rudolf. Personally I'd rather sit down and talk to a rattlesnake."

"He had to find out what game Rudolf was playing," said the girl shortly; and at that moment a shadow fell across them and they both turned round.

Simon Templar stood before them—the Saint himself, with one long arm reaching to the luggage rack and his feet braced against the preliminary jolting of the train, gazing down at them with a wide, reckless grin. Even so it was a second or two before they recognized him. A white straw hat was tilted onto the back of his head, and a monocle in his right

eye completed the amazing work of wiping every
fragment of character from his face and reducing the
features to amiable vacuity. A large carnation
burgeoned in his buttonhole, and his tie was pulled
into a tight knot and sprung foppishly forward from
his neck. Patricia had actually seen him at the far end
of the platform and dismissed him without further
thought.

"Hail, Columbia," said the Saint.

Monty Hayward recovered magnificently from
his surprise.

"Go away," he said. "I thought we'd got rid of you.
We were just getting along splendidly."

The Saint stared at him rudely.

"Hullo," he said. "What's happened to your little
soup strainer? I always told you something would
happen if you didn't keep moth balls in it."

"It was removed by special request," said Monty,
with some dignity. "Pat told me it tickled."

"But what have you been doing?" asked the girl
breathlessly.

The Saint laughed and kissed her. He chucked his
straw hat up on the rack, loosened his tie, put the
monocle away in his pocket, removed the flower
from his coat and presented it exquisitely to Monty,
and flung himself loosely into a corner seat, long-
limbed, and piratical and unchangeably
disturbing—taking Patricia's cigarette from her lips
and inhaling from it between merry lips.

"I've been keeping the ball rolling and adding
another felony to our charge sheet. Rudolf knows
that the boodle is now in the post—he'd done a few
calories of hot thinking and spooned the confirmation out of the head porter. I didn't dispute it. Then
he offered to join forces and halve the kitty—told me

we hadn't a hailstone's break in hell of making the grade alone. Well, the time was getting on, and I'd got to shake him off somehow. He told me his car was outside and it was mine if I cared to go in cahoots with him, so I told him quite truthfully I should love to borrow it. I think he must have misunderstood me, somehow, because we went out together, and he was quite shocked when I simply stepped in and drove away. I ran around a couple of blocks into a quiet street behind the station, and bailed out when no one was looking. Then I went through a shop and brought that lid, and an old woman sold me the veg for two marks because she said I'd a lucky face. And—do you know, Monty?—I believe I have!"

Monty nodded.

"You'll need it," he said decisively. "If Rudolf catches you again I should think he'll roast you over a slow fire."

"He's likely to try it," said the Saint lightly. "But d'you know what it was worth? . . . My villains, think of the situation! Right now we've got Rudolf —got him as he's never been got in his life before. He knows the boodle hasn't gone out of Germany—I couldn't have risked it, because it might have been opened by the Customs. His one hope is to trail me and watch me collect my mail. *And the worst thing that could possibly happen to him would be to get us into more trouble with the police!* Whatever we said to his proposition, he was doomed to move heaven and earth to keep the paws of the police from our coat collars, because once we were in jug the boodle'd be lost forever. He's got to take everything we give him. We can shoot up his staff—pinch his cars—pour plates of soup down his dicky—and he's got to open his face from ear to ear and tell the world how he loves a good joke!" Simon rolled over on one elbow and thumped Monty in the stomach. "Boys and girls—do you like it?"

The other two sorted his meaning gradually out of that jubilant cataract of words. They analyzed and absorbed it while he laughed at them; and then, before they could marshal their thoughts for a reply, he was raiding and scattering them again with a fresh twist of mountebank's magic.

"You two were followed to the station. Rudolf's pals were snooping round the hotel, even if they thought it was safer to stop outside. You can take it that a guy who could deduce the whole idea of shooting boodle into the post office would have his own notions about fire escapes. That little runt we laid out in the Königshof last night is on the train, and I'll bet he trod in on your heels. The one thing I'm wondering is whether he had time to get a message back before we pulled out." Simon was radiant. "And now try some more. Have you heard the new scream about the bishop?"

"Bishop?" repeated Monty feebly.

"Yep. And for once there's no actress in it——"

He broke off as a large-bosomed female burdened with two travelling rugs, a Pekinese, and the words of Ethel M. Dell threaded herself through the door and deposited herself in the vacant corner. The Saint glared at Monty and waved his arms wildly in the air. He raved on as if he had not noticed the intrusion.

". . . and you *would* be locked up if I had my way. You ought to have gone to the hospital. I should think if the authorities knew you were tearing around like this with a dose of scarlet fever they'd clap you straight into an asylum. And what about me? Did I tell you I wanted to catch all your diseases——"

A muffled yelp wheezed out of the strong, silent corner, and the Saint started round in time to see a black bombazine rump undulating agitatedly out of view. Simon settled himself back and grinned again.

"Bishop?" Monty encored hazily. The pace was a bit rapid for him.

"Or something like it. But you must have seen him. Bloke with a face like a prawn and white fur round his ears. Damn it, he was rubbering in here a few minutes back! I was dodging him in and out of lavatories all down the train, which is why I didn't join you before—him and Rudolf's five feet of stickphast. Well, I can tell you where I last saw Prawn-face. He was lashed to a chair in the Crown Prince's *schloss* with that hellish screw tightening into his skull—being invited to open his strong-box and disclose the sparklers. That parson is Comrade Krauss, the bird who first lifted that packet of jewels and began the stampede!"

Patricia recaptured the remains of her cigarette.

"One minute, boy. . . . No—he couldn't have recognized Monty and me. He's never been near us in his life. And you dodged him. . . . But how did he get here?"

"Made his getaway in the confusion, as I expected he would. And if any man's got a right to be thirsting for Rudolf's blood, he has. Why he should be on this particular *schnellzug* is still more than we know— unless maybe he overshot the mark thinking we'd got farther ahead than we have. We shall know soon enough. If this journey is peaceful I shall have lived in vain."

The prospect appeared to please him. Nothing

was more certain than that he was in the one element for which he had been born: the delight of it danced in those rakehell blue eyes—the eyes of a king in his own kingdom.

"What do we do?" asked Patricia.

She asked it from her own corner, with her hands tucked in the broad leather belt of her tweed costume. It was a swashbuckler's belt with a great silver buckle, an outrageous belt, a belt that no lady would have dreamed of wearing; and she looked like a scapegrace Diana. She asked her question with long, slim legs stretched out and her fair head tilted rather lazily back on the cushions, with a hint of the same laziness in her voice—perhaps the most obvious thing she could have said, but it made Monty Hayward fill his eyes with her, belt and all. And the Saint pulled her hair.

"What do we do, lass?" he challenged. "Well, what's wrong with a little tour of inspection? I could just do with a glimpse of the ungodly gnashing their teeth to give me an appetite for lunch."

"What's wrong with sitting where we are?" replied Monty reasonably. "We aren't getting into mischief. You could spend several hours working out how you're going to get me across the next frontier and take the jewels with you as well. And by the way, where *are* the ruddy things?"

"They'll be waiting for us at the *poste restante* in Cologne—where moth and rust may corrupt, but Rudolfs will have a job to break through and steal."

Monty scratched his head.

"I'm still trying to get that clear," he said. "What have you done with them?"

"Bunged 'em into the post, laddie—all done up in brown paper, with bits of string and sealing wax and everything. As I told Rudolf. They're on their way now—they might even be on this very train—but there's no detective on earth who could prove now that I've ever had anything to do with them. Even if he thought of looking for them in the right place. In this game the great idea is to have brains," said the Saint modestly.

Monty digested the pronouncement with becoming gravity. And then Patricia stood up.

"Let's go, boy," she said recklessly; and the Saint hauled himself up with a laugh.

"And shall we dally with the archdeacon or gambol with the gun artist?"

He framed the question in a tone that required no answer, balancing himself easily in the swaying carriage, with a cigarette between his lips and one hand shielding his lighter—he was as unanswerable as a laughing whirlwind with hell-for-leather blue eyes. He was not even thinking of alternatives.

And then he saw the hole that had been bored through the partition on his left—just an inch or two below the mesh of the luggage grid.

The raw, white edges of it seemed to blaze into his vision out of the smooth, drab surface of the varnished woodwork, pinning him where he stood in a sudden hush of corrosive immobility. Then his gaze flicked down to the half-dozen fresh white splinters that lay on the seat, and the smile in his eyes hardened to a narrow glitter of steel.

"Or should we just sit here and behave ourselves?" he murmured; and the change in his voice was so contrasting that the other two stared at him.

Monty recovered the use of his tongue first.

"That's the most sensible thing I've heard you say for a long time," he remarked, as if he still doubted whether he should believe his ears. "You can't be feeling well."

"But, *Simon*—"

Patricia broke in with a different incredulity. And the Saint dropped a hand on her shoulder.

His other hand went out in a grim gesture that travelled straight to the hole in the partition.

"Let's keep our heads, Pat." The smile was filtering back into his voice, but it was so gentle that only the most sensitive ear could have picked it out. "Monty's the moderating influence—and he may be right. We don't want to make things unnecessarily difficult. There's a long journey in front of us, and I'm not sure that I should object to a little rest. I'm not so young as I was."

He subsided heavily into his corner with a profound sigh; and the visible part of his audience tore their eyes from the tell-tale perforation in the wall and looked at him in the tense dawning of comprehension.

"Good-night, my children," said the Saint sleepily.

But he was reaching to his feet again as he said it, and there was not a trace of sleepiness in one inch of the movement. It was like the measured straightening of a bent spring. And it was just as he came dead upright that a dull thud seemed to bump itself on the partition, clearly audible above the monotonous rattling of the wheels.

"And happy dreams," said the Saint, in the softest of all whispers.

He slid out soundlessly into the corridor. Down towards the end of it he saw the back of a man lurching from side to side in a clumsy attempt to run, and instinctively the Saint's step quickened. Then he glanced sidelong into the next compartment as he passed it—he was merely satisfying a professional desire to see the other end of the listening-hole which had tapped through into his private business, but what he saw there made him pull up with his fingers hooking round the edge of the sliding door. Without another thought he shot it back along its grooves and let himself in. He went in quietly and without fear, for the eyes of the man who was crumpled up in the far corner looked at him with the calm greeting of one who has already seen beyond the Curtain. It was Josef Krauss, with one hand clutched to his side and the grey pallor of death in his face.

8

HOW SIMON TEMPLAR CONTINUED TO BE DISCREET, AND MONTY HAYWARD IMPROVED THE SHINING HOUR

SIMON TEMPLAR pulled the door shut behind him and went over to the dying man. He started to fumble with the buttons of the stained black waistcoat, but Krauss only smiled.

"*Lassen Sie es nur*," he said huskily. "It is not worth the time. The old fox has finished his journey."

Simon nodded. The first glance had told him that there was nothing he could do. He sat down beside the stricken thief and supported him with an arm round his shoulders; and Krauss looked at him with the same calm and patient eyes.

"I have only seen you once before, Herr Templar. That was when you saved me from the screw." A shiver passed over the man's bulky frame. "If I had lived, I should have repaid that kindness by robbing you. You know that?"

"Does it matter?" asked the Saint.

Krauss shook his head. There were beads of perspiration starting through the pink grease paint on his face, and each breath cost him an effort.

"Now the time is too short for these things," he said.

Simon eased him up a few inches, settling him

more comfortably into the corner. He knew that the end could be no more than a few minutes away, and he had time to spare. The man who had fired the shot, whose back he had seen scuttling down the corridor, could wait those few minutes for his turn. However the killer might choose to dispose of himself meanwhile, he would still be available when he was wanted unless he elected to step right off the train and break his neck. And the Saint would watch the old fox creep into the last covert, according to the rules of the game as he knew them. It had never occurred to him to refuse the unspoken appeal that had leapt at him out of the doomed man's weary eyes as he sidled that casual glance into the compartment; and yet he never guessed on what a strange twist of the trail that unthinking chivalry was to lead him.

He looked at the litter of curled wood shavings on the opposite seat, and then up at the partition.

"I suppose you heard all you wanted to?" he said.

The reply came as a surprise to him, in a wry grin that warped its way across the man's face of bitter fatalism.

"I heard nothing, *mein lieber Freund.* Marcovitch heard—that little cub of the young jackal. If my gun had not stuck in my pocket you would have found him here instead of me."

"He was listening here when you found him?"

"*Ja.* And I think he has heard too much. You had better kill him quickly, Herr Templar—he will be troublesome."

Krauss coughed painfully; and there was blood on his handkerchief. Then he raised his eyes and saw the uniform of another ticket inspector in the corridor outside, and he seemed to smile cynically under his make-up. As the door grated open again he pulled himself together with an effort of will that must have been almost superhuman. It was the most eerie performance that the Saint had ever seen, and it left him dumb with wonder at the magnificent sardonic courage of it.

Krauss jerked himself almost upright in his corner and sat there unsupported, with his hands clasped calmly on his lap. He met the Saint's eyes expressionlessly, and spoke in a voice that rang out oddly with the iron strength of his self-control—a voice that hadn't the minutest tremor in it—as if he were merely setting the trivial capstone on an ephemeral argument.

"After all," he said, "when one is confronted with a summons, one can still pay one's debts with a good grace."

Simon groped around for his ticket and offered it to be clipped.

And Josef Krauss did the same. That was the one simple act with which he paid his debt in the only way that was left to him. He did it with an unflinching rendering of the benevolent and rather fatuous smile that belonged to his disguise, playing out the last lines of his part without a fault, while the hot stab of death seared bitterly into his lungs.

He received his ticket back, and beamed at the inspector.

"We come at half past-eleven to Köln, *nicht wahr?*"

"At eleven thirty-eight, *mein Herr*."

"So. Now I am very tired. Will you have to disturb me at Wurzburg and Mainz?"

A note rustled in his hand, and the inspector accepted it graciously.

"If you will allow me to keep your ticket until after

we have left Mainz, *hochehrwürdener Herr,* I will
see that your sleep is not interrupted."

"Herzlichen Dank!"

The official bowed his way out respectfully—he
had pocketed a tip that would have been notable at
any time, and which became almost an epoch-
making event when the donor's garb confessed to a
vocation whose members are rarely able to compete
with millionaires in purchasing the small luxuries of
travel. The door closed after him; and Simon turned
slowly from watching him go, and saw the dour
fatalism grinning again from Krauss's eyes.

"At least, my death will put you to no inconvenience," he said.

Then the supernatural endurance which had
shored him up through those last minutes seemed to
fall away as if the king-pins had been wiped out of it,
and he sagged back with a little sigh.

Simon leaned over and dried a thin trickle of
blood from one corner of the relaxed mouth. The
glazing eyes stared at him mockingly, and Krauss
fought for breath. He spoke once more, but his voice
was so low that the Saint only just caught the words.

*"Sehen Sie gut nach . . . dem blauen Diamant.
. . . Er ist . . . wirklich . . . preislos . . ."*

Then he was silent.

Simon Templar rose quietly to his feet. He put out
a steady hand and pressed the lids down over the
derisive eyes that had gone suddenly blind and rigid
in their orbits; and then he looked round and saw
Monty Hayward in the doorway. Patricia Holm
came in behind him.

"You know, Simon," said Monty, after a moment's
eloquent stillness, "if you show me a few more stiffs,
I believe I shall begin to get quite used to it."

"I shouldn't be surprised," said the Saint laconically.

He took out his cigarette case and canted a cigarette gently into his mouth, facing the others soberly, while they searched for the meaning of his terseness.

"Did you have trouble with that ticket inspector?" hazarded Patricia.

"Not one little bit." The Saint looked at her straightly. "There wasn't any cause for it. You see, Josef figured he had a bill to pay. He told the inspector he wanted to go to sleep, and tipped him like a prince not to be disturbed till we get to Cologne."

Slowly the other two built up in their minds the full significance of that curt explanation, while the only sound in the compartment was the harsh rattle and jar of their race over the metals. It was a silence which paid its inevitable tribute to the code by which the man in the corner had ordered his grim passing.

"Did Josef make that hole?" queried Monty Hayward presently.

"No. Marcovitch did that—the boy friend who tailed you on board. Josef walked in on him, and lost the draw. The last I saw of Marcovitch, he was busting all records down towards the brake van. And 'I guess he's my next stop."

The Saint pushed his hands into his trouser pockets and walked past, out into the corridor. Patricia and Monty followed him. They lined up outside; and the Saint drew at his cigarette and gazed through a window into the unrolling landscape.

"Not the three of us," he said. "We aren't muscling in. Pat—I think it's your turn for a show. There may be trouble; and the ungodly are liable to be smooth guys before the Lord. I'd like to have you a carriage length behind me. Keep out of sight—and watch your corners. If the party looks tough, beat it quietly back and flag Monty."

"O.K., Chief."

"Monty, you stay around here till you're sent for. Get talking to someone—*and keep talking*. Then you'll be in balk. You're the reserve line. If we aren't back in twenty minutes, try and find out what's wrong. And see your gun's working!"

"Right you are, old sportsman."

"And remember your wife and children," said the Saint piously.

He turned on his heel and went roaming down the train, humming an operatic aria under his breath. The decks were clearing for action in fresh earnest, and that suited him down to the ground. And yet a little bug of vague perplexity was starting to nose around in the dark backgrounds of his brain, nibbling about in the impenetrable hinterlands of intuition like the fret of a tiny whetstone. It blurred fitfully on the tenuous outfringings of a deep-buried nerve, sending dim flitters of irritation telegraphing up into the obscure recesses of his consciousness; and every one of those messages feathered up a replica of the same ragged little question mark into the sleek line of his serenity. Ten times in a minute he glossed the line down again, and ten times in a minute the identical finicky interrogation smudged through it like a wisp of fabric trailed across an edge of wet paint.

Still humming the same imperturbable tune, he came to the end of a coach and eased himself cautiously round into the connection tunnel. With equal caution he stepped across the swaying platforms and emerged circumspectly into the foyer of the next car. Down the length of the alleyway ahead he saw only a small female infant with platinum blonde pigtails, and continued on his way with unruffled watchfulness.

The dying words of Josef Krauss were ticking over in his mind as a kind of monotonous accompaniment to the melody that carolled contentedly along with him as he walked. They repeated themselves in a dozen different languages, word by word and letter by letter, wheeling and countermarching and forming fours in an infinite variety of restless patterns with all the aimless efficiency of a demonstration platoon of trained soldiers—and with precisely as much intelligence. They went through their repertoire of evolutions like a clockwork machine; and it just didn't mean a thing. They ended up exactly where they started: two simple sentences spoken in a voice that had been so weak as to be incapable of expression, qualified by nothing but the enigmatical derision in the doomed man's eyes. Simon could still see those eyes as vividly as if they had been photographed on the air a yard beyond his nose, and the bland, flat gibe in them was the most baffling riddle he had encountered since he began wondering why the female corset should almost invariably be made in the same grisly shade of pink.

Hands still resting loosely in his pockets, Simon Templar continued on his gentle promenade. Nearly every compartment he peered into yielded its quota of specimens for observation, but Marcovitch was not among them. Apart from that serious omission, any philanthropist in the widest sense would have found ample material on which to test the stamina of his eccentric virtue. All along the panorama which unfolded to the Saint's roving eye, other excrescences upon the cosmos roosted at regular intervals in their upholstered pens, each tending his own little candle of witness to God's patronage of the almost human race. Simon looked at them all, and felt his share of the milk of human kindness curdling under the strain. But the second most important question in his mind remained unanswered. It was still probable that Marcovitch was not alone. And if he was not alone, the amount of support he had with him was still an entirely nebulous quantity. The Saint had received no clue by which he could pick out the problematical units of that support from the array of smug bipeds which had passed under his eyes. They might have been there in dozens; or he mightn't have seen one of them yet. There was no evidence. It was a gamble on blind odds, and the Lord would have to provide.

Thus the Saint came through to the end of the last carriage, and still he had not seen Marcovitch. He stopped there for a moment, drawing the last puff from his cigarette and flattening the butt under his toe. One episode in his last adventure in England was still far from fading out of his memory, and the remembrance of it sent a sudden ripple of anticipation pulsing through his muscles. He knew that he had not lost Marcovitch. On the contrary—he was just going to meet him. And most assuredly there would be trouble. . . .

A gay glimmer of the Saintly fighting smile touched his lips. The pain which had afflicted him during his patient survey of so much unbeautiful humanity was gone altogether. He had forgotten the very existence of those anonymous boils on the universe. Just one more stage south of him was the

brake van, and Simon Templar went towards it with
a new unlighted cigarette in his mouth and his hands
transferred to his coat pockets. He could have
reached out and touched the handle when he saw it
jerk and twist under his eyes, and leapt back round
the corner. He had one glimpse of the man who
came stumbling out—a man in the railroad uniform,
capless, with a gash over his temple and his face
straining to a shout of terror. It didn't require any
genius to reconstruct the whole inside history of that
frantic apparition: Simon had no time to think about
it anyway, but he guessed enough without thinking.
The thud of a silenced gun was one of the diverse
incidents that tumbled hectically into one crowded
second of lightning action in which there was positively no time for meditation. In the same second
Simon caught the brakeman by the arm as he flung
past.

"*Verweile doch–du bist zu schnell,*" said the Saint
gently. They were face to face for an instant of time;
and Simon saw the man's eyes wide and staring,
"Let's take a walk," said the Saint.

He screwed the wrist he was holding up into the
nape of the brakeman's neck, and pushed him back
into the van. There was another shot as they came
through, and the man flopped forward like a dead
weight. Simon let go and let him fall sideways. Then
he kicked the door shut behind him and stood with
his shoulders lined up square against it, with his feet
spaced apart and three quarters of his weight balancing on his toes. The cigarette slanted up into a
filibustering angle as he smiled.

"Hullo, Uglyvitch," he said.

Marcovitch showed his teeth over the barrel of an

automatic. There were four other men round him; and the blithe Saintly gaze swept over them in an arc of affectionate greeting.

"Feelin' happy, boys?" drawled the Saint. "It's a grand day for fireworks." He looked past them at the piles of litter on the floor of the van. Every mailbag had been ripped open, and the contents were strewn across the scenery like the landmark of a megalomaniac's paper-chase. Letters had been torn through and parcels slit across and discarded in a search that had winnowed that vanload of mail through a fine-meshed sieve. "Somebody getting married?" asked the Saint interestedly. "Or is the confetti for me?"

There was a tantalizing invitation in the slow lift of his eyebrows that matched the interrogative inflexion of his voice. Quite coolly he sized up the strength of the man before him, and just as coolly he posed himself in the limelight for them to return the compliment. And he saw them hesitate. If he had been blindfolded he could have deduced that hesitation equally well from the one vital fact that he was still alive. The wide smiling insolence of his unblinking candour, the barefaced effrontery of his very artlessness, walked them into that standstill in a way that no other approach could have done. While it lasted, it held them up as effectively as a regiment of Thomson guns. They couldn't bring themselves to believe that there was no more in it than met the eye. It dangled them on red-hot tenterhooks of uncertainty, peeling their eyes sore with suspicion of the trap they couldn't see.

"Well?"

Marcovitch forced the monosyllable out of his

throat in a hoarse challenge that indexed his embarrassment to the last decimal point; and the Saint smiled again.

"This is an auspicious occasion, brother," he remarked amiably. "I've always wanted to know just what it feels like to be a slab-faced little squirt of dill-water with a dirty neck and no birth certificate; and here you are—the very man to tell me. Could you unbosom for us, little flower?"

Marcovitch licked his lips. He was still casting around for the one necessary hint that would give him confidence to tighten up on the trigger of his gun and send an ounce of swift and unanswerable death snarling into the easy target in front of him. His knuckle was white for the pull-off, the automatic trembling ever so slightly in the suppressed tension of his hand.

"What else have you got to say, Templar?"

"Lots. Have you heard the one about the old farmer named Giles, who suffered acutely——"

"Perhaps you were looking for something?"

The question came in a vicious monotone that dared a direct reply. And the Saint knew that his margin of time for stalling was wearing thin as a wafer under the impatient rasp of the Russian's overstressed nerves.

"Sure—I was taking a look round."

He flaunted Marcovitch eye to eye, with that heedless little smile playing up encloudedly to the tilt of his cigarette, and his fingers curling evenly round the grip of his own gun. The twitch of a muscle would have roared finish for Marcovitch in the middle of any one of those sentences; but Simon Templar knew when he was deadlocked. He knew he was deadlocked then, and he had known it ever since he stepped into the van. He could have dropped Marcovitch at his pleasure, but the remaining four men represented just so many odds against any human chance of surviving to boast about it. And the Saint was not yet tired of life. He bluffed the deadlock without turning a hair—smiled calmly at it and asked it to play ball—because that was the only thing to do. Any other line would have sung his requiem without further debate. But he knew that his only way out was along the precarious alleyways of peace with honour—with black italics for the peace, if anything. It was unfortunate, admittedly, but it was one of the immutable verities of the situation. He had breezed in to take a peek at the odds, and there they were in all their mathematical scaliness. A tactful and strategic withdrawal announced itself as the order of the day.

"I just thought I might find some crown jewels," said the Saint; and Marcovitch steadied his automatic.

"Did you?"

Simon nodded. His level gaze slid down the other's coat and detected a bulge in one pocket that signified as much as he required to know.

"Yeah. Only you got here first." Lower down, he caught a gleam of reflected light from the floor. "Excuse me—I think you missed something."

He took a pace forward and stooped as if to pick up the stone.

Then he hurled himself at the knees of the nearest man like the bolt from a crossbow. Marcovitch fired at the same moment, but the Saint's luck held. His impetus somersaulted him clean over the sprawling body of his victim, and he rolled over like a scalded eel and ducked behind the struggling breastwork.

His left hand whipped round the man's waist and fastened on the man's gun wrist, holding him in position by the sheer strength of one arm.

"Sorry about this," said the Saint.

The others paused for a second, and in that breathing space the Saint got to his feet again, bringing his human shield up with him in a heave of eruptive effort. He backed toward the door, reached it, and got it open; then the man half broke from his hold in a flurry of cursing fight, and Simon flung him away and leapt through the door with a bullet crashing past his ear. Patricia Holm was outside, and the Saint caught her in his arms and spun her round before she could speak.

"Run for it!" he rapped. "This is why angels have wings!"

He thrust her on; and then his eye fell on the emergency rescue outfit in its glass-fronted case on the wall beside him. He let go his gun and put his elbow through the glass, snatching the light axe from its braket, and ran backwards with it swinging in his hand. Everything was a matter of split seconds in that extraordinarily discreet getaway, and no one knew better than Simon Templar that only an exhibition of agility that would make cats look silly was going to skin a ninth life out of the hornets' nest that had blown up under his feet. He had been labelled for the long ride from the moment he had entered that raided brake van: the urgent menace of it had been flaming at him through the atmosphere as plainly as if it had been chalked up on the wall. And the Saint felt appropriately self-effacing. . . . As the leading gunman came out of the van, Simon drew back his hand and sent the axe whistling down the corridor in a long, murderous parabola. The man let out an oath and threw up his arms to save his skull —short of committing suicide, he had no option in the matter—and that distraction gave Simon the few seconds' start he needed. He raced up behind the girl and swung her into the nearest compartment, and its solitary occupant looked up from her Ethel M. Dell and displayed a familiar face freezing into a glare of indignant horror.

"Must you follow me everywhere?" she squeaked. "You and your filthy germs——"

"Madam, we were just having a little bug hunt," said the Saint soothingly; and then the woman saw the gun in his hand and rushed to the communication cord with a shrill scream.

Simon grinned faintly and glanced past her out of the window. They were running over a low embankment at the foot of which was a thick wood; he couldn't have arranged it better if he had tried—it was the one slice of luck that had come to him without a string on it that day.

"Saved us the trouble," murmured the Saint philosophically.

He was wedging his automatic at an angle between the sliding door and its frame, so that it pointed slantingly down the corridor. The train was slowing down rapidly, and he prayed that that whiskered gag would get by for as long as they took to stop. Also he had an idea that the alarm given by the frightened lady would push a hairier fly into that ointment of the ungodly than anything else that could have happened.

He looked round and saw the shadow of puzzlement on Patricia's forehead.

"Has anything gone wrong, lad?" she asked; and the question struck him as so comic that he had to laugh.

"Nothing to speak of," he said. "It's only a few rough men trying to kill us, but we've had people try that before."

"Then why did you want the train stopped?"

"Because I want to back Bugle Call for the Derby, and I've heard no news of totes in heaven. I can't think when we've been so unpopular. It seems a lot of fuss to make over one little blue diamond, but I suppose Rudolf knows best."

He went over to the other side of the compartment and opened the window wide. The train was grinding itself to a standstill, and once it came to rest there would be very little time to spare. In one corner, the apostle of strength and silence was clutching her Pekinese and moaning hysterically at intervals. Simon ruffled the dog's ears, hauled himself up with his hands on the two luggage racks, and swung his legs acrobatically over the sill.

2

Monty Hayward was a couple of coaches farther north when the train stopped.

He had begun to drift thoughtfully southward a minute or two after Patricia Holm left him. The Saint's instructions to engage someone in conversation appealed to him. He felt that a spot of light-hearted relaxation was just what he needed. And the orders he had been given seemed to leave him as free a hand as he could have desired. The prospect lifted up his spirits like an exile's dream of home.

He squeezed past a group of chattering Italians

and came up beside the girl who was gazing pensively through a window near the end of the corridor. She moved aside abstractedly to let him pass, but Monty had other ideas.

"Don't you know that policemen get their flat feet from standing about all day?" he said reproachfully.

The girl looked at him critically for several seconds, and Monty endured the scrutiny without blinking. There was a curl of soft gold escaping from under one side of her rakish little hat, and her lips had a sweet curve. And then she smiled.

"Can you tell me what that station was that we just went through?" she asked.

"Ausgang," said Monty. "I saw it written up."

She laughed.

"Idiot! That means 'Way Out.' "

"Does it?" said Monty innocently. "Then I must have been thinking of some other place." He offered his cigarette case. "I gather that this isn't your first visit to these parts."

She accepted a cigarette and a light with an entire absence of self-consciousness, which was one of the most refreshing and at the same time one of the most complimentary gestures that he had seen for a long time.

"I ought to know the language," she said. "My father was born in Munich—he didn't become an American citizen until he was three years old. But still, they say it's a young country." She had a frank carelessness of conventional snobbery that matched her natural grace of manner. "As a matter of fact, I've just finished spending a fortnight with his family. That was the excuse I made for coming over, so I couldn't get out of it."

"My father was a Plymouth Brother," said Monty

reminiscently. "He once thought of going abroad to convert the heathen, but Mother didn't trust him. Now, if he'd been a Bavarian, I might have been your cousin—and that would have been a quite different story."

"Why?"

"I should have refused to allow you to leave us without a chaperon."

"Would you?"

"I would. And then I'd have proposed myself for the job. I'm not sure that it's too late even now. Could I interest you in a thoroughly good watchdog, guaranteed house-trained and very good with children?"

She glanced at him mischievously.

"I should want to see your references."

"I was four years in my last place, lady."

"That's a long time."

"Yes, mum. I was supposed to be in for seven, but there was a riot, and I climbed over a wall."

He was confirmed in an early impression that her laugh was like a ripple of crystal bells. She had very white teeth, and eyes like amethysts, and he thought that she was far too nice to be travelling alone.

She turned back her sleeve and consulted a tiny gold watch.

"Do you think they'll ever serve tea?" she said. "I've got one of the world's great thirsts, and Germany doesn't care."

Monty had a saddening sense of anticlimax. He was starting to realize the sordid disadvantages of being a buccaneer. You can take a beauteous damsel's acquaintance by storm, but you can't offer her a cup of tea. He felt that the twentieth century was uncommonly inconsiderate to its outlaws. He tried to picture Captain Kidd in a similar predicament. "I'd love to buy you a glass of milk, my dear, but Grandma's walking the plank at five. . . ."

"I'm afraid you've beaten me," he said. "I'm not allowed to move from here until Simon gets back."

"And what's Simon doing?"

"Well, he's trying to find some crown jewels; and if he gets shot at I'm supposed to go along and get shot as well."

The girl looked at him with a slight frown.

"That one's a bit too deep for me," she said.

"It's much too deep for me," Monty confessed. "But I've given up worrying about it. I don't look like a desperate character, do I?"

She contemplated him with a renewal of the detached curiosity with which she had estimated his first advance. Her ancestry might have been German, but her quiet self-possession belonged wholly to the American tradition. Monty would have counted the day well spent if he had been free to take her under his wing; but his ears were straining through the continuous clatter of the train for the first warnings of the violent and unlawful things that must soon be happening somewhere in the south, and he knew that that pleasant interlude could not last for long. He returned her gaze without embarrassment, wondering what she would say if she knew that he was wanted for murder.

"You look fairly sane," she said.

"I used to think so myself," said Monty amusedly. "It's only when I come out in a rash and find myself biting postmen in the leg that I have my doubts."

"Then you might let me share the joke."

"My dear, I'd like to share lots of things with you. But that one isn't my own property."

The full blaze of her unaffected loveliness would have dazzled a lesser man.

"Weren't you ever warned that it's dangerous to tease an inquisitive woman?"

Monty laughed.

"Why not have half my shirt instead?" he suggested cheerfully; and then the sudden check of the train as the brakes came on literally threw her into his arms.

He restored her gently to her balance, and found himself abstractedly fingering the butt of the gun in his pocket while she apologized. He needed the concrete reminder of that cold, metallic contact to fetch him back to the outlook from which he had been trying to escape—the view of his corner of the world as a place where murder and sudden death were common-places, and freedom continued only as the reward of a ceaseless vigilance.

"That's all right," he said absently. "You didn't have to help yourself to it. If you'd asked me for it I'd have given it to you."

He kept his hand in his pocket and stared out of a window at the finest angle that he could manage. Instinct alone told him that the stoppage had nothing to do with any ordinary incident of the journey—it was the hint that he had been waiting for, the zero signal that strung up his nerves to the last brittle ounce of expectation. Beside him, the girl was saying something; but he never had the vaguest idea what it was. He was listening for an intimation of how the typhoon would burst, knowing beyond all possibility of evasion that the breakup was as inevitable as the collapse of a house of cards. For a moment he felt like a man who has just seen the tail of a slow fuse vanishing into a cask of gunpowder: the uncanny hush that had settled down after the train pulled up seemed to span out to the cracking brink of eternity. He heard the sibilant hiss of the Westinghouse valves, the subdued mutter of voices from a dozen compartments, the distant clank of a coupling shaking down into equilibrium; but his brain was striving to tune through those normal sounds to the first whisper of the abnormal—speculating whether it would come as a babel of enraged throats or the unequivocal stammer of artillery.

Then a door was flung open up at the northward end of the carriage, and the heavy tread of official-sounding boots made his heart miss a beat. Out of the corner of his eye he saw two men in uniform advancing down the passage. They stopped at the first compartment and barked a question; and the chattering of the group of Italians farther up died away abruptly. A deeper stillness lapped down on the perspective, and through it Monty heard the question repeated and the boots moving on.

He felt the girl gripping his arm and heard her speaking again.

"Say, don't you Englishmen ever get excited? Somebody's pulled the communication cord. Boy, isn't that thrilling?"

Monty nodded. The officials came nearer, interrogating each compartment as they reached it. One of them turned aside to accost him with the same standardized inquiry, and Monty schooled his features to the requisite expression of sheep-like repudiation.

"Nein–ich habe nichts gehört."

The inquisition passed on, and the group of Italians trailed gaping after them. A fresh buzz of conversation broke out along the carriage.

Monty found the girl eyeing him indignantly.

"Were you trying to kid me you didn't speak German?" she demanded.

He faced her shamelessly.

"I must have forgotten it for the moment."

"Anyway," she affirmed, "I'm going to see what it's all about. This is much too good to miss."

Monty looked at her steadily. He realized that he had put his foot in it from nearly every conceivable aspect, but it was too late to draw back.

"I should keep out of it if I were you," he said quietly, and there was that in his tone which ought to have told her that he was in earnest.

He walked past her without giving her time to reply, and went through to the tiny lobby at the end of the coach. It was pure intuition, again, which told him that the stopping of the train must have its repercussions outside—whoever had given the alarm. He opened the door at one side and looked out, but he could discover no exterior symptoms of a disturbance; then he crossed to the other side, and the first thing he saw was Simon Templar skidding elegantly down the embankment towards the trees. A second later he saw that Patricia Holm was already at the foot of the slope: the Saint was taking his time, glancing back over his shoulder as he went.

It was Monty Hayward that the Saint was looking for, and the sight he had of him was a considerable relief.

"If you stayed well back among that timber, Pat, you might live a long time," he murmured. "I don't think Marcovitch'll run the risk of taking pot shots at us now, but it's best to be on the safe side."

He waved to the figure in the doorway and strolled along the bottom of the embankment to meet him. It was not entirely typical of the Saint that he scorned to follow his own advice and take cover, but Simon was beginning to feel that he had done a lot of work that day with his rudder to the wind, and that unheroic position had lost a great deal of its charm. He waited until Monty had scrambled down to the low level before he turned off and steered him through a narrow path into the shelter of the wood; and his recklessness was justified by the fact that there was no more shooting.

"I'm afraid this is good-bye to our luggage," said the Saint, by way of explanation, "but let's think what we've saved in death duties."

"Was it as bad as that?" asked Monty; and Simon laughed.

"I reckon a swell time was had by all."

They came out into a small clearing around the roots of a giant elm, and at the same time Patricia Holm threaded her way through the shrubbery on the opposite side and joined them under the tree.

From where they stood they could get a strip view of the train without being seen. An assortment of passengers from various carriages had climbed out and scattered themselves along the permanent way; a few of them were dislocating their necks in the attempt to peer through into the depths of the wood, but the majority were heading excitedly down to add their personalities to the knot of gesticulating orators who were thumping the air beside the brake van. The principal performers appeared to be Marcovitch, the two uniformed officials, and the lady with the Pekinese. Flourishing their arms wildly towards the unresponsive heavens on the rare occasions when words failed them, they were engaged in shouting each other down with a tireless vociferous-

ness that would have gladdened the heart of an
argumentative Frenchman. It was several minutes
before the lady in black bombazine began to turn
purple for lack of breath; and then the Pekinese,
seizing its chance, rushed into the conference with a
series of strident yaps which worthily maintained
the standard of uproar. Simon gathered that Marcovitch was keeping his end up with no great difficulty. His voice, when it rose above the oratorio,
could be heard speaking passionately of bandits,
thieves, robbers, murderers, battles, perils, pur-
suits, escapes, and his own remarkable perspicacity
and valour; and the generous pantomime of his
hands supplied everything that was drowned by the
persistence of the other speakers. From time to time
the other members of his party chimed in with their
corroboration.

"That little skunk'll qualify himself for a medal
before he's through," said the Saint fascinatedly.
"He's the loveliest liar since Ulysses."

"What was the truth of it?" asked Monty.

Simon put his hands on his hips and continued to
gaze up at the drama on the line.

"We were bounced off," he said simply. "Marcovitch rode us out on a rail. I'm not bragging about
it. He'd cleaned up the van when I got there—and
my guess was right. The jewels were travelling with
us. His pockets were stuffed with 'em, and I saw a
diamond he'd dropped wedged between the floor
boards to make it a cinch. And right there when I
blew in it was a choice of death or get from under.
We got from under—just."

The smile on the Saint's lips was as superficial as a
reflection in burnished bronze. There was something of the implacable immobility of a watching

Indian about him as he stood at gaze with his eyes narrowed against the sun. The staccato sentences of his synopsis broke off like a melody cut short in the middle of a bar, leaving his listeners in midair; but the conclusion was carved deep into the unforgetting contours of his face. He wasn't complaining. He wasn't saying a word about the run of the cards. He wasn't even elaborating one single vaporous prophecy about what might happen when he and Marcovitch got together again over a bottle of vodka to yarn over old times. Not just at that moment. But the indomitable purpose of it was etched into every facet of his unnatural quiescence, sheathing him like a skin of invisible steel. And once again the parting riddle of Josef Krauss went ticking through the core of his stillness like a gramophone record that has jammed its needle into one hard worn groove. . . .

And then the gas picnic up on the track began to sort itself out. One of the officials tore himself away from the centre of rhetoric and started to urge the passengers back into their carriages. The empurpled lady lifted her yapping paladin tenderly into the last coach, and was in her turn assisted steatopygously upwards. The second official, brandishing a large notebook vaguely in his left hand, pressed the still voluble Marcovitch after her. Gradually the train re-absorbed its jabbering débris like a large and sedate vacuum cleaner. The locomotive, succumbing at last to the force of overwhelming example, let out a mighty cloud of steam and wagged its tail triumphantly. Somebody blew a whistle; and the northbound express resumed its interrupted journey.

Simon Templar turned away from the emptying landscape with an imperceptible shrug. He had not expected any impromptu search party to be organized. A trio of armed and desperate male bandits would have very few attractions as a quarry to a trainload of agitated tourists, and transcontinental expresses cannot be left lying about the track while their passengers play a game of hare and hounds. The incident would be reported at the next station twenty miles up the line, and the whole responsibility turned over to the police. And the getaway would have to find its own way on.

The Saint threw himself down on a bank of grass, and lay back with his hands behind his head, staring up into the sky through the soft green tracery of the leaves.

"After all," he said profoundly, "life is just a bowl of cherries."

Patricia leaned on the trunk of the great tree and kicked at a stone.

"You might have borrowed Monty's gun and plugged Marcovitch while he was talking," she said wistfully.

"Sure. And then I don't suppose they'd even have had to bother to turn out his pockets. The minute he became horizontal he'd've cascaded diamonds like a dream come true. I don't know how you feel about it, old girl, but I should just hate those jools to fall into the hands of the police. It might be kind of difficult to establish our claim and get 'em back."

Monty Hayward produced a pipe and began to scrape it out with his penknife.

"Getting them back from Marcovitch," he observed, "will be comparatively child's play."

"As Simon said," murmured Patricia softly, "it seems a lot of fuss to make over one little blue diamond."

She spoke almost without thinking; and after she had spoken there was a silence.

And then, very firmly and distinctly, the Saint said: *"Hell! . . ."*

"I know how you feel about it, old man," said Monty Hayward sympathetically; and there he stopped, with the rest of his speech drying up in a hiatus of blank bewilderment. For the Saint had rolled over on one elbow in a sudden leap of volcanic energy, and his eyes were blazing.

"But that's just what you don't know!" he cried. "We've been bounced off a train—chucked out on our ears and darned glad to be let off as lightly as that. And why? God of battles, what have we been thinking about all this time? What have we been daydreaming about Rudolf?"

"I thought he was a crook," said Monty rationally.

"I know! That's the mistake we've all been making. And yet you can't say you ever heard me speak of Rudolf as a crook. He never had to be. It wasn't so long ago when Rudolf could have bought us both up every day for a week and never missed it. It wasn't so long ago when Rudolf and Rayt Marius were playing for bigger chips than a few coloured stones. It was war in those days, Monty—death rays and secret Service men, spies and Bolsheviks and assassinations—all the fun of the fair. Naturally there was money in it, but that was all coming to Rayt Marius. Marius was a crook, even if he was dealing in millions. But Rudolf was something that seems much stranger in these days. Something a damned sight more dangerous."

"And what's that?"

"A patriot," said the Saint.

Patricia kicked at her stone again, and it tumbled

out of reach. She hardly noticed it.

"Then when we found we were up against Rudolf again——"

"We ought to have been wide awake. And we weren't. We've been fast asleep! We've watched Rudolf moving heaven and earth to get his hands on those jewels—killing and torturing for them—even coming down to offering me a partnership while his men had orders to shoot us on sight—and we took it all as part of the game. We've been on the spot ever since Stanislaus went home with us. Up in that brake van—I've never seen anything so flat-and-be-damned in my life! Marcovitch was primed to put me out of the way from the beginning. It was written all over his face. And after that he'd've shot up anyone else who butted in for a witness, and taken you and Monty for a dessert—made a clean sweep of it, and shovelled the whole mortuary out onto the line." The Saint's voice was tense and vital with his excitement. "I thought of it once myself, right in the first act; but since then there doesn't seem to have been much spare time. When Rudolf walked into our rooms at the Königshof, I was wondering what new devilment we'd stumbled across. I was telling myself that there was one thing we weren't going to find in this adventure—and that was ordinary boodle in any shape or form. And then, just because a quarter of a million pounds' worth of crystallized minerals fell out of that sardine tin, I went soft through the skull. I forgot everything I ever knew."

"Do you know any more now?" asked Monty skeptically.

Simon looked at him straightly.

"I know one thing more, which I was going to tell you," he answered. "Josef Krauss gave me the hint before he died. He said: 'Take great care of the blue diamond. It is really priceless.' And just for the last few minutes, Monty, I've been thinking that when we know what he meant by that we shall know why Rudolf has made up his mind that you and I are too dangerous to live.''

10

HOW SIMON HAD AN INSPIRATION, AND TRESPASSED IN THE GARDEN OF EDEN

MONTY HAYWARD dug out his tobacco pouch and investigated the contents composedly. His deliberately practical intelligence refused to be stampeded into any Saintly flights of fancy.

"If it's any use to you," he said, "I should suggest that Josef was trying to be helpful. Perhaps he didn't know you were a connoisseur of blue diamonds."

"Perhaps," said the Saint.

He came to his feet with the lithe swiftness of an animal, settling his belt with one hand and sweeping back the other over his smooth hair. The cold winds of incredulity and common sense flowed past his head like summer zephyrs. He had his inspiration. The flame of unquenchable optimism in his eyes was electric, an irresistible resurgence of the old Saintly exaltation that would always find a new power and hope in the darkest thunders of defeat. He laughed. The stillness had fallen from him like a cloak—fallen away as if it had never existed. He didn't care.

"Let's be moving," he said; and Monty Hayward stowed his pipe away again with a sigh.

"Where do you think we could move to?" he asked.

And once again it seemed to Patricia Holm that the breath of Saintly laughter in the air was like the

164

sound of distant trumpets rallying a forlorn venture on the last frontiers of outlawry.

"We can move out of here. It won't be fifteen minutes after that train gets into Treuchtlingen before there'll be a cordon of gendarmerie packing around this neighbourhood closer than fat women round a remnant counter. And I've got a date with Marcovitch that they mightn't want me to keep."

He flicked the automatic adroitly out of Monty's pocket and dropped it into his own, and then a blur of colour moved in the borders of his vision, and his glance shot suddenly across Monty's shoulder.

"Holy smoke!" said the Saint. "What's this?"

Monty turned round.

It may be chronicled as a matter of solemn historical fact that the second in which he saw what had provoked the Saint's awed ejaculation was one of the most pregnant moments of his life. It was a backhander from the gods which zoomed clean under his guard and knocked the power of protest out of him. To a man who had laboured so long and steadfastly to uphold the principles of a righteous and sober life in the face of unlimited discouragement, it was the most unkindest cut of all.

He stood and stared at the approaching nucleus of his Waterloo with all the emotions of a temperance agitator who discovers that some practical joker has replenished with neat gin the glass of water from which he has just gulped an ostentatious draught of strength for his concluding peroration. He felt that Providence had gone out of its way to plant a banana skin directly under his inoffensive heel. If his guardian angel had bobbed up smirking at that moment with any chatty remarks about the weather, Monty would unhesitatingly have socked him under the

jaw. And yet the slim girl who was walking towards
them across the clearing seemed brazenly unaware
that she was making Nemesis look like a decrepit
washerwoman going berserk on a couple of small
ports. She was actually smiling at him; and the un-
blushing impudence of her put the finishing touch
to Monty Hayward's débâcle.

"It's—it's someone I met on the train," he said
faintly, and knew that Patricia Holm and the Saint
were leaning on each other's shoulders in a convulsion of Homeric mirth.

It was Monty's only consolation that his Waterloo
could scarcely have overtaken him in a more attrac-
tive guise. The awful glare with which he regarded
her arrival almost sprained the muscles of his conscience, but it disconcerted her even less than the
deplorable exhibition that was going on behind him.

"Hullo, Mr. Bandit," she said calmly.

The Saint freed himself unsteadily from Patricia's
embrace. He staggered up alongside the stricken
prophet.

"Shall we have her money or her life?" he
crooned. "Or aren't we going to be introduced?"

"I think that would be a good idea," said the girl;
and Monty called up all his battered reserves of
self-control.

He glanced truculently around him.

"I'm Monty Hayward," he said. "This is Patricia
Holm; and that nasty mess is Simon Templar. You
can take it that they're both very pleased to meet
you. Now, are we allowed to know who you are?"

"I'm Nina Walden." The girl's introspective survey considered Simon interestedly. "Aren't you the
Saint?"

Simon bowed.

"Lady, you must move in distinguished circles."

"I do. I'm on the crime staff of the *Evening Gazette*–New York—and there's nothing more distinguished than that outside a jail. I thought I recognized your name."

She took a packet of cigarettes from her bag, placed one in her mouth, and raised her eyebrows impersonally for a light. The Saint supplied it.

"And did you get left behind in the excitement?" he murmured.

"I arranged to be left. Your friend told me there was a story coming—he didn't mean to give away any secrets, but he said one word too many when the train stopped. And then when he jumped out and left me floating, I just couldn't resist it. It was like having a murder committed on your own doorstep. Everyone was hanging out on this side of the track, so I stepped out on the other side while they were busy and lay low under the embankment. I walked over as soon as the train pulled out, but I certainly thought I should have to chase you a long way. It was nice of you to wait for me." She smiled at him shamelessly, without a quiver of those downright eyes. "Gee—I knew I was going to get a story, but I never guessed it'd be anything like this!"

The Saint brought his lighter slowly back to his pocket. On his left, Monty Hayward was stomaching that final pulverizing wallop of revelation with a look of pained reproach on his face which was far more eloquent than any flow of speech; on his right, Patricia Holm was standing a little aloof, with her hands tucked into the slack of that swashbuckling belt of hers, silently enjoying the humorous flavour of the scene; but the Saint had flashed on far beyond those things. A wave of the inspired opportunism which could never let any situation become static under the ceaseless play of his imagination had lifted him up to a new level of audacity that the others had yet to reach. The downfall of Monty Hayward was complete: so be it: the Saint saw no need to ask for further details—he had thrust back that supreme moment into the index of episodes which might be chortled over in later years, and he was working on to the object which was just then so much more urgently important. Nina Walden was there—and the Saint liked her nerve.

"So you're a dyed-in-the-wool reporter?" he drawled, and the girl nodded bewitchingly.

"Yes, sir."

"And you've got all your papers—everything you need to guarantee you as many facilities as a foreign journalist can corner in this country?"

"I think so."

"And you want the biggest story of your life—a front-page three-column splash with banner lines and black type?"

"I'm hoping to get it."

The Saint gave her smile for smile. And the Saintly smile was impetuous with a mercurial resolve that paralleled the swaggering alignment of his shoulders.

"Nina, the story's yours. I've always wanted to make one newspaper get its facts about me right before I die. But the story isn't quite finished yet, and it never will be if you're in too much of a hurry for it. We were just pushing on to finish it—and we've wasted enough time already. Come on with us—leave the interviews till afterwards—and I'll give you the scoop of the year. I don't know what it is, but I know it'll be a scoop. Wipe all your moral scruples off the map—help me as much as I'll help you—and it's a monopoly. Would you like it?"

The girl picked a loose flake of tobacco from the edge of her red mouth.

"Reporters are born without moral scruples," she said candidly. "You're on."

"We're leaving now," said the Saint.

He flung an arm round Patricia's waist and turned her towards a path which led out of the clearing away from the embankment, a grass-paved ride broad enough for them to walk abreast; and if she had been a few pounds lighter his exuberance would have swung her off her feet. Even after all those years of adventure in which they had been together he would never cease to amaze her: his incredible resilience could conceive nothing more fantastic than the idea of ultimate failure. In him it had none of the qualities of mere humdrum doggedness that it would have had in anyone of a more dull and commonplace fibre; it was as swift as a steel blade, a gay challenge to disaster that never doubted the abiding favour of the stars. If it had been anything less he could never have set forth in such a vein to find the end of that chequered story. Marcovitch was gone. The jewels were gone. Prince Rudolf had become an incalculable quantity whose contact with the current march of events might weave in anywhere between Munich and the North Pole. And three tarnished brigands plus a magazine-cover historian, who had been lucky to escape from the last skirmish with their lives, were left high and dry in an area of strange country that would shortly be seething with armed hostility. The task in front of them might have made hunting needles in haystacks seem like an idle pastime for blind octogenerians; but the Saint saw it only as a side road to victory.

"Pat, when this jaunt is over I think we must go back to England. You've no idea how I miss Claud Eustace Teal and all those jolly games we used to have with Scotland Yard."

She knew that he was perfectly serious—as the Saint understood seriousness. He had never changed. She did not have to look at him to see the sunny glint in his eyes, the careless faith in a joyously spendthrift destiny.

She said: "What about Monty?"

The Saint gazed ahead down the widening lane of trees.

"I should like to have kept him, but I suppose he isn't ours."

Westwards as they walked the trees were thinning out, opening tall windows into a landscape of green fields and homely cottages. The golden daylight broke through the laced boughs overhead and dappled their shady path with pools of luminance. A lark dived out of the clear infinity of blue and drifted earthwards like an autumn leaf. Way over on a distant slope the midget silhouettes of a ploughing team moved placidly against the sky, the tinkle of bells and the crack of the ploughman's whip coming vividly through the still air. It seemed almost unbelievable that that peaceful scene could be overrun with grey-clad men combing inexorably through the hedgerows and hollows for a scent of the irreverent corsair who had tweaked their illustrious beards; but the Saint stopped suddenly at a turn of the path, halting Patricia with him, and she also had seen the road and heard the voices.

"Wait here while I take a look," he murmured.

He flitted in among the trees like a shadow, and the girl stood motionless in the shelter of a clump of bushes with her heart beating a little faster. Monty Hayward and the *Evening Gazette* were closing up in an interrogative silence; and Patricia had a numbing sense of the magnitude of the feat which Simon Templar had set himself to perform. Escape would have seemed difficult enough for one man alone—a mere modest getaway that was satisfied with a whole skin for its reward—but the Saint was cheerfully booking passengers for the tour and announcing his unalterable intention of collecting a quarter of a million pounds' worth of expenses *en route*. That was the measure of his genius, the squandered greatness that created its own worlds to conquer.

He came back in a few moments; and he was smiling.

"Down there," he said, "there's a covered wagon. And the crew are having an early tea. I ordered them specially to meet us here, and they look good enough to me. Let's take 'em."

He turned back with a swing of lean, venturous limbs; and Monty Hayward followed him in a mood of unwonted lightheadedness. Something inside Monty Hayward was reacting vengefully against the continued impact of circumstance. He felt that he had taken as much dragooning from circumstance as he could stand, and his capacity for meek long-suffering was wearing out. A malicious freak of fate had thrown up an unceremonious slip of a girl to let the Saint acclaim him hilariously as a fullfledged buccaneer, and that was the last straw. Buccaneer he would be—and let the blood flow in buckets.

They reached a narrow gap in the undergrowth,

and there the Saint touched Monty's shoulder, pointing down to the road. A six-wheeled lorry was drawn up close to the side, and just below where they had paused two weatherbeaten men in overalls were reclining against the low bank. Each of them held a massive sandwich of bread and sausage in one hand and a steaming cup in the other; and Monty's eyes fastened on one of those cups fascinatedly. It occurred to him that a twentieth-century buccaneer might not necessarily be at such a disadvantage as he had once thought. . . .

"Make it snappy," said the Saint.

He went over the bank in a flying dive, and Monty was only a second behind him. Patricia heard one muffled howl, an eddy of whirling effort, and the smack of bone against bone; then she also came over the bank and saw Simon already starting to strip the overalls from his victim. Monty was dusting his trousers, and in his right hand he held like a captured banner the unspilt cup which he would always estimate as one of the outstanding achievements of his life. He raised it dramatically to Nina Walden as she came through the trees.

"Madam," he said, "your tea."

It was a moment which atoned to him for everything that had gone before; and the girl stepped down smiling into the road and accepted his triumph in the same way as Queen Elizabeth might have accepted the Armada.

"You boys certainly know how to work," she said; and Monty shrugged.

"We do this sort of thing every day," he stated aggressively.

The Saint laughed.

"You're getting the spirit of the business, Monty,"

he said. "Now if you can hustle into those jeans
before anyone else comes along we might call the
boat pushed out. Pat, you take a peep under the
tarpaulins and find out what the cargo is. They might
be carrying some more crown jewels!"

"They're carrying engine castings," Patricia reported.

"O.K., lass. There ought to be room for you girls
to pack between them. I'm sorry it wasn't eider-
downs, but, after all, it's a warm day."

The Saint was completing one of those lightning
changes which had always been the envious wonder
of his select audiences. The immaculate draperies of
Savile Row and St. James's had disappeared under a
soiled blue boiler suit as if he had never worn them;
the shoes of Lobb were stuffed into his pockets and
replaced by the dusty boots of toil; the patent-
leather hair was tousled into negligent curls. Those
who knew him best had asserted that Simon Templar could parade more miracles in the way of disguise
with a dab of treacle and a length of string than most
men could have accomplished with the largest
make-up box in Hollywood. To him the outward
paraphernalia of costume was merely the show case
for a perfect cameo of character study—an inimita-
ble transformation of personality in which no living
man could equal him.

"What you boys and girls have got to remember,
now and forevermore," he said, "is that the bushiest
false whiskers on earth won't help you unless you
can put on the authentic pride of whiskeredness.
The hair has got to enter into your soul."

He was working in front of the open bonnet of the
lorry while he talked, rubbing a judicious blend of
grease and grime into his hands and finger-nails and

smearing artistic stains of it across his face. It seems a simple thing to write, and yet the bare truth of it is that when he turned round again he had literally annihilated Simon Templar—he *was* a German truckdriver, with a past and a present and a future and an aged aunt in Frankfurt to whom he faithfully sent a card every Christmas.

Monty Hayward was just securing the last button of his own overalls, and the Saint lugged him boisterously over and smudged his immaculate face and hands with half a dozen similarly rapid masterstrokes.

"Sit quiet and blow your nose on your sleeve occasionally," he said, "and we can't go wrong."

He ran a hawk-like eye over the details of his protégé's attire; and then he grinned boyishly and smote Monty a detonating blow between the shoulder blades.

"C'mon! Let's push these birds out of the way."

They carried the two unconscious men into the wood and hid them in a thicket, after the Saint had bound and gagged them with strips of their own clothing. Simon's departing flourish was to pin a hundred-mark note to each of their shirtfronts—the assault on their persons had been a regrettable necessity, but it was one of those little debts which the Saint never forgot. And in the corner of each note he sketched the quaint little haloed figure which had been the signature of more rollicking outrages than Scotland Yard could discuss in polite language. It was a long time since the Saint had last used that flippant symbol, and the chance appealed to him as an omen that could not be passed by.

He returned jauntily to the road, and saw that Patricia and the *Evening Gazette* had already taken

up their positions. Simon pulled up the starting
handle and vaulted into the driving seat.

As they lumbered clangorously round the next
bend a car that was speeding towards them swerved
peremptorily across their path and stopped broadside on. An officer in field grey climbed out and
marched authoritatively over to the Saint's side. The
stamp of his commission was branded all over him,
and the flap of his revoler holster was unstrapped
and turned back into his belt.

"*Woher kommen Sie, bitte?*" he demanded curtly;
and the Saint drew a grubby hand across an even
grubbier forehead.

"*Aus Ingolstadt, Herr Hauptmann.*"

"*So. Haben Sie auf diesem Wege nicht zwei Män-
ner und eine Frau gesehen? Der grössere Mann trägt
einen hellgrauen Anzug, die Frau ist ganz hübsch
und gut gekleidet—*"

"*Doch!*"

"*Kolossal!*" The officer whipped out a notebook
and signalled vehemently to his men. "*Welche
Richtung haben sie eingeschlagen?*"

Simon took one hand from the wheel and pointed
back over the fields.

"*Sie sind soeben dort über die Wiesen gegangen.
Ich begreife es jetzt noch immer nicht, dass ich das
Mädchen nicht überfahren habe, denn sie ist mir
gerade aus der Hecke unter die Vorderräder
gelaufen—*"

"*Ihr Name?*"

"*Franz Schneider.*"

"*Adresse?*"

"*Nürnberg, Juliusstrasse, seibzehn.*"

The police car rushed up alongside, and the officer stepped on the running board and called out a

volley of instructions. He turned and shouted to Simon as the driver let in the clutch.

"Wenn wir diese Verbrecher fangen, bekommen Sie vielleicht eine hohe Belohnung!"

Simon slewed round in his seat and watched the police car vanishing in a cloud of dust.

And then, very gravely, he leaned forward and engaged the gears. . . .

They had travelled less than a quarter of a mile up the road before Monty Hayward could contain himself no longer. He sat forward on his perch, that imperturbable and law-abiding gentleman, and flung the bruised fragments of his conscience over the horizon with a stentorian bellow of jubilation that drowned even the ear-splitting racket of the six-wheeler's entrails.

"Kolossal!" he bawled ecstatically. "Tremendous affair! They legged it over the fields, they did, and we nearly ran over one of them. Tally-ho! And if they're caught we may qualify for a reward. *Yoi!"* Monty let out another whoop of rhapsody that should have made the welkin turn pale. "Well, dear old sportsman and skipper—where shall we go and file our claim?"

"Treuchtlingen is the next stop, dear old mate and bloke," said the Saint, raising his voice more modestly above the uproar of the engine. "They must have kept Marcovitch there to get his statement, but the train wouldn't wait for him. He'll have to wait for another—and we might be in time to buy him a bouquet!"

2

The lorry crashed on to the northwest at a sonorous twenty-five miles an hour; and Simon Templar settled himself as comfortably as he could on the hard seat and pondered the problem of the two girls behind.

He knew exactly what he had taken on, even if he refused to allow the knowledge to depress him. Hairbreadth odysseys had been made through hostile country before—by desperate men whose superlatively virile strength and speed and cunning kept them moving in a tireless rush that never let up until sanctuary was reached. He could remember no similar instance in which a woman had taken part. It had been tried often enough, and always it had been the woman who had proved the fugitive's undoing. Always it had been the woman's inferior wieldiness that had damped the spark of ruthless primitive momentum without which no such enterprise could ever succeed. It was she who negatived all the man's resources of strength and speed and left him with cunning as his only asset; and every time his wits had failed to carry the load.

Simon Templar reckoned himself something unique in the way of outlaws, and his restless imagination was bearing around the handicap as optimistically as if it had been thrust upon him in a friendly game of hide-and-seek. One thing at least was certain, and that was that Patricia Holm couldn't ride into Treuchtlingen on the lorry. Quite apart from the risk that they might be stopped again and subjected to a search, the rare spectacle of a Bond Street three-piece crawling out from under the tarpaulin of a six-wheeler in the middle of the main street could scarcely escape attention. Marcovitch would doubtless have given a photographic description of her in which the musical-comedy American disguise that had sailed her through the barriers at Munich Hauptbahnhof must have received due credit; therefore it was time for something bright and new to be thought up, and the Saint drove with one eye on the road and the other questing for his opportunity.

From time to time the gentle undulations of the scene gave him a vista of the Altmühl winding like a silver snake between the meadows; and twelve miles farther on it was that same river which provided him with his solution. It caught his wandering eye through a girdle of trees that ringed round a sheltered fold in the broad valley, and if he had not been in Germany he might have believed for a moment that some sorcery had transported him into a pastoral of Ancient Greece. The glimpse lasted for less than a second, but it looked promising enough. He ran the truck another hundred yards up the road, kicked it out of gear, and jumped lightly down to the tarmac.

"Hold the fort for a minute, Monty," he said. "I've just seen a girl."

Monty Hayward rolled over and grabbed the wheel. The elevation of his eyebrows was a five-furlong speech in itself.

"You've just seen a *what?*" he blurted, and the Saint chuckled.

"A girl," said the Saint. "But she's much too nice for a married man like you."

He flagged Monty a debonair au revoir, and slipped hopefully off the road down a shallow bank that led round towards the hollow where he had seen his vision. It really was a very charming little scene; and in any other circumstances, not being afflicted with the Teutonic temperament, he could have waxed poetic over it for some time. It says much for his stern devotion to duty that he was back

within ten minutes, saddened to think that the ser-
pent of Eden would probably have viewed such
vandalism as his with loathing, but bringing with
him nevertheless a large bundle which he tossed
into Monty's arms before he climbed back onto the
cockpit.

The lorry groaned in its intestines and moved on;
and Monty Hayward gazed at the trophies on his lap
and appeared to sigh.

"You don't mean to say these are her clothes?" he
croaked, and felt that the difficulty of making himself heard robbed the utterance of much of its deli-
cacy.

"I'm afraid they are," answered the Saint, with
similar emotions. "And her girl friend's as well. You
see, she wasn't using them. . . . And Greta was
divine, Monty. It'd be worth taking up this *Freikör-
perkultur* just on the chance of meeting her again."

Another three miles nearer Treuchtlingen, when
he decided that they were temporarily safe from any
immediate pursuit, he braked the lorry again beside
a small spinney and hopped out. The road was clear;
and he threw back the tarpaulins and lifted Patricia
down to the grass verge. Nina Walden followed her
unconcernedly, and the Saint reclaimed his booty
and dumped it into Patricia's hands.

"You two are going to be a couple of *Wandervögel*
with great open faces," he said. "Take this stuff into
the jungle and get on with it. The things you're
wearing will go in the rucksacks. And don't carry on
as if you were dressing to go to a dance—we can't
stay here more than week."

His lady stared suspiciously at the collection of
garments which he had thrust upon her.

"But where did you get these things from?" she

demanded; and Simon propelled her towards the
coppice with a laugh.

"Now don't waste time asking indiscreet questions. I found them lying in a field, and the actress
never told the bishop a smoother one than that."

He paced up and down beside the lorry, smoking
a cigarette, while he waited for the girls to return.
An open touring car jolted past with its springs
labouring under the avoirdupois of a healthy Prus-
sian commercial traveller and his Frau, but beyond
that the prospect had no reason to complain that
only man was vile. It was an almost miraculous
stroke of fortune for the Saint, and he rendered
thanks accordingly. The accident which had enabled
him to misdirect the pursuit had been a bonanza in
itself: it meant that the plight of the truck's crew
might not be discovered for several hours, and
meantime the hue and cry would be spreading away
at right angles to the course he was taking. The last
place in which any policeman would expect to see
him was Treuchtlingen—the very town from which
the alarm had emanated. The hunt would be deploying westward to intercept him at the French frontier, but Simon Templar was not going that way.

His cigarette had still half an inch to go when
Patricia Holm emerged from the spinney and presented herself for his inspection.

"If we've got the rest of a week to spare," she said
blandly, "I think I might have a smoke too."

Simon offered his packet. She had put on a brief
leather skirt and a plain cotton jumper, and her legs
were bare to the rawhide sandals. Her nose was
definitely shiny, and the fair hair was pushed
carelessly back from her forehead as if the wind had
been rumpling it all day. She had even remembered

to take off her gold wrist watch; and the Saint noted that touch with a slow smile of appreciation.

"There isn't much more I can teach you, old Pat," he said.

Nina Walden joined them a few moments later, and her garb was much the same. Simon showed her how to adjust the rucksack; and then he took her in his arms and kissed her heartily. For at least three seconds she was too thunderstruck to move, and then her voice returned.

"Are you getting fresh?" she demanded huskily; and Simon Templar laughed.

"I was just taking off some of your lipstick, darling. It's not being worn on great open faces these days, and it seemed a shame to mess up your hankie."

He whirled expeditiously up to the cockpit and sat on the edge of it to give his orders, leaning over with one forearm on his knee and his eyes dancing.

"You two'll have to make it on foot from here—it's under seven kilometres by the milestones, and you couldn't have a better day for a walk. Besides which, this lorry alibi mayn't last forever, and we don't all need to ride in one basket with the eggs. Go into Treuchtlingen and look for the station. Pat goes into the nearest *Konditorei* and buys herself a cup of chocolate to pass the time; Nina, you shunt into the *Bahnhof* and take a return ticket to Ansbach. Slide through the door marked *Damen* and make yourself at home. Change back into your ordinary clothes, wrap the other things into a parcel with some brown paper which you'll get on the way, wait till you hear the next train through, cross the line, and walk out the other side as if you owned the railroad—giving up the return half of your ticket. All clear so far?"

"I think so," said the American girl slowly. "But what's it all for?"

"I've got a job for you," said the Saint steadily. "You wanted the complete story of those crown jewels, and this is part of it. Your next move is the police station. You're a perfectly honest American journalist on vacation who's got wind of the attempted mail robbery and general commotion. We must know definitely what's happened to Marcovitch and his troupe of performing gorillas, and there's only one way to find out. Someone's got to jazz into the lion's den—and ask."

Simon looked down at her quietly; but the hell-for-leather twinkle was still dancing way down in his eyes. Sitting up there beside him, Monty Hayward began to understand the spell which the Saint must have woven around those cynical young freebooters of death who had followed him in the old days—the days which Monty Hayward knew only from hearsay and almost legendary record. He began to understand the fanatical loyalty which must have welded that little band together when they flung their quixotic defiance in the teeth of Law and Underworld alike, when every man's hand was against them and only the inspired devilry of their leader stood between them and the wrath of a drab civilization. And it came to Monty Hayward, that phlegmatic and unimpressionable man, in a sudden absurd flash of blind surrender, that if ever that little band should be gathered once more in the sound of the trumpet he would ask for no prouder fate than to be among their company. . . .

"I'm not asking you to do anything disreputable," said the Saint. "As a reporter, it's your job to get all the news; and if you happen to share some of it with a friend—well, who's going to lose their sleep?"

"I should worry. But when do I get the rest of the story?"

"When we've got it ourselves. I've promised you shall have it, and I shan't forget. But this has got to come first. I told you I'd help you as much as you helped me. I wouldn't give you the run-around for worlds—I couldn't afford to. We need that piece of news. It's the one thing that'll lead us to the only climax that's any use to anyone. If we lose Marcovitch, I lose my crown jewels—and your story's up the pole. You're the only one who can save the game. You're a journalist—will you go on and journalize?"

The others went still and silent in a heart-stopping moment of revelation. The preposterous surmise that had been tapping at the doors of their belief ever since the Saint began speaking burst in on them as an eternal fact. And with it came a realization of all that hung from the Saint's madness and that crazy instant of inspiration back in the woods by the railroad.

The Saint had never been thinking of defeat. With the hunt hard behind him and a price on his head, when he should have been thinking of nothing but escape, he had still been able to play with a madcap idea that fortune had thrown into his path. There was something about it which stunned all logic and all questions—a sense of the joyously inevitable which swept every sane criticism aside. It stirred something in the heart which was beyond reach of reason, like the cheering of a thousand throats or the swing of a regiment moving as one man—something that was rooted in the core of all human impulse, a primeval passion of victory that lifted the head higher and sent the blood tingling through the veins. . . . And the Saint was almost laughing.

"Will you try it?" he asked.

And Nina Walden said, with her marvellous amethyst eyes full upon his: "I can do that for you— Saint."

The Saint reached down and put out a brown hand.

"Good girl. . . . And when you've got the dope, all you have to do is rustle back to the *Konditorei* where you left Pat. Monty and I will park the lorry and be around. We'll find you somewhere. And it'll be a swell story." He smiled. "And thanks, Nina," he said.

The girl smiled back.

Then the Saint spilled over into his seat. He caught Patricia up to him and kissed her on the lips. The six-wheeler's engine raced with a protesting scream, and the huge truck jolted on up the road.

10

HOW SIMON TEMPLAR DISCOURSED ABOUT PROHIBITION, AND PATRICIA HOLM WALKED LIKE A PRINCESS

SIMON drove the lorry clear through Treuchtlingen and out the other side. Pressed hard on its elephantine second gear, it rumbled through the streets with a din that shook the town on its foundations, and several scores of the population turned away from their jobs with representative emotions to see it go. Simon Templar had no objection. That part of the journey was one of those master strokes of strategy which multiplied in his fertile inventiveness like a colony of rabbits with their souls in the business. He had plenty of time to give it rein, and the system of tactics tickled his sense of fun. Two policemen had marked his noisy passage; and if the theft of the lorry were prematurely discovered their statements ought to give the pursuit a fresh start in the wrong direction. Whatever happened, Treuchtlingen would still be the last place on earth in which the hue and cry would search for them.

He went eight kilometres beyond Treuchtlingen on the Ansbach road, and abandoned the truck within sight of a crossroads which would annoy the pursuit still more. They doubled back across country, for there were other travellers on the road, and the alarm would soon be spreading like a forest fire.

"This police force will just hate me before I'm through," said the Saint lightly; and then he laughed. "What'll you do with you share of the boodle, Monty?"

For once it never occurred to Monty Hayward to question whether that share would ever materialize.

"I haven't had time to think about it," he said. "I suppose I shall spend most of it on fares—trying to keep out of jail."

The list of crimes for which he could be tried and almost certainly convicted had faded into the dim outskirts of his consciousness like a tally of old scars. The prospects for his future had gone the same way, like a distant appointment with the dentist. And yet he knew, from the swift sidelong glance which answered his thoughtless remark, that the Saint had not forgotten. The Saint was thinking of the same thing, even then.

Monty fell into a kind of reverie as he walked. He knew that the Saint was quietly searching for a scheme that would clear up the tangle and allow Monty Hayward at least to go free, and for a while he allowed himself to fancy that even such a forlorn hope as that might be carried through by a man to whom no hope seemed too forlorn for a dice with the gods. Suppose the miracle had been worked, and the hue and cry spumed past him like a turning tide, leaving him to dry his wings far up on the shore? . . . Then there would be silence for a week or so, broken at length by a characteristic message of salutation to announce that a worthy proportion of the boodle, mysteriously converted into sterling, had been credited to him through his bank—and tell Ann to have a large plateful of those cakes hot from the oven for him next time he called. That would be the Saintly method—a conclusive share-out that precluded all possibility of refusal. And an unregenerate patchwork of a letter in which every vigorous line would bring back the tang of a ridiculous glamour. . . . And what then? The Consolidated Press, the snug office, the regular hours, the respectable week-ends, the everlasting discussion of rough-neck plots with swan-necked authors, the barometric eye on the circulation figures every Monday. Or an even deadlier retirement, with a sports car and a yacht for toys, Mediterranean summers, luxury cruises, and the bromidic gossip of other douce, unambitious parasites who had the whole world for their playground and could only see it as a race track or a tennis court. In either alternative, the same endless quest for a meaning in life that he had come near to grasping on one wild drive through the Bavarian hills. It gave him a queer feeling of emptiness and futility; and he said very little more during that walk back into the town.

Simon Templar also was silent. There had been times when he had deliberately tried to shut out from his mind the responsibility for Monty Hayward's predicament, and yet it had never been very far below the surface of his thoughts. He had ignored it, joked with it, passed it over; but now, with the tightening of the net round them, it was brought home to him as another debt that was still to be paid.

He picked their route with an unerring instinct: to Monty Hayward it seemed almost inconceivable that such a journey could be made in broad daylight without at least one casual observer to see them pass, but the Saint achieved it. There was a spring in his stride and a fighting line to his mouth that told their own tale. For him the story could have only one dénouement; but the precious minutes were ticking up against them, and the time he had to play with was hacked sharp and square out of the schedule of destiny. Three hours, perhaps, he might allow for the local gendarmerie to amuse themselves with their squad cars and bloodhounds; but inside that limit the Higher Command would get its circus licked into shape. The Higher Command, with its coat off and the arrears of Löwenbräu oozing out of its stagnant pores, would be fusing telephone wires in all directions with the coödinating groundwork of a cordon that would demand identification papers from a migrating tapeworm. The Higher Command, with its ineffable moustachios fairly bristling to avenge the affronts which had been sprayed upon them, would be winnowing through the enclosed area in an almighty clean-up that would fan the pants of every citizen in that peaceful community. The Higher Command, in short, would be taking a personal interest in the gala; and when that time came Simon Templar had no desire to be around.

It was six o'clock when Treuchtlingen received them again, letting them into its back streets through a narrow path between two houses—less than fourteen hours since that moment by the bridge in Innsbruck when Monty Hayward of his own unsuspecting free will had launched them on that harebrained steeplechase. The town seemed quiet enough. Like the core of a cyclone, it was a paradoxical oasis of tranquillity within the belt of official spleen that must have been raging round it. The Saint and Monty plunged into it as if the mayor were their personal friend, and no one paid any attention to them; but the Saint had expected that much immunity. Doubtless the next day's newspapers would inform him that his exploits had roused the neighbourhood to a fever of indignation, but if he had hoped to be regaled with the magnificent spectacle of Treuchtlingen's aldermen woofling up and down the main street with their ties under their ears and the veins standing out on the backs of their necks he would have been disappointed. Treuchtlingen went about its daily business, and left any woofling that might be called for to the authorities who were paid to woofle on suitable occasions. It was a sidelight on the social system which deputes its emotions to a handful of salaried wooflers that had stood the Saint in good stead before; and yet perhaps only Simon knew how thin was the veneer of apathy on which his bluff was based.

But once they were inside the town concealment was impossible, and the only way to proceed was by that sheer arrogance of brass-neckedness in which the Saint's nerve had never failed him. They located the police station without difficulty and walked past it. Farther on, a heaven-sent *Weinstube* swam into their ken; and Monty Hayward realized that his throat had been parched for hours. He glared at the temptation like a starving rabbi resisting a fat slice of ham, but the Saint saw no objection.

"Why shouldn't we?" drawled the Saint. "We don't want to roam about the streets. We can't go into a *Konditorei*—they'd think there was something wrong with us. Why not?"

Their trail turned through the doors. It was Simon who called for beer and sausages, and produced a packet of evil-smelling cigarettes from his overalls. Monty began to wish that he had suffered his thirst in silence: he had caught a smile in the Saint's eye which forboded more mischief.

"I have been thinking," said the Saint.

He broke off while their order was placed on the stained wooden table in front of them. To fill up the interval he smiled winningly at the barmaid. She smiled back, disclosing a faceful of teeth that jutted out over her lower lip like a frozen Niagara of ivory. The Saint watched her departure with some emotion; and then he turned to Monty again and raised his glass. They were in an isolated corner of the room where their conversation could not be overheard.

"Great thoughts, Monty," said the Saint.

"I suppose you must think sometimes," conceded Monty discouragingly, without any visible eagerness to probe deeper into the matter. He swilled some Nürnberger round his palate with great concentration. "Why can't they make beer like this in England?" he asked, pulling out the best red herring he could think of.

"Because of your Aunt Emily," said the Saint, whose patience could be inexhaustible when once he had made up his mind. "In America they have total prohibition, and the beer is lousy. In England they have semi-prohibition, in the shape of your Aunt Emily's wall-eyed Licensing Laws, and the beer is mostly muck. This is a free country where they take a proper pride in their beer, and if you tried to put any filthy chemicals in it you'd find yourself in the can. The idea of your Aunt Emily is that beer-drinkers are depraved anyway, and therefore any poison is good enough to pump into their stomachs—and the rest is a question of degree. Now let's get back to business. I have been thinking."

Monty sighed.

"Tell me the worst."

"I've been thinking," said the Saint, with his

mouth full of sausage, "that we ought to do a job of work."

He took another draught from his glass and went on mercilessly.

"We are disguised as workmen, Monty," he said, "and therefore we ought to work. We can't stay here indefinitely, and Nina'll only just have got started on the pump-handle. That police station looked lonely to me, and I'd feel happier if we were on the spot."

"But what d'you think you're going to do?" protested Monty half-heartedly. "You can't go to the door and ask if they've got any chairs to mend."

The Saint grinned.

"I don't think I could ever mend a chair," he said. "But I know something else I could do, and I've always wanted to do it. I noticed a swell site for it right opposite that police station. We'll be moving as soon as you're ready."

Monty Hayward finished his beer with rather less enthusiasm than he had started it, while Simon clinked money on the table and treated himself to another yard of the barmaid's teeth. It was on the tip of Monty's tongue to spread out a barrage of other and less half-hearted protests—to say that the jam was tight enough as they were without giving it any gratuitous chances—but something else rose up in his mind and stopped him. And he knew at the same time that nothing would have stopped the Saint. He caught that smile in the Saint's eye again; but now it was aimed straight at him, with a sprinkling of banter in it, cutting clean as a rapier thrust to his inmost thoughts. It stripped the meaningless habit of lukewarm criticism clear away from him, taking him back to other moments in those fourteen crowded hours which he had lately been remembering with a contentment that he could not have explained in words. It brought him face to face with a self that was still unfamiliar to him, but which would never be unfamiliar again. In that instant of utter self-knowledge he felt as if he had broken out of a bondage of heavy darkness; he was a free man for the first time in his life.

"O.K.," he said.

They went out into the streets again, finding them softened by the first shadows of twilight. Monty was still wondering what new lunacy had brewed itself in the Saint's brain, but he asked no more questions.

Men and women passed them on the pavements, sparing them no more than a vacant glance which observed nothing. Monty began to feel the flush of a growing confidence. After all, there was nothing about him which could legitimately induce a sane population to stand still and gape at him. He looked again at the Saint, detachedly, and saw a subtle change in his leader which increased that assurance. The Saint was slouching a little, putting his weight more ruggedly on his heels, with his shoulders rounded and the half-smoked cigarette drooping negligently from one corner of his mouth: he was just a plain, unaspiring artisan, with Socialistic opinions and an immoderate family. Again the picture was perfect; and Monty knew that if he played his own rôle half as well he would pass muster in any ordinary crowd.

A miscellaneous junk store showed up on the other side of the road, with its wares overflowing onto benches set out on the sidewalk. Simon crossed the road and invaded the gloomily odorous interior. He emerged with a large and shabby secondhand bag, with which they continued their journey. A hardware store was the next stop, and there Simon proceeded to acquire an outfit of tools. The purchase taxed his German to the utmost, for the layman's technical vocabularies may be sketchy enough in his own language, without venturing into the complexities of a specialized foreign jargon. The Saint, who could carry on any everyday conversation in half a dozen different dialects, could no more have trusted himself to ask for a centre-bit or a handspike than he could have knitted himself a suit of combinations. He explained that his kit had been stolen, and bluffed his way through, wandering round the shop and collecting likely-looking instruments here and there, while he kept the proprietor occupied with a flow of patter that was coarse enough to keep any laughter-loving Boche amused for hours. It was finished at last, and they hit the footway again while the storekeeper was still wheezing over the Saint's final sally.

"Well—what are we supposed to be?" inquired Monty Hayward interestedly, as they turned their steps back towards the police station; and the Saint shrugged at him skew-eyed.

"I haven't the vaguest idea, old lad. But if we don't look impressively energetic it won't be my fault."

They stopped directly opposite the station, and Simon laid his bag down carefully in the road. Gazing about rather blankly, Monty noticed for the first time that there was a rectangular metal plate let into the cobbles at his feet. Simon fished a hooked implement out of his bag, inserted it in a sort of keyhole, and yanked up the slab. They got their fingers under the edge and lifted it out onto the road beside the chasm which it disclosed. Without batting an eyelid, the Saint deliberately spread out an imposing array of tools all round him, sat down in the road with his legs dangling through the hole, and stared down at the maze of lead tubes and insulated wiring which he had uncovered, with an expression of owlish sagacity illuminating his face.

2

"It's not so good if you happen to open up a sewer by mistake," Simon remarked solemnly, "but this looks all right."

He hauled up a length of wire and inspected its broken end with the absorbed concentration of a monkey that has scratched up a bonanza in its cousin's scalp. He tapped Monty on the shoulder and required him also to examine the frayed strands of copper, pointing them out one by one in a dumb-show that registered a Wagnerian crescendo of distress and disapproval. Monty knelt down beside the hole and shook his head in manifest sympathy. Rousing himself from his grief, the Saint picked up a hammer and launched a frenzied assault on the nearest length of lead pipe. It lasted for the best part of a minute; and then the Saint sat back and surveyed the dents he had made with an air of professional satisfaction.

"Gimme that file," he grunted.

Monty passed it over; and the Saint bowed his head and began to saw furiously at the angles of a joint that he had spotted lower down in the pit.

If there had been any genuine experts in the vicinity that performance would never have got by for ten seconds; but no one seemed sufficiently inquisitive to make a lengthy study of the Saint's original methods. Hardly anyone gave them a second glance. Planted right out there in the naked expanse of the highway, they were hidden as effectively as if they had buried themselves under the ground. And the necks of Treuchtlingen were innocent of the taint of rubber. An occasional automobile honked round them, and a dray backed up close to Monty's posterior and parked there while the driver went into a good pull-up for carmen. Apart from the infrequent sounds of plodding boots or grinding machinery going past them, they might have been a couple of ancient lights for all the sensation they provoked. So long as he didn't electrocute himself or carve into a gas main and blow the windows out of the street, the Saint figured that he was on velvet.

And if he had wanted to be near the scene of action, he couldn't have got much closer without walking in and introducing himself. As he bent down over his improvised program of free services to the Treuchtlingen municipality, he could study the whole architecture of the police station under his left arm—a drab, two-storied building to which not even the kindly shades of the evening could lend any mystery. It stood up as squat and unimaginative as the laws behind it, a monument of prosaic modernity wedged in among the random houses of a more leisurely age. Simon looked up at the regular squares of window that divided the stark façade in geometric symmetry, and saw the first of them light up.

"Six-thirty," he said to Monty. "Nina must be getting them warmed."

Monty fiddled with a spanner.

"There's no chance that she left before we arrived, is there? She might have got what she wanted quicker than we expected."

"Not here or anywhere else, in a blockhouse like that. There isn't a government official anywhere in the world who could get anything done in less than seventy-nine times as long as it'd take you or me to

do it. They're all born with moss under their feet—
it's one of the qualifications."

The Saint lugged out another line of cable and
battered it ferociously with a chisel. Underneath the
triviality of his words ran a thin, taut thread of strain.
Monty heard it then for the first time, hardening the
edges of Simon's voice. There was no weakness
about it, no trace of fear: it was the strain of a man
whose faculties were strung up to a singing intensity
of alertness, the cold expectancy of a boxer waiting
to enter the ring. It showed up something that
Monty alone had overlooked during those fourteen
hours of his adventure. The Saint's own optimism
had made it all seem so easy, even in its craziest
gyrations; and yet that very smoothness had derived
itself from nothing but the steel core of inflexible
purpose behind the whimsical blue eyes that had
unconsciously slitted themselves down for a moment into two splinters of the same steel. And the
story had still to be brought to the only possible
end. . . .

Simon snapped his cable in the middle, tied the
pieces together again, wrapped a strip of insulating
tape round the connection, and hammered it out
flat. His movements had the gritty restraint of fet-
tered impatience. Inside that cubist's bellyache of a
fortress the real work was being done for him by a
girl; and as the time went on he knew that he would
rather have done it himself—shot up the police station in person and extracted his information at the
snout of a Webley. Anything would have been better than that period of nerve-rasping inaction. He
knew that he was thinking like a fool—that any such
course would have been nothing short of a high road
to suicide—but he couldn't help thinking it. The

suspense had started to tug at the muscles of his stomach in an intermittent discharge of hampered energy. Somehow it shook up the cool flow of his mind, when he should have been focusing solely on the task that was coming to him as soon as the information was obtained. It was as if he had been trying to see down into a pool of clear water, and every now and then something in the depths stirred up a cloud of silt and swallowed up his objective in a turbid fog. Somewhere in that fog Marcovitch was sneering at him, capering farther and farther beyond his reach. . . .

A chilled drop of moisture trickled clammily down his side, and the Saint shook himself in the sudden astonishment of finding that he was sweating. The pale eyes of Josef Krauss loomed up before him again, glazed with that unforgettable film of bitter mockery. Simon set his lips. He couldn't understand himself. In everything physical he was the same as he had always required himself to be; his hand was steady, his sight was clear, his heart beat normally. The rhythm of his aimless hammering still gave him the joy of perfect bodily fitness, trained to the last ounce. And there he was behaving like a frightened schoolboy, losing control of his mind just at the point where it should have been tuning itself up to concert pitch for the showdown.

He forced himself back into the train of thought that kept slipping away from him. How much ground had Marcovitch been able to put between them during those three hours since the carnival in the brake van? Simon tried to work it out again. Half an hour to get to Treuchtlingen; at least another half hour to get through to the local police chief; then an hour of romancing and circumstantial fiction. Leaving another hour in which anything might have happened. And meanwhile, what had become of Rudolf? The stolen Rolls would have been recovered before long, once the theft had been notified— certainly before the departure of the next northbound express at five-thirty—and Rudolf would probably elect to follow up by road. He would have to make contact with Marcovitch again somewhere, and Marcovitch was an unstable quantity. The Saint made an effort to put himself in the enemy's place. What would he do if he were Rudolf? He'd have every possible route out of Munich measured out, with points of communication arranged for on all of them. If Marcovitch had succeeded in getting a message back from the station before the train left, which seemed very probable, he would know what road to take as soon as he could find a conveyance; and the rest would simply be a matter of making inquiries at the prearranged points along the route to which news might be telephoned. Sooner or later that system would link them up again; and in view of the spare hour with which Simon had to credit Marcovitch, the vote went to sooner. Marcovitch would have made the wires sizzle with the narrative of his accomplishment at the earliest opportunity, and the panegyric would already be waiting for Rudolf to catch it up. Ingolstadt seemed a likely junction. . . . Which meant that Rudolf might even then be speeding on to Treuchtlingen to take over the command. . . . And if Marcovitch and his aviary of jailbirds were actually holding on in Treuchtlingen, waiting for Rudolf to meet them there . . .

The Saint took a grim hold on himself. Once again the thread had slipped through a loophole in his mind at that point, as it had done every time before.

The fog swirled up again, blotting it out in a maddening haze. He wrestled against it in a moment of frozen savagery, but the mists only swelled thicker. The thread had gone back on him for good, and his own efforts to recapture it only seemed to drive the loose end into a more infuriating obscurity. He felt as if his brain had chosen that moment to fall into a sluggist conflict of cross-purposes with itself—as if one part of it had mutinied and disordered the clean running of the rest, jarring through insubordinately with a shapeless idea of its own. And it was not until many weeks afterwards, when he recalled that span of unaccountable impotence, that he could see in it the interference of some psychic power which was beyond understanding.

He looked up at the flat, concrete face of the police station. Other windows were lighting up as the dusk overtook them, slashing their mathematical squares of luminousness out of the grey blankness of the wall. The low rectangle of doorway was still dark, like a cuneiform rat's hole.

Simon passed a hand over his eyes.

"If we knew which of these things were telephone wires, we might cut 'em," he said, without a change in the cool level of his voice. "I'm not sure that we mayn't have disorganized something already—those were two very classy-looking bits of wire before I repaired 'em."

That was all he said. And he left off speaking so naturally that for several seconds Monty Hayward guessed nothing of what had happened.

And yet before the last words were out of his mouth Simon Templar had seen a thing which crushed every other thought out of his head. It burst in on his senses with the stupefying concussion of an exploded bomb, gripping his brain in an icy constriction of sheer paralysis, so that for one heart-stopping instant the whole world seemed to stand still all round him. And then the full torrent of comprehension weltered down on him like a landslide and shattered the fragile stillness as though it had been held in a gigantic bubble of glass, blasting the shredded fragments of his universe into a swimming vortex of incoherence that made the blood roar in his ears like a hundred dynamos.

It had started so very quietly and gently that he had watched its approach without the slightest flicker of suspicion. His eyes had taken it in exactly as they took in the details of the surrounding houses, or an individual cobblestone among the scores that lay all around him—merely as one uneventful item of the general street scene with no particular significance in itself. He sat there and spread himself wide open to it, wide open as a new-born babe crowing innocently at the distended hood of a cobra.

Three people were coming down the road.

The Saint gazed at them merely because he happened to be looking in their direction. They were sixty or seventy yards up the street when he first noticed them, too far away for him to see them as anything but shadowy figures in the failing light; and they meant nothing more to him than any of the other figures that had passed and repassed since he had been sitting there. He watched them without seeing them, while his mind was wholly occupied with other things. The thread of his deductions was still eluding him at the most vital knot, baffling him again in that murky whirlpool of disjointed ideas which persisted in deflecting the straight trajectory of his thoughts, and he was bullying himself back to the fence which his imagination steadily refused to take. *If Marcovitch was waiting for Rudolf in Treuchtlingen* . . . The figures came nearer: he made out that one of them was a woman, and somewhere beside her he seemed to catch a sheen of bright metal, but even then he thought nothing of it. The fog had balked him again. He glanced up at the police station—began speaking to Monty, giving no hint of the struggle within himself. . . .

And then the street lights went on suddenly, leaping into yellow orbs of incandescence that studded the dusk with moons. The rays of one of them fell clearly over the three figures less than twenty yards away, striking full on the pale, proud face of the girl in the middle; and Simon saw that it was Patricia Holm.

The Saint went numb. Dully he made out the features of the two men—the policeman on one side, holding her by the arm: Marcovitch on the other, viciously jubilant. The deadly unexpectedness of it stunned him. He felt as if destiny had slammed a door in his face and turned a key, and he was helplessly watching the bolts sinking home into their sockets, one by one. It was the one thing that he had never even found a place for in his calculations. He tried stupidly to find a reason for it, as if only a logical interpretation could confirm the evidence of his eyes. The lost end of the thread that he had been pursuing whisked through his brain again like a streak of hot quicksilver: *"If Marcovitch was waiting for Rudolf in Treuchtlingen—"* It snapped off there like an overstrained wire, splitting under the shock of a boiling inrush of realization. The facts were there. Patricia was caught, disarmed, locked in the iron clutch of the Law as surely as if the door of a cell had already been closed upon her; and Marcovitch was going with her to the station to clinch

the charge. The machinery was in motion, clamping
its bars round her, dragging her inexorably into the
relentless mill. The bubble had burst.

Dimly Monty Hayward became aware of the ter-
rible stillness beside him, and raised his eyes. The
Saint was rigid to his fingertips, staring across the
road like a man in a nightmare. Turning to follow
that stare, Monty Hayward also saw; and in the next
searing instant he also understood.

Then the Saint came to life. A red mist drove
across his eyes, and the pent-up desperation of his
stillness smithereened into a reckless blood-lust.
His right hand leapt to his hip pocket; and then
Monty Hayward pulled himself together in a blaze of
strength that he had not known he possessed and
caught at the flying wrist.

"Simon—that won't help you!"

For a second he thought the Saint would shoot
him while he spoke. The Saint's eyes drilled through
him sightlessly, as if he had been a stranger, with
those pin-points of red fire smouldering behind brittle flakes of blue. There was no vestige of reason or
humanity in them—nothing but the insensate flare
of a barbaric vengefulness that would have gone up
against an army with its bare hands. For that second the Saint was mad—raving blind and deaf
with a different madness from any that Monty had
seen in him before. Monty looked death in the face,
but he held his ground without flinching. He
gripped the Saint's wrist like a vise, forcing his
words through the dead walls of the Saint's stark
insanity. And slowing, infinitely slowly, he saw
them groping to their mark. The Saint's wrist relaxed, ounce by ounce, and the red glare sank
deeper into his eyes. The eyes wavered from their
blind stare for the first time.

"Maybe you're right."

The Saint's voice was almost a whisper; but Monty saw his mouth frame the syllables, and watched a trace of colour creeping back into the lips which had been pressed up into thin ridges of white stone. He let go the Saint's wrist, and Simon picked up a wire and twisted it mechanically.

The street was undisturbed. In all those tense seconds there had only been two violent movements, and neither of those would have impressed any but the closest observer in that faint light. And the pavements were practically deserted, except for the three figures passing under another lamp-post, only half a dozen yards now from the doors of the police station. The curious glances of the few pedestrians in sight were centred exclusively on the girl: none of them had any attention to spare for the commonplace counter attraction of two workmen squatting over a hole in the road tinkering with wires. Marcovitch never knew how near he had been to extinction. He was gloating over his triumph, oblivious of everything else around him, walking straight for the entrance of the police station without a glance to right or left. It was he who led the way up the steps; and then Simon had one more glimpse of the girl, a glimpse that he would remember all his life, with her fair head fearlessly tilted and the grace of a princess in her unfaltering stride. And then she also was gone, and the dark doorway sprang into empty brilliance after her.

"I think Marcovitch will have to die," said the Saint.

The wire broke in the twisting of his fingers like a piece of rotten thread, and he dropped it without noticing that it had broken.

He stared expressionlessly up and down the road.

The scattering of people near by were resuming their affairs as if nothing had happened; but at either end of the street he could see more of them, drifting in desultory mosaics under lamp-posts and lighted windows. Monty had been right—bitterly right. They could never have got away. There wasn't a vehicle of any kind in sight—nothing that they could have commandeered for such an escape as they would have had to make. The first shot would have hemmed them in with a human wall.

Simon felt as if an arctic wind had blown through him, turning his stomach to ice. He sat with his fists clenched in a spasm that ached up his arms, with his eyes fixed on nothing, tasting the dregs of humiliation.

And then he saw a new shaft of luminance swimming round into the street. It fanned out along the line of houses, lifting them in turn into a garish oval of illumination and dropping them back into the dark. For a moment the Saint was caught squarely in the beam, but he had bent his head instinctively and commenced to play with the wires. Then the beam went past him, settling into a long, low stream of light that swept straight down the road and turned the cobblestones into gleaming mountains with black pits behind them. The car sped down the oppposite side of the road with the soft hiss of a perfectly balanced engine, and braked to an effortless stop outside the police station.

Then a wave of gloom rolled back on it as the headlights were switched off; and the Saint looked at it over his shoulder in a throb of incredulous expectation. The chauffeur was running round to open the door, and as the passenger stood up Simon saw his profile clean-cut against the light in the station doorway. It was the Crown Prince Rudolf.

11

HOW MONTY HAYWARD RECITED POETRY, AND SIMON TEMPLAR TREATED HIMSELF TO A WASH

THE Crown Prince dusted his sleeve and walked up the steps of the police station, exquisite and inscrutable as ever. He disappeared into the gaunt building. Simon watched him go.

And then something seemed to crack in the Saint's brain. Something had to give way under the tearing impact of the desperation that had engulfed him, and the thing that gave way was the desperation itself. A great weight lifted off his shoulders, and his lungs opened to a mighty breath of life. The heaving earth steadied itself under him. He felt like a strong swimmer who has been trapped in a clinging entanglement of weed, who has fought back out of the choking darkness into a blaze of sunlight and blessed air. The horrible constriction of helplessness broke away from his head, and he felt the wheels of his mind spinning sweet and true again, unhindered even by the disorder which had been throwing them out of gear before the bomb burst. He could have given no reason for that strange reawakening: he only knew that the old fighting courage had come back, sending the blood racing warm along his veins and filling his muscles with the old unconquerable sense of power. He stretched himself like a cat in the exultant gathering of that flame of indomitable strength. And already he knew how the story was going to end.

Monty Hayward looked at him, and was amazed. The bleakness was still in the Saint's eyes, but suddenly there was a twinkle with it as if the sun had glinted over two chips of blue ice. There was the phantom of a smile on the Saint's lips—a smile that had still to reach the careless glory of pure Saintliness, but yet a smile that had not been there before. And the Saint spoke in a voice that shared his smile.

"Could anything be better?"

Monty shied away from that voice as if a thunderbolt had hit the ground in front of him. He could hardly believe that it came from the man whom he had seen reaching for his gun a few seconds earlier. It was lilting—positively lilting.

"I don't see what you mean, old chap," he said awkwardly.

"Don't you see what's happened?" The lilt in the Saint's voice was stronger—and the Saint was still smiling at him. "Marcovitch was waiting for Rudolf in Treuchtlingen! He saw Pat somewhere, we don't know where, and put the cop onto her. Then when he came along here with her he had to leave a message at the rendezvous to say where he'd gone. Rudolf must have arrived a couple of minutes later, and he naturally followed straight on. *And here they are!*"

Again Monty Hayward felt as he had done in the hotel in Munich—that the Saint must have gone bughouse under the strain. Only this time the feeling verged on an awful certainty.

"What about it?" he said quietly.

The Saint laughed under his breath.

"This about it! They're here—Pat, Rudolf,

Marcovitch—the whole all-star cast of unparagoned palukas! And the crown jewels are with them somewhere—I'll bet you a million dollars. Marcovitch would never dare to let them out of his sight. The whole bag of tricks, Monty, packed up and sealed for delivery in that futurist abomination of a *Polizeiamt!* Just as if we'd fetched 'em together on purpose for the reunion. And only a skeleton staff inside. Every ablebodied man they can lay their hands on is out in the wide county chasing our trail through the cowslips. And here we are as well— wearing out our sterns on this goddam field of bricks while the ungodly are collected for us twenty feet away. We've got 'em cold!"

Monty stared at him.

"What's your idea?" he articulated slowly; and the Saint answered with five syllables that leapt back at him like bullets.

"Go in and get 'em!"

A couple of working girls went past them, giggling over the crytic gossip that working girls giggle over in every country in the world; and Monty Hayward looked into the twinkling icicles of the Saint's eyes, and knew what he would find there before he looked. The Saint meant every crackling consonant of it. Monty had the dubious consolation of knowing that his diagnosis was a bull's-eye. The Saint was as mad as a hatter's March hare. But it was not the red, homicidal ferocity of a moment ago—it was the madness of the bridge in Innsbruck and the ride into Treuchtlingen, a thing against which Monty couldn't argue any more.

"I'll go with you," he said.

It never occurred to him to question why he said it. Hell!—he was damned anyway. Why worry?

There was still a good scrap waiting, and retribution
would follow soon enough. He hadn't discovered his
new self such a short while ago only to throw it away
unused.

He heard the quick rippling voice of the tempter
in his ear. Simon was leaning over towards him,
scraping a chisel about somewhere among the pipes.

"It's the only thing we can do, Monty. We'll never
get a chance like this again. And it's got to be done
right now, while they're all busy. Death or glory,
Mont!"

"Lead on, son and brother."

The Saint grinned.

He inspected the road sideways under his arm.
The chauffeur was patrolling comatosely up and
down the road beside the cream-coloured Rolls,
with the mystic neutrality of chauffeurs; but Simon
recognized him as the man whose nose he had been
privileged to pull a few hours before.

"We shall have to remove the grease ball," he
said. "I may want his car. And you'll have to remove
him, Monty, because he knows me."

He gave further instructions.

And thereupon a number of remarkable experi-
ences began to enliven the daily round of Herr
Bruno Plez, chauffeur extraordinary to His Inde-
scribable Pulchritude the Crown Prince Rudolf.

They initiated themselves harmlessly enough
with the deceptively commonplace incident of an
overalled workman levering himself out of the hole
in the road where he had been engaged in his own
abstruse travail, and walking across towards him.
They continued in the same deceptively commonplace manner with the workman approaching
Herr Pelz and politely requesting the loan of a match
for his cigarette. And they went on with Herr Pelz

providing the required light; whch was also a very commonplace event in itself, for Herr Pelz was not yet submerged in such abysses of indiscriminate churlishness as to revolt against the custom of a country where fire is as free as air. But at that point in Herr Pelz's history the ordinariness of the affair ended for ever.

He struck a match and held it to the workman's cigarette, glancing at him casually as he did so. And that casual glance gave him the shock of his life.

Over the uncertain flame the workman was ogling him with the most horrifying squint that he had ever seen. The round, goggling eyes swivelled over him with a repulsive significance that was as nauseating as the leer of a bloated harpy in a lecher's delirium. Herr Pelz recoiled from it in an involuntary convulsion of disgust. He felt the hairs rising on the nape of his neck, as if those odiously astigmatic eyes had stretched out of their orbits and laid their slimy contact on his flesh. But the workman seemed utterly unconscious of the repugnance which he aroused. He muttered his thanks, and turned away with a final hideous wink that warped his whole face into one ghastly deformity of innuendo.

Herr Pelz's head revolved in a perfect mesmerism of loathing to watch him hobbling down the street. He couldn't even tear his gaze away from the man's back while his memory was still crawling with the impressions of that repellent stare. And thus it came about that Herr Pelz saw what he might not otherwise have noticed; that as the workman passed under the next street lamp he pulled a filthy handkerchief out of his pocket, and a scrap of paper was dragged out with it and fluttered down to the pavement.

Herr Pelz could no more have resisted that scrap

of paper than he could have vowed himself into a monastery. He started towards it without a second thought, impelled solely by the degenerate curiosity which the experience had aroused. Then as he came nearer, he saw that the scrap of paper was a hundred-mark note.

He picked it up, and turned it over suspiciously in the lamplight. It was unquestionably genuine.

Curiosity gave way to an even more deeply rooted cupidity. Herr Pelz flashed a furtive glance around him to see if anyone else had observed the accident. But no one seemed to be paying any attention to him, and the other workman was hammering away at his pipes with uninterrupted vigour. Herr Pelz returned his gaze with a little less revulsion to the beneficent ogre's retreating figure. And as Herr Pelz looked, the ogre replaced the handkerchief in his pocket—and a second hundred-mark note drifted down onto the pavement.

If there was any manifestation of Providence at which Herr Bruno Pelz had ever prayed to be a witness, it was the phenomenon of an endless flood of hundred-mark notes pouring down at his feet; and at that moment he seemed to be spectating the nearest approach to such a prodigy that he was ever likely to see. While he stared up the street with bulging eyes, a third scrap of paper fell from the workman's pocket and floated down into the gutter—closely followed by a fourth. A fifth, a sixth, and seventh joined them with incredible rapidity. The workman was shedding money all over the road like a perambulating mint. And then he turned off into a dark side alley with the eight hundred marks flopping down to the paving stones behind him.

Herr Pelz didn't even hesitate. He plunged on to

his doom with his mouth hanging open, as fast as his legs would carry him. Prince Rudolf was still inside the police station, and even if he came out unexpectedly, an excuse should be easy to find. And meanwhile Fortune was opening her cornucopia and decanting largesse with a liberality which it would have been a sin to ignore. Whether the workman was a thief, an escaped lunatic, or an eccentric millionaire—if he could be caught in that dark alley . . . Herr Pelz's black eyes gleamed like marbles. There had been days when he had ruled a minor underworld as master of the precarious trade of the garotte, and his hand had not lost its cunning. It would be over and finished in ten seconds, without a sound.

He hurried down the pavement, snatching up hundred-mark notes as he went. His fingers grasped the last one as he turned into the alley, and few yards down the lane he saw another. He stooped to pick it up. . . .

And then a massive lump of metal wielded with masterly precision crashed into the back of his head. For one blissful second he gaped at a complete free fireworks display that would have been the making of any Fourth of July; and then a hospitable darkness came down and folded him in his dreams.

Monty Hayward returned like a paladin from the wars.

He lowered himself to the cobbles beside the hole in the road, and looked at the Saint with eyes that were no longer squinting. There was the seed of a smile in them—a seed such as can only be sown by the force of a doughty blow struck for the honour of lawlessness. And the Saint smiled back.

"Oke?" he drawled.

"Oke," said Monty Hayward. "I hid in a doorway and dotted him a peach. There was a sort of van close by, and a bloke was just starting it up. I heard him say they'd have to hustle to get to Nürnberg by dinner time, so I picked up your pal and heaved him in with the greens." He looked round as an antique Ford swung into the street and clattered past. "And there he goes!"

Simon Templar nodded; and the nod spoke volumes.

He stood up and stretched his legs.

"Then he won't bother us for some time," he said. "I guess we can begin."

"Suits me, Saint."

The Saint gazed down at him steadily. In fewer years than the other man had lived, he had come to know the game from every angle, and grown used to its insidious allurements. Its seductive charms held him no less than they had always done; but he knew their treachery. Even then, he hesitated to take advantage of Monty's surrender.

"There's no need for you to come inside," he said. "This isn't quite like anything we've done before. We may be running into a trap. If you'd like to hang on here for a bit——"

"Why not get on with it?" said Monty Hayward shortly. "I wouldn't miss a show like this for a thousand pounds."

The Saint smiled ruefully.

"On your own head be it," he said; but his hand rested on Monty's shoulder for a moment.

And then he turned and walked across the road.

He had no illusions about what he was trying to do. Before it was finished there might easily be a miniature war storming in that peaceful street. He had to take the risk. And if necessary, he'd have to fight the war. It was the only way. Patricia Holm was inside that police station, irreparably meshed in the ponderous dragnet of the Law; and even if he had been a free man, that would have seemed hopeless enough—to sit scheming with lawyers, pulling the sticky threads of bail and remand, pitting miserable atoms of truth against the massed batteries of intrigue and influence that Rudolf could command, knowing that the scales were weighted against him from the beginning. With the police offering rewards for his own capture it couldn't be thought of. He was taking the one chance that the fall of the cards gave him—a clean fighting chance to win the game as he had fought it from the start, as he had won such games before, with the honest steel of a gun butt in his hands, clearing the tangled chess board with a challenge of death.

He ran up the station steps and entered the bare vestibule. On his left was a corridor; farther down he came to a pair of glass doors opening into a microscopic space where the common citizen could stand and lean over a counter to hold converse with the Law. Beyond the counter was an untidy sort of office, in which he could see one bald-headed policeman writing laboriously at a desk and another thoughtfully picking his teeth.

Simon burst in unceremoniously, with one quick glance backwards to make sure that Monty was following. The game had to be played fast—taken at a rush that would allow the enemy no time to ponder over details or gaze too closely at his own charming features. He fell breathlessly on the counter with his face a mask of agitation under the grime.

"*Machen Sie schnell!*" he panted. "*Ein Kind ist von einem Motorrad angefahren worden!*"

The toothpicking officer might not have been sentimentally moved by the thought of a child being knocked down by a motor-bicycle, but he had a commendable devotion to duty.

He picked up his cap and came through a flap in the counter, buttoning the neck of his tunic. Simon stood aside to let him pass. As the policeman stepped out of sight of his colleague in the office, Simon hit him twice on the back of the neck—two slaughterous ju-jitsu blows delivered with the edge of his hand. The policeman slumped forward soundlessly—straight into Monty's arms.

"Hold him up and talk to him!" rapped the Saint. "You can be seen from outside. I'll just get the other one. . . ."

Monty propped the policeman against the wall and clung to him dazedly. He had never been called upon to do anything like that, even in his wildest dreams of buccaneering. But the daylight lamps in the vestibule were beating down on him like a battery of limes, and he knew that to anyone glancing in from outside he was as conspicuous as the central figure on a lighted stage. In a kind of stage fright he began to recite "The Wreck of the *Hesperus*," with violent gesticulations. . . .

Simon raced back into the office, and the clerkly constable looked up. The Saint gave him no more time to think than he had given the first man.

"*Wollen Sie hinauskommen, bitte? Der andere Schupo bedarf Hilfe—*"

The scribe rose from his chair grumbling. Simon caught him with the same blow as he came through the counter, and left him where he fell.

He went back and found Monty returning hoarsely to the first stanza, having lost his memory after three verses.

"And the skipper had taken his little daugh*ter* to bear him——"

"All clear," said the Saint.

He closed in on the other side of Monty's *vis-à-vis*. Together they bore the unconscious man into the office and laid him on the floor, dragging the clerkly one farther in to join him. Simon rummaged round and discovered handcuffs with which they fastened the two policemen's wrists and ankles; then he improvised gags with their handkerchiefs and screwed-up balls of blotting paper. It was all done with amazing speed and in perfect silence.

The Saint jerked his head toward a door on the far side of the office, through which came the murmur of voices.

"I think that must be the charge room," he whispered, in Monty's ear. "Don't make a sound—we aren't ready for the alarm yet——"

A subdued clicking noise blurred into his speech, and he looked round swiftly. It came from a private telephone exchange in one corner, where a tiny red bulb was blinking its impatient summons.

The Saint dropped into the operator's stool and plugged in on the calling circuit. Monty listened tensely, trying to make out the brief words which were clacking through the receiver diaphragm. Only a couple of sentences were spoken; and then he saw the Saint smile and clip out a single word of reply.

"*Sofort!*"

Simon came out of the stool and searched round for the main lead-in wire. He found it and broke it loose with one jerk. Then he spoke a second time in Monty's ear.

"The Big Cheese is somewhere upstairs. That was

him—asking for Pat and the witnesses to be taken up
to his office. Keep things quiet while I look after
him—there are guns on those stiffs which you can
take, and there's sure to be another way out of the
charge room which you'll have to watch for. Don't
shoot if you can possibly help it. I'll be right back."

He vanished into the vestibule and turned into
the corridor which he had already observed. A short
way down it there was a door on the right, through
which he heard the same voices talking—the second
entrance to the charge room which he had already
guessed of. Simon would have given much to listen
there for a while, but the ticking seconds were vital. The dusk was now well advanced, and at any
moment the squad cars which had depleted the
station staff to a negligible fraction would be snoring
up the street again with the reports of their fruitless
chase. And when that happened the slugs would be
fairly spawning in the salad. . . . The Saint closed
his lips grimly and tiptoed past the door without a
backward glance.

He came through to a flight of stone stairs and
went up them. On the landing above there were
doors all around him. He sank to one knee and
scanned the floor for a sign of the room from which
the telephone call had come. Only one door showed
a tell-tale streak of light close to the ground. His luck
was holding magnificently. He walked up to the
door and knocked, instantly receiving the curt
command to enter.

A white-haired man with a square jaw and military
shoulders, and a middle-aged man with a typical
bullet head, both in plain clothes, looked up from a
desk littered with maps and papers as the Saint came
in.

Simon let them see his gun and his smile, and
reverted to his very best German.

"I believe you were looking for me," he said.

2

The two men coagulated where they stood, staring at him whitely in the dumb startlement of his
arrival. If the door had opened to admit a herd of
emerald-green hippopotami they could scarcely
have been more flabbergasted. But beyond the involuntary swelling of their eyes and the limp fall of
their chins they made no movement. Whatever they
may have lacked as shining lights of the Law, they
were not deficient in human courage.

Several seconds went by before the elder of the
two spoke.

"What do you want?" he asked calmly.

"A little talk," said the Saint. He gestured with his
automatic towards the chief's right hand, which was
sliding stealthily across the desk towards a row of
bell pushes. "You can save yourself the trouble of
ringing—all the wires are disconnected, and in any
case no one would answer."

Perhaps he was guilty of stretching the truth,
but the chief did not know it. And the warning was
spoken with such an air of quiet conviction that it
went home as effectively as a shot from the Saint's
steady gun. The chief's hand relaxed.

"How did you get in?"

"I walked in. The door was open."

The two men remained motionless, continuing to
stare. It was the Saint's gun and the Saintly smile
that had paralyzed them at first—their first thought
had been that they were dealing with a maniac, and

the Saint knew that after the initial shock of his appearance had worn off they were both weighing the chances of his touching off the trigger if either of them made an incautious movement. Against that they were balancing the alternative potentialities of a tactful submission until they could distract the attention of those unwavering blue eyes.

Then Simon observed that the younger man was studying his face intently; he sensed the incredulous understanding before it was fully formed in the man's own mind and forestalled it cheerfully:

"I am Simon Templar—the Saint."

The two men remained motionless—and now the reason for their stillness was concentrated entirely in his gun hand. He could feel every phase of the struggle that went on in their minds. The most wanted man in Europe—the man for whom the whole German police force was scouring the country—the man on whose head extravagant rewards had been placed—was standing coolly before them in that room. The prize that every man in the force would have given his right hand to win was tempting them from a range of four yards. And the automatic in his hand was held in the tremorless grip of a steel robot. The terse information they had received had magnified itself in their imaginations to something almost fabulous. Whichever of them made the first threatening move would be doomed—the other might possibly survive to win the glory. The atmosphere stifled with the terrific pressure of their inward battle.

"I shall have to handcuff you," said the Saint quietly. "You will turn your backs and put your hands behind you—and keep them well away from your bodies." He saw their limbs go tense as the full meaning of his order became plain to them, and went on swiftly, with his voice tightened up in a crisp urgency of menace: "You think that any risk would be preferable to the disgrace of having been made prisoners in your own stronghold. You would be wrong. Both of you would die before you could take a step towards me. You have heard of me—you can estimate your own prospects. I give you my word that no harm will come to you."

It was a war of wills, fought out silently in that confined space over the thrusting swords of their eyes. The Saint had no wish to shoot. And yet, if it had been forced upon him, he would have dropped those two men as mercifully as he could. To him there was a bigger issue at stake even than the lives of two innocent martyrs to duty.

Perhaps the two men, by some strange telepathy carried on that clash of opposing wills, felt what was on the Saint's mind. But the elder man bowed his head and turned slowly round. His subordinate paused a moment before following his example, and turned round at last with an unswerving glare of defiance.

Simon sensed all the galling bitterness of their surrender as he fastened handcuffs on their wrists and linked their ankles similarly together; but he breathed again. He pocketed his gun and allowed them to turn round to their former positions. In another corner of the room he saw an enormous steel cabinet, with plenty of room for two men to stand between the shelves of documents that lined the walls. He went over and examined it more closely; but, as he had feared, the great door would seal it hermetically.

He faced his prisoners again.

"I do not want to make your position more painful than my own safety demands," he said. "If you will give me your paroles as gentlemen that you will make no attempt to escape, or to attract attention in any way, whatever happens, I shall be able to spare you further indignity."

The chief gazed at him sombrely.

"You could scarcely do more than you have done already," he remarked, with a trace of irony; "and it seems that you have taken effective measures to protect yourself. What else do you want?"

"I have still to enjoy the little talk I spoke of," said the Saint. "But your part in it is silent. You must not be allowed to interrupt. I assure you, it would distress me to have to stun you while you are defenseless, and then gag you, before I placed you in that cabinet. The alternative is in your own hands. I shall require you to stand inside the cabinet during my conversation. You will do nothing to betray your presence, whatever you hear, until five minutes after I have finally left the room."

"May I know your object?"

"You will realize it soon enough."

The white-haired soldier hesitated, and in his hesitation, the younger man let loose a string of snarling protests.

The chief cut him short with a movement of his head.

"We do not help ourselves by inviting injury, *Inspektor*," he said. "I shall give my parole."

The Saint bowed. In that self-possessed white-haired chief of police he recognized a quality of manhood which he would have been glad to meet at any time.

"I am in your debt, *Herr Oberst*," he said. "And you, *Inspektor?*"

The younger man drew himself up stiffly.

"Since I am commanded," he replied shortly, "I have no choice. I give you my word of honour."

"You are very wise," murmured the chief.

Simon smiled. He opened the door of the cabinet wide and ushered the two men in. As soon as they had settled themselves he closed it again, leaving only a two-inch gap which would give them plenty of air to breathe. He left them with a final warning:

"Remember that you have given your paroles. I shall be back in a few moments. Whatever happens, you will remain hidden."

Then he left the room and went down the stairs again to relieve Monty Hayward's vigil. His arteries were playing an angelic symphony, and there was a new brightness in his eyes. Perhaps after all the running fight could become a triumph. Thus far he had no complaints to make. The gods were spilling Eldorados on him with both hands. If only the breaks held. . . . It would be a worthy finish to one story and a merry overture to many more. Admittedly there was a price to pay, and those lost few minutes would have boosted the bill against him to heights that would have made most men giddy to think of, but he had learned that in his chosen way of life there were no bargain sales. It was wine while it lasted. And he had never really wanted to be good.

He came upon Monty Hayward with a swinging step and the Saintly smile still on his lips. The automatic spun on his first finger by the trigger guard.

"I have cleaned up, Monty," he said. "Let's make it a party."

He burrowed through his overalls and produced
his own cigarette case. As he opened it, the polished
interior showed him a reflection of his own face. He
grinned and closed the case again.

"Back along the corridor," he said, "I think I
heard the swishing song of a gents' toilet. I should
hate Rudy to see us like this—and we can still keep
an ear on the charge room from there."

If there was anything which finally emerged as
supremely nightmarish out of Monty Hayward's
memories of the cumulative palpitations of that day,
it was the wash and brush-up which the Saint thereupon ordained. Monty hadn't proposed himself for
anything quite so hair-raising as that. Battle, murder, and sudden death were things immutable in
themselves; but to make oneself free of the
lavatories of a captured police station in which an
uncertain number of the personnel were still at large
called for a granitic quality of nerve to which only a
Simon Templar could have aspired. To the Saint it
was a pleasure with a pungent spice. He stripped off
his greasy overalls, threw them into a corner, and
abandoned himself to the delights of warm water
and yellow soap as if he were in his own home. As far
as he was concerned, the only visible reminiscence
of the things that waited a couple of walls away was
the blue-black shape of the automatic pistol placed
carefully on the marble top of the wash basin beside
him.

Monty sighed and made the best of it. Now that he
saw himself in a mirror for the first time, he began to
understand how he had been able to travel so far
without being identified. It was some relief to be
able to divest himself of the stained blue jeans and
feel himself in a more accustomed garb; it was even
better to be able to scrub the oil and grime from his

face and hands and feel clean. He looked up presently with a sort of indefinite optimism—and saw the Saint coolly manicuring his nails.

"Ready for more, Monty?"

The Saint's piratical eyes rested on him humorously. Monty nodded.

"Surely."

They went back towards the office. The two policemen still slept. Simon expected them to be out to the world for all of another ten minutes—the handcuffs and gags were an additional precaution. He knew where he was when the blade of his hand got home with those tricky blows.

He took out his cigarette case again, offered it to Monty, and helped himself. The ratchet of his lighter scraped a flame out of the shielded wick. He stood there for a moment, drawing the mellow smoke gratefully into his lungs to wipe away the last dry harshness of the stuff that he had had to inhale in his former rôle. Monty watched him releasing the smoke again through his lips and nostrils with a slow widening of that newborn Saintly smile. The tanned, rakish contours of that lean face, cleared now from their coating of dust and dirt, were more reckless than he had ever seen them before. The black hair was brushed back in one smooth swashbuckling sweep. No one else in the world could have been so steady-nerved and at ease, so trim and immaculate after the rough handling of his clothes, so alive with the laughing promise of danger, so careless and debonair in every way. The Saint was going to his destiny.

"You take the corridor," he said. "Stand outside the door and listen. Come in as soon as you hear my voice."

"Right."

Monty walked away.

Simon Templar drew at his cigarette again, gazing back the way Monty had gone. He was still smiling.

Then he turned back to the office. He gave it one more glance round to make certain that everything was in order—policemen securely bound, telephone disconnected, windows barred. He went rapidly through the drawers of the desks, taking over a bunch of keys and a couple of spare automatics. Then he went to the door of the charge room.

With his ear pressed to the panels, he could make words out of the murmur that he had heard before. The conversation was in English—he heard Prince Rudolf's silkily faultless accent, commanding the scene as interpreter.

"Would it not be unusual, Miss Holm, if our friend showed no interest in your whereabouts?"

Then Patricia's unfaltering stone-wall:

"I really don't know."

"And yet you insist that he had made no arrangements about meeting you again."

"He isn't a nursemaid."

"But, my dear lady! You must remember that we have met before. I have had my experience of the esteem in which Mr. Templar holds you. Are we to understand that he has transferred his affections elsewhere? I must confess I had heard rumours——"

"As a matter of fact," said Patricia calmly, "we did quarrel."

"Ah! And was it because of another woman?"

"No."

"Will you tell us the reason?"

"Certainly. He said you were a slimy baboon, and I told him I wouldn't have him insulting baboons."

A guttural voice broke in with a rattle of short-tempered German. Prince Rudolf replied soothingly; then he spoke again in English, imperturbably as ever, but with the suave malignity razoring even more clearly through his voice.

"Miss Holm, you will be unwise to attempt to imitate your—er—friend's celebrated gift of repartee. Perhaps you have not yet realized the seriousness of your position. You are charged with being an accessory to three crimes. It would be a pity for you to waste your beauty in prison."

"Is that so?"

"I am instructed to tell you that there are two ways of turning State's Evidence, and only one of them is voluntary—or pleasant. One can be—persuaded."

There was a brief silence; and then another voice entered the discussion with the confidence of its own personality. It was Nina Walden's.

"Now you're getting interesting, Prince," she remarked. "That'll make a grand story at the trial. It'll be front page stuff. 'Crown Prince Practices Third Degree—Lady Killer In Real Life—Royal Exile Retains Torture Chamber!' Say, wait till I get this all down!"

"Miss Walden, I should advise you——"

"I didn't ask for advice," said the American girl coldly. "I'm here as a reporter. If it's your job to find three men to bully a woman, it's my job to tell the world."

There was another silence.

Then the German officer muttered something vicious and impatient. Simon heard a faint gasp—then the smack of a flat palm and a startled oath.

He turned the handle and kicked open the door.

The figures in that charge-room scene printed

themselves on his eyes one by one in a second of unbroken immobility, just as his own image was stamped forever on their memories. They spun round together at the sound of his entry, those of them who had their backs to him, and froze on their feet all at once. His eyes went over them bleakly, like a camera panning round a group set. The sergeant standing by a high desk at the end of the room. The policeman who had brought Patricia in, with her wrist still half twisted in the grasp of one hand, while his other hand moved unbelievingly over the red brand of fingers on his cheek. Nina Walden standing close to him, just as she had been when she hit him. Marcovitch in the background, caught in the middle of his gloating as if he had taken a bullet in the stomach. The Crown Prince, poised with his unfailing grace, with his pale delicate features as reposeful as an alabaster mask, raising his long jade cigarette holder in tapering fingers that were as steady as a statue's. And Patricia Holm staring, with the leap of a bewildered hope coming to her lips. . . .

"Good-evening, boys and girls," said the Saint softly.

They gazed at him speechlessly, striving to orient their intelligences to the astounding fact of his presence. And the Saint gave them all the time they needed. He lounged against the jamb of the doorway, smiling at them, circling his gun over them in a gentle arc. He was enjoying his moment. Such instances as that were the skysigns of his career, the caviare that made all the rest of it worth while. He liked to linger over them, tasting every shade and subtlety of their rare flavour, writing them into the mental memoirs that would shed their light over his declining years—if he lived long enough to decline.

And then Patricia Holm broke the stillness with his name.

"Simon!"

The Saint nodded, looking at her. The conversation that he had heard before he came through the door was still in his mind. He saw the blind happiness in her face, the faith in her eyes, the eager courage of her slim body; and he knew that, whatever happened, whatever the price to be paid, he had taken the very best of life.

"I'm here, lass," he said.

The man who had hold of her roused out of his stupor. He let go the girl's wrist and grabbed for the Luger in his belt. . . .

Crack!

Simon's automatic spat from a half-charged cartridge with a sound like two thin planks of wood slapped smartly together, and the Luger banged down to the stone floor. The policeman, with a limp right arm, stared foolishly at a dribble of blood that was running out of his sleeve down the back of his hand.

The Saint glanced aside and saw that Monty had advanced through the other door. Then he faced the group again.

"So long as you all behave yourselves," he murmured, "everything will be hunky dory. Rudolf, I've been looking for you everywhere!"

12

HOW NINA WALDEN SPOKE, AND MONTY HAYWARD LOOKED OUT OF A WINDOW

COMPARED with the silence there had been before, the taciturnity that greeted the Saint's affable announcement swelled up to deafening proportions. No one who might by any chance have associated himself with its scope succumbed to any irresistible desire to step forward and offer an illuminated address of welcome in reply. An aura of obstinate bashfulness draped itself over the scene like a pall—suspended from the swinging muzzle of the Saint's gun, and trimmed at its edges with the crimson smudge on the back of the policeman's hand. The sergeant at the desk shamelessly took the lesson of that single shot into his well nourished bosom and allowed it to incubate. He went puce to the end of his nose, and his neck flowed wrathfully over his collar, but he made no movement. Marcovitch tried to sidle away behind him. Even the prince said nothing. And the Saint's blue eyes flitted over them mockingly.

"Pat, you'd better take the Luger and toddle out of the line of fire."

Patricia picked up the fallen gun and came over to him. His left arm slipped around her shoulders, and for a moment he held her close to him. Then he set her quietly aside.

"Marcovitch, you mop that gaffed cod mouth off your face and keep well out in the open. I don't like being able to see you, but I don't feel safe when I can't. Jump to it! . . . Hands up over your head— and keep 'em there till your spine cracks! . . . That's better. Monty, you can go round behind 'em and take their artillery. Pat and I'll take care of any acrobatics they're thinking of."

Monty Hayward dropped his guns into his side pockets and went on the round. Simon looked at the American girl.

"I heard Rudy call you Miss Walden," he said, "and you mentioned being a reporter. Are those details correct?"

Nina Walden understood. He was not implicating her at all. She accepted her cue easily.

"That's right."

"What's the job here?"

"I came in for the story of your mail robbery, Mr. Templar. Maybe you can tell me some more about it."

The Saint swept her a bow.

"Sister, you came in at the right time. You're going out with more thrills than you ever thought you'd get. But I'm afraid this news isn't released yet. You can stay on if you give me your word not to interfere—or do anything else that might bother me."

The girl smiled.

"I guess I haven't much choice."

Simon's left hand saluted her. He had time to play Claude Duval with the most charming reporter he had ever met, but even while he did it he was wondering how much grace the gods were going to give him to gather up the loose ends. His glance transferred itself to the clock over the sergeant's desk. Twenty minutes after seven—and almost dark outside. . . . Yet it never occurred to him to doubt whether the wash and brush-up that had done so much to enhance his beauty had been a wise expenditure of time. That power of thinking ahead, almost intuitively, into the most distant possibilities, and preparing for them long before they arose, was the gift which had made the grand moguls of the Law gnash their teeth over him for so many years in vain. And that night he might need it all.

The tableau remained mute while Monty passed from one man to the next, making a collection of their weapons. The sergeant was unarmed. Marcovitch yielded an automatic and a long thin-bladed knife. The Crown Prince had a tiny nickel-plated pistol. Simon frowned a little—he was expecting something else. He waited until Monty had retired again to his position with his pockets weighted down by the load of armoury, and then he crooked a coaxing finger.

"Marcovitch—little   blossom—come   hither! You're too retiring—and we want to know all the secrets of your underwear."

The Russian came forward sullenly. Monty Hayward and Patricia were covering the other men, and the Saint's automatic had suddenly taken entire charge of him. Its round gleaming barrel had slanted up and settled in a dead line with the bridge of his nose, so that he stared down the black tunnel from which sudden death could spurt into his brain at a touch.

"Right here—right up close to papa, sweetheart!"

The Saint's voice rapped at him with a ring that made him start. And Marcovitch came on. He fought every inch of the way, with his lips snarling—but he came on. The single black eye of the gun dragged him inexorably across the room, step by step—that and the living bleak blue eyes behind it.

He stopped in front of the Saint, a yard away; and the blue eyes looked him over slowly and thoughtfully.

Then the Saint's left hand flashed out at him. Marcovitch cringed from the blow that he could not avoid. But the mistake was his—the blow never materialized. Simon had done his job before Marcovitch knew what was happening. There was the sharp splitting tear of rending cloth, and one half of Marcovitch's coat hung off him down to the elbow. In another second it was joined by half of his shirt. And the Saint grinned amiably.

"Wool next the skin, Uglyvitch?" he murmured. "Dear me! And I thought you were a tough guy. . . ."

Something else was revealed besides the woolen vest, and that was a band of tape that stretched across the man's chest and disappeared under his armpit. A neat little bundle hung there, tied in a soiled linen handkerchief slung from the tape which passed over the opposite shoulder.

Simon ripped it off. There was another similar bundle concealed under the man's left arm.

"An old game—which you ought to have remembered, Monty," said the Saint. "He might just as well have had a gun there. . . . You can go back to your place in the bread line now, Comrade."

He pushed Marcovitch away. The man's face was white with fury, but Simon Templar could endure hardships like that with singular fortitude. The two knotted handkerchiefs filled his spread hand, and their contents crunched juicily when he squeezed them in his fingers.

He gave the Crown Prince a broadside of his most seraphic smile.

"Dear old Gaffer Rudolf!" he drawled. "So that's the simple end of an awful lot of fuss. Well, well, well! We none of us grow younger, do we?—as we've been telling each other several times to-day."

The prince gazed at him passionlessly.

"Would it be in order to congratulate you?" he murmured; and the Saint laughed.

"Perhaps—when we've finished."

Simon turned to Monty.

"If you'd like something more to do, old dear," he said, "you might try and find some more handcuffs. We shall want six pairs—if the station'll run to it. Hands only for Rudolf and Marcovitch—they've got to walk. Hands and feet for the Law—we don't want them at all. And mind how you go around that sergeant. He looks as if he might burst at any moment, and you wouldn't want to get splashed with his supper."

Monty searched around. After a few moments he discovered a locker that was plentifully stocked with both hand and leg irons; he came back trailing the chains behind him. Under the Saint's directions the two police officers were efficiently manacled together; and finally an extra pair of handcuffs fastened them to a ringbolt set in the wall, which had apparently been used before for the restraint of refractory prisoners.

The prince smoked tranquilly until his turn came; and then he detached the cigarette end from the long jade holder, placed the holder leisurely in an inside pocket, and extended his own hands for the bracelets.

"This is a unique experience," he remarked, as Monty locked the cuffs on his wrists. "May I ask where we are to go?"

"Upstairs," said the Saint coolly. "We've got a little talk coming, and the air's better up there."

The prince raised his sensitive eyebrows, but he made no reply.

They went up the stairs in a strange procession: Patricia and Nina Walden leading, the Saint going up backwards after them and covering the cortège, Prince Rudolf and Marcovitch following him, and Monty Hayward bringing up the rear. The prince's face remained impassive. Simon knew that that impassivity belied the workings of that quiet ruthless brain; but the prince and Marcovitch were firmly sandwiched between two fires, and they could do nothing—at the moment. And the Saint didn't care. The prince must have known it—even as the two men in the room above must have known. It was significant that Rudolf had been very silent, ever since that playful séance in the charge room had received its staggering interruption.

"This way, boys."

Simon opened the door of the police chief's office and let the caravan file past him. He went in last—closed the door and leaned back on it.

"Sit down."

Prince Rudolf sank into a chair. Monty prodded Marcovitch into another with the nose of his Luger. And the Saint cleared a space on the desk and sat there, dumping the two knotted handkerchiefs beside him. He put away his gun and opened the bundles, pouring the contents of both onto a single handkerchief in a shimmer of rainbow flames that seemed to light up the whole dingy room.

"The time has come, Rudolf, for us to have a little reckoning," he said; and once again, for no reason that the others could think of, he was speaking in German. And yet to Monty Hayward there was no difference, for the man who spoke was still the Saint, making even that stodgy language as vivid and pliable as his own native tongue. "We have a few things to learn—and you can tell us about them. And we'll have all the jewels out to encourage you. Fill your eyes with them, Rudolf. You used to be a rich man. But just for this quarter of a million pounds worth of stones you were ready to kill men and torture them; you were ready to run up a list of murders that'd get anyone hanged three times—and frame them onto Monty and me. Which was very unkind of you, Rudy, after all the fun we had together in the old days. But you aren't denying any of it, are you?"

The prince shrugged.

"Why should I? It was unfortunate that you personally should be the victim, but——"

"Highness!"

Marcovitch sprang up from his chair. And at the same instant the Saint came off the desk like a streak of lightning. His fist smashed into the Russian's mouth and sent him reeling back.

"I never have liked your voice, Uglyvitch," said the Saint evenly. "And it's rude to butt in like that. Gag him, Monty."

Simon lighted another cigarette while the order was being carried out. It had been a close call, that; but his face showed no sign of it. He had been watching Marcovitch from the start. It was odd how an inferior mentality might sometimes feel brute suspicions before they came to the more highly geared intelligence.

He sat down in the police chief's chair behind the desk and laid his automatic on the papers in front of him.

"As you say, it was unfortunate that I should have been the victim," he murmured, as if nothing had happened. "I've never been a very successful victim, and I suppose habits are hard to break. But there were others who weren't so lucky. It was all the same to you."

"My dear young friend, we are not playing a game for children——"

"No. We're playing a game for savages. We've come down in the world. Once upon a time it was a game for soldiers—in the old days. I liked you because you were a patriot—and a sportsman—even though we were fighting on opposite sides. Now it's only a game of hunting for sacrifices to put on the altar of your bank account." The Saint's eyes were cold splinters of blue light across the table. "Two men died because they stood between you and these jewels. An agent of yours—didn't you refer to him as 'the egregious Emilio?'—murdered Heinrich Weissmann in my hotel bedroom in Innsbruck after I rescued him from three detectives whom we mistook for bandits. He was taking the jewels to Josef Krauss, whom you had allowed to pull the chestnuts out of the fire for you. You tortured Krauss last night; and to-day, when he had escaped, Marcovitch murdered him on the train between Munich and here. And Marcovitch would also have murdered all three of us if we'd given him the chance."

"My dear Mr. Templar——"

"I haven't quite finished yet," said the Saint

quietly. "Marcovitch was the man who raided the
brake van on that train, with four more of your hired
thugs, to regain those jewels after I'd taken them off
you. And when we had to jump off to save our lives,
he told the officials that it was I who stole the mail.
That also meant nothing to you. You were ready to
have all your crimes charged against us—just as you
were ready to have them actually committed by your
dirty hirelings. You hadn't even the courage to do
any of the work yourself, before it was framed onto
me. But only a few minutes ago you were ready to
apply your torturing methods to a girl, to make
certain that there would be more blood on those
jewels before you'd done with them. The methods of
a patriot and a gentleman!"

For the first time Simon saw a flush of passion
come into the pale face opposite him. The taunt had
gone to its mark like a barbed arrow.

"My dear Mr. Templar!" The prince still con-
trolled his voice, but a little of the suavity had gone
from it. "Since when have your own methods been
above reproach?"

"I'm not thinking of only myself," answered the
Saint coldly. "I'm only alleged to have robbed a
train. Monty Hayward here is accused of murdering
Weissmann as well, and he's the most innocent one
of us all. The only thing he ever did was to help me
rescue Weissmann in the first place, through a mistake which anyone might have made. And since
then, of course, he's helped me to hold up this police
station in order to see justice done, for which no one
could blame him. But you know as well as I do that
he isn't a criminal."

"His character fails to interest me."

"But you know that what I've said is the truth."

"Have I denied it?"

The Saint leaned forward over the desk.

"Will you deny that Weissmann was murdered by an agent of yours and by your orders; that Josef Krauss died in the same way; and that it was Marcovitch and other agents of yours who robbed the mail?"

The prince lifted one eyebrow. He was recovering his self-control again. His face was calm and satirical.

"I believe you once headed an organization which purported to administer a justice above the law," he said. "Do I understand that I am assisting at its renaissance?"

"Do you deny the charge?"

"And supposing I admit it?"

"I'm asking a question," said the Saint, with a face of stone. *"Do you deny the charge?"*

A long, tense silence came down on the room. Marcovitch moved again, and Monty's hand caught him round the neck. The significance of it all was beyond Monty Hayward's understanding, but the drama of the scene held him spellbound. He also had begun to fall into the error that was deluding the Crown Prince. The Saint's face was as inexorable as a judge's. The humour and humanity had frozen out of it, leaving the rakish lines graven into a grim pitilessness in which the eyes were mere glints of steel. They stared over the table into the depths of the prince's soul, holding him impaled on their merciless gaze like a butterfly on a pin. The tension piled up between them till the very air seemed to grow hot and heavy with it.

"Do you deny the charge?"

Again those five words dropped through the room like separate particles of white-hot metal, driving

one after another with ruthless precision into the
same cell of the prince's brain. They had about them
the adamantine patience of doom itself. And the
prince must have known that that question was
going to receive a direct answer if it waited till the
end of the world. He had come up against a force
that he could no more fight against than he could
fight against the changing of the tides, a force that
would wear through his resistance as the continual
dripping of water wears through a rock.

And then the Saint moved one hand, and quietly
picked up his gun.

"*Do you deny the charge?*"

The prince stirred slightly.

"No."

He answered unemotionally, without turning his
eyes a fraction from the relentless gaze that went on
boring into them. There was the stoical defiance of a
Chinese mandarin in the almost imperceptible lift of
his head.

"Does your worship propose to pronounce sentence?" he inquired mockingly.

The Saint's mouth relaxed in a hard little smile.

Every word had been registered on the ears of the
two captive police officers whom he had hidden in
the corner cabinet. The gods fought on his side, and
the star of the Crown Prince had fallen at last.
Otherwise such an old snare as that could never have
caught its bird. Marcovitch had smelt it—but Marcovitch was silenced, and now he had gone white
and still. The prince had been a little too clever. And
Monty Hayward was free. . . .

"Your punishment is not in my hands," said the
Saint. "It will overtake you in the course of legal
justice, and I see no need to interfere."

He ran his fingers again through the heap of
jewels, letting them trickle through his fingers in
rivulets of coloured splendour that caught the light
on a hundred cunning facets.

"Pretty toys," said the Saint, "but they tempted
you. And you could have bought them. You could
have had them all for no more trouble than it would
have taken you to write a cheque. I shall often
wonder why you did it. Was it a kink of yours,
Rudolf, that told you you couldn't enjoy them unless
they were christened in blood? The Maloresco
emeralds—the Ullsteinbach blue diamond——"

"What did you say?"

It was Nina Walden who spoke, starting forward
suddenly from her place in the background.

Simon looked at her curiously. He picked up the
great blue stone and held it in the light.

"The Ullsteinbach blue diamond," he said.
"Wedding gift of the late Franz Josef to the Archduke Michel of Presc—according to information in
The Times. Josef Krauss tried to tell me something
about it before he died, but he didn't get far. Do you
know anything about it?"

The American girl took the stone from his fingers
and turned it over and over. Then she looked at the
Saint again.

"I know this much," she said. "It's a——"

"Look out!" yelled Monty.

He had seen the prince's hand move casually to
his sleeve, as if in search of a handkerchief, and had
thought nothing of it. Then the hand came out again
with a jerk, and the knife that came with it went
spinning across the desk in a vicious streak of silver.
The Saint hurled himself sideways, and it skimmed
past his neck and clattered against the wall. The

prince flung himself after it like a madman, clawing at the Saint's gun.

Simon stood up and met him with a straight left that smashed blood out of the contorted face and sent the man staggering back against his chair.

"Keep your gun in his ribs, Monty," ordered the Saint crisply. "This is getting interesting. What were you going to tell me, Miss Walden."

The girl gave him back the stone.

"It's a piece of coloured glass," she said.

2

Simon Templar subsided on to the desk as if his legs had given out under him. The room danced round him in a drunken tango. And once again he heard the dying jest of Josef Krauss ringing in his ears: *"Sehen Sie gut nach . . . dem blauen Diamant. . . . Er ist . . . wirklich . . . preislos. . . ."* And the bitter derisive eyes of the man. . . .

"The Ullsteinbach diamond is in America." Nina Walden went on speaking without a glance at the prince. "It was sold to Wilbur G. Tully, the straw hat millionaire, just before the war. The owners were hard up, and they had to raise money somehow: their treasurers wouldn't give them any more, so they raided the crown jewels. This imitation was made, and the real stone was sold to Tully under a vow of secrecy. He keeps it in his private collection. I don't think any living person knows the story besides Tully and myself. But my grandfather made the imitation. I've known about it for years, and I've been saving the scoop for a good occasion. The Archduke Michel did that when he was sowing wild oats in his fifties—*and he's Prince Rudolf's father, at present the King of*—"

"Great God in Heaven!"

The Saint leapt up again. He understood. The mystery was solved in a flash that almost blinded him. He cursed himself for not having thought of it before. And he was half laughing at the same time, shaking with the sublime perfection of the truth.

"Let me get this straight!" he gasped. "It wasn't the other crown jewels that Rudolf gave a damn about. They just happened to be among the spoils. What he wanted was the Ullsteinbach blue diamond. And he didn't want it because it was valuable, but because it wasn't—because it was literally priceless! He couldn't let the jewels come into any ordinary market, because someone would certainly have discovered the fraud, and the whole deception would have been shown up from the beginning. The old Archduke would probably have been booted off the throne, and Rudolf would have gone with him. He had to let Josef Krauss pinch the jewels, and then take them off Josef. Josef had discovered the secret when he handled the stones, so he had to go. And then I got hold of them by a fluke, and I might have discovered it—so I was a marked man. And everyone with me was in the same boat. Hell!. . ."

The Saint flung out his arms.

"I said it wasn't ordinary boodle—and it isn't! It's the most priceless collection of boodle that's ever been knocked off! There were men dying and being tortured for it—mail vans broken—policemen sweating—thrones tottering—and all because the star turn of it wasn't worth more than an empty beer bottle! My God—why didn't I know that joke hours ago? Why wasn't I told till now?"

He hugged Nina Walden weakly.

Monty swallowed. He didn't know what to say. He realized dimly that he had just heard the unravelling of the most amazing story he was ever likely to hear, but it was all too crushingly simple. For the moment his brain refused to absorb the elementary enormity of it.

In the same daze he saw Simon Templar pick up the glittering blue crystal from the carpet where he had dropped it and advance solemnly towards the Crown Prince. And the Saint's voice spoke uncertainly.

"Rudolf—my cherub—you may have it as the souvenir I promised you."

Monty saw the prince's livid face. . . .

And then a new sound broke into the room—faint and distant at first, swelling gradually until it seemed to pierce the eardrums like a rusty needle. The Saint stiffened up and stood still. And he heard it again—the mournful rising and falling wail of a police siren. It shrilled into his brain eerily, mounting up to its climax like the shriek of a lost soul, moaning round the room at its height like the scream of a tormented ghost. It was so clear that it might have been actually under his feet.

Simon sprang to the window and flung it up. Down in the street below he saw two squad cars pulling into the curb, spilling their loads of uniformed men. Among them, under a street lamp, he could recognize the officer whom he had misdirected on the road. The pursuit squadron had come home.

The Saint turned and faced the room. In his heart he had expected no less. He was quite calm.

"Will you hold the fort again, Monty?" he said.

He ran quickly down the stairs and the corridor leading to the vesitbule. As he came out of the corridor he saw the officer mounting the steps. For an instant they stared at each other across the doorway.

Then Simon slammed the great doors in the officer's face, and dropped the bar across them.

He heard a muffled shout from outside, and then the thumping of fists and gun butts on the massive woodwork; but he was dashing into the nearest room with a window on the street. He looked out and saw a third squad car driving up; then a bullet slapped through the glass beside him and combed his hair with flying splinters. He ducked, and grappled with the heavy steel shuttering that was rolled away on one side of the window. He unfolded it and slammed it into place, and went to the next window. A hail of shot wiped the glass out of existence as he reached it, but the next volley spattered against the plates of armour steel. He had been right about that police station—it was built like a fortress. Simon sprinted from room to room like a demon, barricading one window after another until the whole of the ground floor on the street side was as solid as the walls in which the windows were set.

Then he went through to the back of the building. A section of armed men detached from the main body nearly forestalled him there: there was a back door opening onto a small square courtyard, and one of them had his foot over the threshold when the Saint came to it. Simon swerved round the levelled Luger: the shot singed his arm before he thrust the man backwards and banged the door after him.

The other windows at the back were barred, and Simon could tell at a glance that the bars would withstand any assault for at least half an hour. A face loomed up in one of the windows while the Saint was making his reconnaissance, and he was barely in time to throw himself to the floor before the man's automatic was spitting lead at him like a machine gun.

Rat-tat-tat-tat-tat!

Simon lay flat on his belly and watched the bullets stringing a ruled line of pock-marks along the plaster of the wall over his head. He crawled out on his stomach and went upstairs again, and when he reached the police chief's office he had a Luger automatic rifle under each arm.

He pushed one of them into Patricia's hands.

"Over the landing, and take any of the rooms opposite. Some of 'em are trying to break in at the back. Keep 'em away from the door. Don't hit anyone if you can help it—and don't get hit yourself!"

He flung himself across to the window which he had opened before. Some of the policemen were keeping back the crowd of civilians who had materialized from nowhere; others were standing in groups watching the police station, and the Saint's appearance was the signal for a scattered fusillade. Another man was running across the street with an axe.

Bullets chipped the window frame and scraped showers of plaster from the ceiling as the Saint took aim. He dropped the man with the axe with a flesh wound in the fleshy part of his leg; another man picked up the axe and rushed for the main doors. Simon spread a curtain of clattering steel along the cobbles in front of the man's feet and checked the rush. It was certain suicide to take a step further into that rain of spattering death. The officer shouted a command, and the man ran back with the Saint slamming bullets round his feet.

The police retired behind the shelter of their cars, and paused. Simon saw the peak of the officer's cap rise up, and sent it flying with a well aimed shot. The man sank down again, and Simon proceeded methodically to plug the tires of the police cars. A couple of volunteers were carrying the wounded man away, and the Saint let them get on with it.

A lull descended on the street side of the battle, and through it Simon heard Patricia's rifle across the landing spitting its syncopated stutter of defiance. He waited, ramming a fresh feeder of ammunition into the clips.

Then another order rang out, and the police leapt up as one man in a second and better organized attack.

One squad charged for the door, headed by the man with the axe. The others covered their advance with a storm of fire that went whistling round the Saint's head like a cloud of angry hornets. Simon made his Luger belch lead till the barrel scalded his hands. It was a miracle that he was not hit himself, while he sprayed shots along the armour of the police cars and sent volleys of ricochets whining away off the cobble stones. One shot clipped his ear and drew blood: he shook his head and crowded a new box of cartridges into the Luger's hungry breech.

Suddenly he found Monty Hayward beside him, automatic raised, taking aim. The Saint caught his wrist and dragged him away.

"You stay out of it!" he snarled. "I didn't take all this trouble just for you to get a bullet through your head, and I didn't clear you of one set of charges so that you could be pinched for shooting policemen."

Monty Hayward looked him in the eyes.

"That be damned for a yarn——"

"And you be damned for a fool. Your job is to look after Rudolf. What're you doing about him?"

"I knocked him out and left him," said Monty calmly.

The Saint looked round. He saw the prince lolling back in his chair with his face turned vacuously to the ceiling—and also he saw that the cabinet door was wide open, and the police chief and his inspector were standing in the room.

"What do you mean—you cleared me?" said Monty Hayward.

Simon turned him round by the shoulders.

"Rudolf's confession was heard. I arranged it like that—that's why I made him answer me, and got rather theatrical in the process. But it worked. You're clear, Monty—and if you do anything silly now those same men will be witnesses against you."

Monty looked at the white-haired police chief and then back to the Saint. His mouth set in a stubborn line.

"I told you I'd see it through with you," he said.

He flung off the Saint's hand and went back to the window. Then he felt the Saint's gun in his back.

"I mean it, Monty. If you don't stay out I'll plug you. Or else I'll lay you out as you laid out Rudolf. Don't be a fool!" They eyed each other steadily, while the guns outside thundered and chattered erratically. The regular thudding of the axe at the front doors resonated up through the building. And the Saint's face softened. "Monty, it's been swell having you. But you've done your share. Leave this to me."

He swung back to the window with his rifle coming up to his shoulder. Again the hysterical rattle of the Luger battered through the room, like a sheet of tin jabbed against a fast-moving fly-wheel. Simon poured the bullets round the knot of men clustered in the doorway, kicking up little spurts of dust and powdered stone from the cobbles. The fury of his fire drove them back for a moment; then a shot from the barrage that rained through the window struck the side of his gun, numbing his hands and hurling him backwards with the impact. When he tried to bring a fresh cartridge into the chamber he found that the action had jammed.

He threw the useless weapon across the room and dashed through the door. Out on the landing the sounds of thudding and smashing timber were louder, and he knew that the minutes of the front door's resistance were numbered. He took no notice. In a moment he was back, hauling a Nordenfeld machine gun behind him.

"They shall have everything but the kitchen sink," he said; and Monty saw that he was smiling.

Monty stood and watched him drag the heavy gun to the window and set it up so that it pointed down at the nearest squad car. A full belt of cartridges was clamped through the slots, and the Saint jerked at the cocking lever to make sure of its smooth running. He fanned a burst along the street; and then he straightened up.

"It's been a great day, Monty," he said.

He glanced round the room.

Prince Rudolf was rousing again, staring as if hypnotized at the police chief and the inspector who were gazing down at him. The meaning of their presence was writing itself over his brain in letters of fire. Then he turned his head and saw the Saint.

He struggled to his feet. One of the things that Simon would always remember was the Crown Prince's last charming smile, and the gesture of those eloquent hands.

"After all, my dear young friend," said the prince gently, "you have not disappointed me."

The Saint looked at him without answering.

Then he turned to the desk and picked up a flat ebony ruler. He went with it to the machine gun and rammed it through the firing handles, locking down the trigger button, and the Nordenfeld started a continuous crackling as the breech sucked in the long belt of ammunition.

Simon left it and faced Monty again.

"Good luck, old lad," he said.

The Saint's hand was out, and the blue eyes smiled. Monty Hayward found himself without words, though there were questions still teeming in his mind. But he took the Saint's hand in a firm grip.

He felt a last strong touch on his shoulder, and the Saint laughed. And then Simon Templar was gone.

Monty Hayward heard him across the landing, calling to Patricia. The firing from the other room ceased. Their footsteps went down the stairs.

Monty stood where he was. He wondered whether those two splendid outlaws were choosing to go out as they had lived, in a blaze of their own glory and the stabbing flames of guns, making one last desperate bid for freedom. And he didn't know. His brain had gone hazy. He saw the Crown Prince fingering a button on his coat, saw the prince's hand go to his mouth; but still he didn't move—not even when Nina Walden cried out, and the prince sat down quietly like a tired man. . . . The door below was breaking in. He could hear every blow pounding through the heart of the seasoned oak, and the hoarse voices of the men working. There was less firing outside, but the Nordenfeld with the jammed trigger still played the crackling message of the man who had gone.

A long time afterwards—it might have been centuries, or it might have been a few seconds—Monty Hayward went to the window and stood beside the gun, looking out.

He saw the front doors give way, and the grey-uniformed men pouring in. He heard their boots clattering up the stairs, heard them pounding on the door of the room where he was, shouting for it to be opened. A bullet crashed through the panels and flattened itself on the wall a yard to his left. Still he did not move. The Saint had locked the door as he went out and taken the key. The police chief bawled something to that effect, and a dozen shoulders tore the door from its hinges. Policemen filled the room.

Monty knew that the gun at his side gave a last expiring cough and went silent; that the room was a babel of voices; that Nina Walden was standing beside him and looking out also; that men were shaking him, barking their questions in his ear. He knew all those things, but they were only vague impressions in the haze of his memories.

What he saw, and saw clearly, was a figure in field grey that came out of the main doors with the limp form of a fair-haired girl slung over his shoulder. Monty saw the crowd surge round them, heard the uniformed man's curt explanation murmured from lip to lip through the crowd, and made out the word *"verwundet"* in it. He saw a passage open up through the mob, and the girl carried through on the shoulder of the grey uniform to the Crown Prince's Rolls. He saw the yellow car begin to move slowly through the milling crowd, gaining speed as it won through the densest part, with the grey uniform at the wheel and the girl beside him in the front seat. And he saw, he would have sworn he saw, that as the yellow car reached the open street and whirled away into the night, the driver raised one hand in gay debonair wave—even before another man appeared on the station steps with a shout of revelation that was taken up in the furious rumbling of a thousand throats.

Still Monty Hayward stood there, not hearing the impatient voices round him, not answering them; a free man, living again the unforgettable hours of his adventure and seeing all his life ahead. So he would go back to his life. And the Saint would go on. For it was thus that their paths led them. There would be a chase, but the police cars had already been disabled. There would be cordons, but the Saint would slip through them. There would be armed men at every frontier, but those two would still get away. He knew they would get away.

WATCH FOR THE SIGN OF THE SAINT.

HE WILL BE BACK.